To Nancy F

Thank you
for being the —
I hope you enjoy the book.

Your Friend,

Tom (Gebeau) Savoy

Class of 1989

t.savoy@insightbb.com

MW01204755

Champions
of the Dead

Tom Savoy

Copyright © 2004 by Thomas Savoy

ISBN 0-7414-1759-6

Published by:

PUBLISHING.COM

519 West Lancaster Avenue
Haverford, PA 19041-1413
Info@buybooksontheweb.com
www.buybooksontheweb.com
Toll-free (877) BUY BOOK
Local Phone (610) 520-2500
Fax (610) 519-0261

Printed in the United States of America

Printed on Recycled Paper

Published January 2004

Table of Contents

Dedications i

Foreword ii

The Blue Widower 1

An Old Man's Funeral 3

The Electronic Parent 12

Two Good Days 20

Thirty-Minute Century 26

Where Do You Get Your Ideas From? 30

A Frenchman's Night Out 39

Champions of the Dead 41

Red Light District 82

The Prisoner Unaware 86

Severed Chains 91

Edgar Henry's Final Lap 103

The Black Pariah: Predators 107

Victims of The System 128

Wesley 144

King of the johnnies 148

Journey Toward the Light 152

Dedications

This book was a long time in coming, and I would like to take this time to thank those who have made a significant impact upon my life and, consequently, my writing:

To God, for granting me this skill that has given my life meaning, and for allowing me an entire lifetime in which to practice it.

To Angela, the woman who stands beside me as a partner, as I stand beside her in our shared trip through Life.

To my sister, Lynn, whose unwavering courage and tenacity in her life's battles shines as an example to all. Take a bow, sis. You've earned it.

To my aunt Betty, who stood by me in my darkest hours. I am eternally grateful.

To David, a dear friend who has been like a brother to me. Thank you for teaching me how to laugh again. No gift could ever be greater.

To Gail Galvan, my friend and fellow author. I can't possibly thank you enough for "discovering" me and for your great help in bringing my work to print.

To Louise, for being a true friend when I needed one the most. When our paths crossed, it was a blessing from God.

To Jim, my friend and mentor. Thank you for putting up with me at a time when I took nothing seriously. The old home town hasn't been the same since we got together.

To Matt, my friend and co-conspirator. A more honorable rogue the world has never known. Go ye forth into merriment and pass along what I have taught thee.

And, last but certainly not least, this book is dedicated to You, dear reader. Without your desire to read and your interest in what these pages have to offer, this book is nothing more than a stack of papers collecting dust. You have my most sincere thanks.

This book is also dedicated in memory to the following irreplaceable people:

John Robert "Bud" Null (1909-1989), my grandfather and my hero, who will always be greatly missed.

John Robert "Jack" Null (1935-1990), my uncle, whose dedication to his family remains unmatched.

Stephanie Ann Jolly (1975-1991), my cousin who was like a sister to me. You left us far too soon, but I'm happy that you were part of my life for sixteen wonderful years.

Foreword

I wrote my first short story when I was seven years old, and I've been in love with the written word ever since. My teachers in grade school, however, found me to be very frustrating. They had a hard time accepting that a student who can tell a good story may not necessarily be good at remembering all the rules of the English language. I flunked nearly every grammar test put in front of me, yet I could ace any essay assignment they handed out. Go figure.

Even though I'm only now making a serious attempt to get my stuff printed, the idea of writing a book is one I've carried with me over the last twenty-five years. Since, at the time of this writing, I'm thirty-two, you could say I'm fulfilling a lifelong dream. Actually, I've written seven or eight full-length swords-and-sorcery manuscripts, but the best of them are (maybe) mediocre. Those books are laying on a shelf somewhere in my house, happily collecting dust.

When I decided in the fall of 2002 to write a book consisting of short stories, I wanted to reach out to as many readers as I could. That meant dabbling in genres I might not have touched otherwise. Its been a rewarding experience, and I hope you have as much fun reading this book as I had writing it.

Believe it or not, I almost left out Champions of the Dead. It was a story I wrote for personal reasons, namely my belief that cemeteries should be treated with respect and reverence. With as much trouble as I had cranking out an acceptable version, I didn't think it was good enough to deserve much attention. It was an editing nightmare, and I've done more revisions and corrections than I dare try to count. Basically, I thought it was as lackluster as Nixon's attempts to get past the Watergate fiasco. Luckily, there are people in my life who believed otherwise and were able to convince me to make it the centerpiece of this book.

My original intention was to go through the individual stories and put down some personal notes regarding each one. I decided not to do that. I'll let you discover them on your own without my interference.

So I'll step aside and let you get on with your reading. Thanks for giving me a chance to share my work with you. Have fun!

Cheers!

Tom Savoy

The Blue Widower

So here we are, sitting at the edge of the river, looking at the water that took my wife, Pauline. I always called her Pauly. Married twenty-six years, you know. Got married at this very spot by the river.

Hey, there's some big air bubbles. Maybe I ought to go back to the truck and get my pole.

Yeah, Pauly was nineteen when we got married. I was twenty-one. She had the brightest green eyes and the shiniest red hair I'd ever seen. She couldn't have looked no more beautiful than she did that day we took our vows. And she always liked my blue eyes and brown hair. I sure miss her.

I've never known a more loving woman. Nope, not even my own mother. No matter how sick she was, she always kept the house clean. Fixed every meal, too. I never wanted her to strain herself so, but she insisted, and…well, you know what they say about redheads and their tempers.

We had three kids inside of five years, two boys and a girl. God bless them, they've all got their mother's red hair. Beautiful kids, one and all.

There goes some more big bubbles. I don't know…the pole sounds mighty tempting right about now.

Anyhow, Pauly always thought it was funny to send the kids to school in red shirts and red pants. Except our daughter, Phyllis. Pauly sent her to school in a red blouse and skirt with red stockings. Not every day, you know. That'd give the kids a complex. Just once in a while. The kids thought it was a swell joke. I thought it was dumb. But they're my family and I love them. Even when they act like they ain't got a lick of sense. I always made sure on those all-red days I wore my blue overalls with my sky blue dress shirt. Pauly never liked that.

I tried to be a good family man. I worked hard, never smoked, never drank, never even looked at another woman, never raised my hand or my voice in anger. Never did any of that stuff. And you know what? I'm proud of myself for that. Gosh, I sure miss Pauly.

I see those ain't as big as the last bubbles. I'm still not sure about the pole. We'll have to wait and see.

Hah! I remember once, Pauly mixed red food dye in with the chicken feed. The chickens ended up laying eggs with red yolks! Did you ever hear of such a thing? First she fixed them to me sunny side up. Let me tell you, it ain't no fun watching your breakfast bleed on your plate. At least I didn't think so. The boys took a peculiar liking to it, though. Kids, go figure. Anyhow, the next day she served me the same kind of eggs, only they were scrambled. Truth to tell, I didn't know whether to eat them eggs or bury them. Pauly thought it was funny, but I didn't. A

1

couple weeks later, I put blue dye in the chicken feed and let Pauly see how much fun it is to crack open a bunch of blue-yolk eggs. This time I was the one smiling. She wasn't. And I ate them eggs, too. I guess that's all in the past now. Nothing'll ever be the same without her.

Yep, I knew it. The big bubbles are all gone. Now it's just some small ones. Guess maybe I'll leave the pole in the truck.

Oh, we had a happy enough marriage. We talked quite a bit, took little trips together, played board games with the kids on rainy days, and so forth. Pauly always picked the red game piece. I always picked blue. And yeah, the winner would always gloat a little bit.

There was never nothing wrong in the romance department, neither. Even after the kids grew up, Pauly was still a beautiful woman. And I always kept in shape, too. Whenever we got...you know, romantic...she'd wear this see-through red negligee. I usually wore a tight blue jock strap.

Uh-huh. One little bubble. It's just as well I left that pole in the truck.

Our 25th anniversary was special. The kids and grandkids threw us a big party. It was really great! I mean, just having all the family together was good enough for me, but everyone really went all out to make the day special. Almost. Well, it's nothing, you know. It's just that I wanted blue icing on the cake, and Pauly ordered the red. Oh well. No big deal. She knew I'd return the favor, and I did.

So on our last anniversary, I just wanted for the two of us to get away by ourselves. Pauly thought that was swell. So we came and camped out here, right by the spot where we got married 26 years ago.

Hmm. I guess that *was* the last air bubble. I guess that means I won't never have to put up with her mouthing off about how red's better'n blue. I really hate the color red now after all these years, and I'd have seen a lot more of it if I'd hit her with my pole. Pole's painted blue, you know. Glad I settled for the chains and big rock instead. Spray-painted them both blue, too.

Well, I'm heading back to camp now. Vacation's over. You know, I sure am going to miss her.

An Old Man's Funeral

Ted hugged his grandmother consolingly. The 76-year-old woman and her 16-year-old grandson watched as the men from the coroner's office wheeled a body on a stretcher out of the old woman's home. It was Harold Blanchet, Ted's grandfather and Laura Blanchet's husband of 60 years. The 83-year-old man had fought a valiant battle against lung cancer. But he was an old man who had smoked for nearly 70 years before his illness forced him to quit. The outcome of this battle hadn't been hard for anyone to figure out.

"I'm sorry, grandma." Ted held her close as he whispered to her.

"I know." The old woman's voice was shaky. "But it was his time to go. He was sick. The good Lord took him home. Now he doesn't hurt anymore."

"I'd better call ma." The young man quietly moved away from his grandmother. Ted walked into the kitchen and picked up the receiver to the wall phone. He dialed his home phone number without even thinking about it. The phone at home rang only twice when Shirley, Ted's mother, answered it. "Ma," Ted said.

The woman knew by the sound of her son's voice what had happened. "It's over." She as much stated as asked.

"Yeah." His voice was tight. "It's over."

"I'll be there soon," the mother said.

"I'm riding my bike home," Ted said.

"Are you sure?" Shirley asked.

"Yeah, I just need to sort things out."

"All right, but tell your grandmother I'm coming by to pick her up."

"I will." Ted hung up the phone and turned to his grandmother. "Mom's coming over."

Only when mother and daughter met each other at the front door did they break down in tears. Ted looked on uncomfortably; he hated to see them cry, especially now. Of course, he understood why. And he knew that he, too, would shed tears when he was ready.

"Was he-" Shirley wasn't sure how to ask. "Was he sleeping when it happened?"

"I was in the kitchen." Laura mopped her eyes and nose with a kerchief. "Fixing lunch. I gave Teddy a bowl of soup and asked him if he'd take it to Harold and see if he felt like eating. Next thing I know, Teddy came in and told me Harold had…"

"I know, mom." Shirley gave her mother another hug. "I know. Look, why don't you come stay with us for a while? We've got plenty of room."

Ted faked a smile, attempting to lighten the mood. "Besides, you can watch Gunsmoke in color at our place."

Laura smiled sadly at the offer. "I'd like that. Just let me pack a few things and we'll go."

Shirley and Ted helped the old woman pack her suitcases. Ted loaded them in the trunk of his father's car. The women got in the front seat. "Aren't you coming with us, Teddy?" Laura asked.

"He's going to ride his bike home," Shirley said. "He'll be fine. Besides, we couldn't get him and the bike both in the backseat."

"Be careful coming home," Laura said. The VW started up and pulled away.

He called after them. "I will!" The tall, well built, brown haired youth got on his bike and pedaled to the end of the long dirt and gravel driveway. He stopped and looked around. The Bug was fading out of sight. Ted looked at his grandparents' home. A three-story house and a barn of equal size sat in the middle of more than 200 acres of prime farmland. Once it had belonged to grandpa Harold, and the five generations before him. But when neither of his daughters married farmers, and he grew too old to run the farm by himself, he sold the land to a neighbor.

Ted smiled as he remembered his granddad bragging about the hard bargain he'd drove. And Harold Blanchet had come out smelling like a rose. He and Laura spent the next two decades doing all the things they'd wanted to do when they were younger. Life had been good to them.

Then grandpa Harold developed a cough. No one thought much of it until he also started to complain of chest pains, and he normally never complained. A single word from the doctor in town brought an end to their happiness and laid a shroud upon the entire family.

Cancer.

Ted looked at the house and barn, the last remnants of six generations of farmers. Before he'd taken ill, Harold kept everything in great shape. Now the roof of the barn sagged and the paint on the house was chipped, almost as if the buildings had gotten sick, too. The first floor was where Harold and Laura had lived. The third floor, and part of the second, housed more than 120 years of heirlooms and antiques. Part of the second floor housed guest rooms.

Ted sighed. This was the very last of what he would someday call The Old Days When Grandpa Harold Was Alive. Things would soon change. Grandma would keep a few of the most treasured antiques, some would be divvied up between the surviving relatives, and the rest would be sold off. Grandma would come live with him and his parents, and the house and barn would be sold, too. Then it would all be so many memories.

Ted wanted to cry, needed to cry. But everything was too fresh, he was too numb. He'd done all he could do for the time being. Now it was time to pedal himself home.

There hadn't been a funeral in the family for nearly ten years. The last one had been for Carl Blanchet, Harold's brother. Heart attack.

Funny thing about funerals, more than one family member mentioned. It was the only occasion for which the entire family attended. But, of course, there was always one less person to show up for each one.

The funeral chapel wasn't as drab and gloomy as Ted had imagined it would be. The atmosphere was pleasant, almost welcoming, though in a subdued manner. Today was the viewing, tomorrow the funeral itself.

Ted looked around from his aisle seat in the third row as more and more family members arrived. Good natured greetings were spoken quietly as handshakes and hugs were liberally passed around. Ted was glad to see that every new visitor made a bee-line for grandma Laura as soon as they came in.

Ted turned to look straight ahead at the still form laying in the cushioned, silver-colored box before him. Grandpa looked calm and peaceful, not at all like the dying old man who gasped for air and couldn't seem to get enough painkillers into his system barely two days ago. The youth had to admit that his grandfather would be embarrassed to see all the make-up the morticians had put on him.

Ted could almost hear him. "The last damn thing I want is for people to see me for the last time looking like some kind of fruit!" Ted chuckled, but his mirth was short-lived. Even from this far back, he could see some of the veins in the old man's hands through the makeup. Thinking about what would happen to his grandpa's body after it was buried brought a lump to his throat. But still, something kept him from grieving openly.

Despite being with his family, some of whom he hadn't seen in years, Ted knew this was going to be a long two days.

Although Grandma Laura was staying with Shirley and her husband, Tim, the entire family met back at the old farm house. It was weird, Ted would later tell his friends. It no longer felt like the old family home. They could feel the absence of a presence they had always associated with the house. In fact, more than one person had mentioned, it was like being in the home of a stranger.

Still, the family made the best of it. Although Shirley tried to convince her mother to let Ted and his father go into town for pizzas,

Laura insisted she cook for everyone as this would probably be the last time she'd ever be able to.

No one said anything, but they silently agreed with Grandma Laura. She was the last living member of her generation of the Blanchet family. The next oldest members were Uncle Edgar and Aunt Ruby, both 59. Shirley and Ted trailed behind at a distant 45 and 49, respectively. Unless an unexpected illness or injury took place, the next funeral in the family would likely be hers. So Grandma Laura, with help from Shirley and Ruby, went into the kitchen and began fixing the kind of home-cooked dinner that people tend to miss so dearly when they're older and living far away from home.

Ted felt like a stranger amongst strangers. He quickly tired of watching the little ones play, so he went into the living room to sit with the men. That was almost as boring. Okay, J. Edgar Hoover just died, so what? Dad's brother, Uncle Charlie, said many times that Hoover had been behind both the Kennedy assassinations. He'd had three beers already, and he was saying it again, a little more loudly with each beer he downed. Ted's cousin Jules, who wasn't over in Vietnam because of a gunshot wound he took in the line of duty as a cop, joined in the shouting match. Ted shook his head and left the room. He knew from past experience where these political discussions always led. Ted wandered into the kitchen doorway.

Aunt Ruby spoke in conspiratorial tones. "So I told Daphne. I said, listen up. If he says he's pulling a lot of overtime, but you don't see any extra cash on Friday night, you know he's up to no good. And I'll just bet it's with that skagg that works at the Laundromat."

"I don't know." Shirley sounded doubtful. "I always thought it was Deanna from the salon."

Grandma Laura joined in. "When I was young, before I married you girls' dad, there were places menfolk went to for that sort of thing, so they wouldn't be out catting around with married women."

"Did Dad ever go to a cathouse?" Ruby dared to ask.

The old woman scoffed. "Heavens, no. I always saw to it your father never had a reason to go to those places."

"Why mama!" Shirley regarded her mother with shocked amusement. "I always thought you were such a lady!"

"And I was." Her voice became an undertone. "At least until the lights went out."

The women shared a good laugh, then shooed Ted out of the room when they heard him laughing, too. Smiling, Ted walked back into the living room, ignoring his grandma's blush. Now his cousin Jules, his father, Uncle Edgar, and Uncle Charlie were all standing up, almost in a huddle despite the slight swaying caused by the alcohol, and almost shouting at each other. Ted saw the numerous empty bottles by the sides of the couch and recliner. He shook his head. It always amazed him how four men who agreed on all things political could still argue over who was *more* right than everyone else. Ted walked around them just in time to hear Uncle Edgar virtually scream his oft-spoken opinion that Nixon should have won the '60 election against "that no-good crooked Mick bastard Kennedy."

The heat in the room suddenly felt overwhelming. Ted walked out onto the front porch. He sat on the top step, letting his mind wander. The evening air, which was mild with a slight breeze, was a welcome relief to the young man whose thoughts soared beyond the darkening horizon. A girlish voice brought him back to reality.

"Hiya Ted!" Amanda, Ted's 11 year old cousin, the closest to him in age out of all the people in the house, stood beside him. "Whatcha doing out here?"

"Thinking."

His voice must have struck a sympathetic chord with the girl, because at once she sat down quietly beside him. "What's wrong?"

"I wish I could tell you," he said. There was no air of superiority in his voice, only sadness.

"Is it true you saw grampa die?" Amanda asked. Ted nodded slowly. "Did you see his spirit go up to Heaven?"

Ted gave a low chuckle. "No, but I'm sure it did."

"You just miss him, huh?"

"Yeah. I just miss him."

The girl didn't say anything else. She sat quietly next to Ted and lay her head upon his shoulder until it was time for bed.

Again, the next day found the family gathered at the funeral home. Again, Ted found himself seated by the aisle in the third row, directly in front of the casket. And again, Ted found his eyes drawn toward his grandfather's hands. The hands that had helped him pick apples, the hands that tucked him in whenever he'd stay overnight, the hands that held his when they went to church together. Those marvelous hands. Now they were still, their veins showing more prominently through the makeup today.

People around Ted were talking, some crying, some even laughing quietly about the "good old days." Apparently, there were no hard feelings among his cousin, dad, and uncles, as they were in the latter group. For Ted, the air felt oppressive. He felt as if someone had forgotten that it was May and turned on the furnace. Grief and sorrow blended with bitter regret and a tinge of shame.

The organ began playing, and Ted felt like vomiting. The music, which was intended to sooth in a solemn fashion, sounded mockingly ghoulish. Ted shook his head. Watching someone die was an awful burden, someone had said once. Those last moments, Grandpa Harold's last moments...

Ted jumped up and quickly walked out of the chapel. He virtually ran into the men's room and retched in a stall. Afterwards, Ted cleaned off his face and pulled a stick of peppermint gum from a pocket to cover up the smell. Now his head ached from the strain of vomiting. Ignoring the throbbing sensation, Ted resumed his seat. A few people gave him sympathetic looks as he sat down.

A man stepped up to a podium that had been placed before the casket. He looked even older than Grandpa Harold had been, but moved with an ease that belied his great age. It was Pastor Samson, the Methodist minister whose church grandma and grandpa had attended since time immemorial. Despite his age, the man's voice was strong and clear and never once faltered as he delivered a heartfelt eulogy to the family of his long-time parishioner and life-long friend.

The eulogy was followed by a short sermon, after which the casket's lid was closed by one of the morticians (Grandma Laura still referred to them as 'undertakers,' a term that caused the funeral directors to grit their teeth as they tried to ignore it). Realizing that that was the last time anyone would ever see Harold Blanchet, more than a few people started mourning, only then acknowledging the finality of the family patriarch's existence.

Ted, along with his father, Uncle Edgar, cousin Jules, and two morticians, were pall bearers. Ted had five older cousins, some by blood, some by marriage, who would have helped with this task, but they were all off to war. Ted felt honored to perform this duty.

The young man was surprised at how heavy the coffin was. Grandpa Harold had been skin and bones when he died. Ted kept up his end of things, hefting the coffin as easily as his father.

The atmosphere at the cemetery seemed incongruous with the events transpiring. The coffin and the people sat underneath a heavy pavilion tent that no light could penetrate. And yet, the noontime sky was cloudless, the wind light, the air warm, and birds could be heard chirping. Outside the tent, it could have been the perfect day. Inside, under the canvas, only grief and sorrow existed.

Another Methodist minister, this one largely unknown to the gathered mourners, led the assembled people in a final prayer before concluding the service.

And then it was over. A large chapter in the family's history had ended, and a new one had begun. To Ted, and many others, it was like having an invisible limb removed. You know the wound will heal in time, but for now all the nerves were raw and tingling.

Before Ted even realized he'd left the huge tent, he was sitting in the banquet room of some ritzy restaurant, sharing a table with his parents and grandmother. It was an old place, and had probably housed thousands of get-togethers like this one. But it was clean and the servers

8

hospitable, and that's all that mattered to the majority in attendance. After this, everyone would go back to their homes and resume their lives. Some of them may not see each other for years, if ever again. After the orders were taken and the drinks served, the stories began pouring forth. Ted took a feeble sip of his soda, barely able to stay composed. To Ted, Harold Blanchet had been only his grandfather, an old man he'd loved dearly. But now, hearing all these people telling story after story, Ted began to see Harold Blanchet also as a father, a husband, a neighbor, an old friend, a business associate, and even as someone else's son a very long time ago. The young man began to view him as he would any other person, someone who had been born, lived a full, long life, and died amongst family members.

A pressure began to build within Ted. It grew, despite his attempts to hold it back. Ted began trembling, thinking he was about to explode. He wasn't even aware that his voice had spoken without his permission until the first few words were out.

"I did it!" Ted silently wished he were the one who had just been buried. "It's my fault! I-oh, God! Oh God! I did it!"

"Did what?" Shirley asked. The room had fallen absolutely silent.

"It was me," Ted said. "I k-I'm the reason we're all here today!"

"What do you mean, son?" his father asked.

"I went in to give grampa h-his lunch." The young man held his arms tight against himself as he fought to keep his voice level. "He couldn't eat. The morphine wasn't working anymore. H-he just lay there crying because of the pain. I could barely hear him, but I saw the tears running down his face. H-he said-he said he couldn't take it anymore! Grampa wanted me to help him make the pain go away. I didn't want to, I swear to God I didn't! And I told him so. But he kept begging me not to let him suffer anymore. Oh God, oh God, I couldn't stand to see him like that!" Ted took a necessary moment to compose himself before going on. "S-s-so I pulled his blanket up to his chin and kiss-kissed his forehead like he used to do with me when I stayed over with him. Then I t-t-took the pillow from the other side of the bed. He smiled at me and said I was a good boy, and I-" He lowered his voice to nearly a whisper. "I made the pain go away."

Ted lay his head down in his folded arms upon the table and sobbed bitterly. He didn't care who saw him. He didn't care what they did to him, he deserved it.

And then a wrinkled, careworn hand lay gently upon one of Ted's bobbing shoulders. He didn't look up, he couldn't bear to. After what seemed an eternity of silence, a voice almost as old as the hills spoke to him, bringing comfort to him now as it had when a thunderstorm would scare him as a little boy.

9

"When I met your grandfather," Grandma Laura said, "he was about your age now. I was just a little girl, not even ten years old. But I knew from that first day I'd make him mine. It took me seven years, but I did it. We were married on St. Patrick's day, 1912.

"So when he started asking me to end his pain for him...I couldn't. I couldn't see it as putting a sick old man out of his misery. I saw it as ending the life of that handsome, strapping young man I fell in love with when I was nine. That's why I couldn't bring myself to do it."

"I'm s-sorry, grandma." Ted whispered the words, feeling absolutely horrible.

"Don't you be sorry." The old woman gave him a slight squeeze. "I loved him enough to keep him with me. You loved him enough to let him go."

"That was a pretty big burden you took upon yourself," Ted's father said. "I don't know what I would have done if it'd been up to me. But I understand he was sick and he wasn't ever going to get better. I think it took a lot of love and courage to do what you did."

"We know it couldn't have been an easy decision, son," Shirley said. "But we want you to know that we don't hate you. Honestly, I'm not sure I agree with your decision, but we all know you loved your grandfather and you did what you thought was best for him."

Grandma Laura sat back down after giving Ted a tight hug. The room stayed silent as everyone considered what had been said. Ted was emotionally drained, but he felt as if an incredible weight had been lifted from his shoulders. Let come what may, he decided.

"I'll never forget the time he put green food coloring in with the chicken feed," Aunt Ruby said. "Remember, Shirley? Remember he told us we had magic chickens that laid green eggs, like in that Dr. Suess book?"

Shirley laughed at the memory. Ruby was old enough to know better, but Shirley had believed it.

"Remember our wedding reception, Rube?" Uncle Edgar spoke up. "He'd gotten into the bar before everyone else." His laugh came out a loud haw-haw kind of sound. "When he made the toast, he got so carried away that he had to be carried away!"

The whole room burst into laughter.

"I remember once," Grandma Laura said, "before we were even courting, he'd said something that got me mad. I forget what it was, but it fired me up something fierce. So I waited until he was in the swimming hole, and I took all his clothes and hid them. He had to walk back into town butt naked."

More laughter erupted, this louder than the last.

Ted felt himself able to enjoy the rest of the wake, even sharing some of his own memories with his family and their friends. The food was served and the camaraderie went unbroken until at last everyone parted. Some made promises to keep in touch, but most knew it wouldn't happen.

As Ted watched them leave, his parents and grandmother staying behind to pay the bill, he felt a sense of relief. Some would agree with what he did, others would not. But at least they knew. They knew his actions had been guided by merciful intentions.

Ted didn't feel ashamed anymore. He had done as his conscience, and an old man he had loved dearly, asked of him. Nothing else mattered.

The Electronic Parent

Saturday. Just the thought of that most wonderful of days made seven year old Todd Caplan antsy. The sandy-haired second grader knew that he could play all day today and tomorrow before going back to school on Monday. That's when he had to sit in Missus Booger-Brain's class.

But things were easier now that he knew his days of the week and months of the year. Now he could easily map out his life's big events. Play on weekends, school Monday through Friday, Halloween, Thanksgiving, Christmas...he had it all down pat.

And now today. He had gotten his very first report card of the year, and Missus Booger-Brain had said he was doing well in school. Now Mommy was taking him to the store to get him the new action figure made after his favorite cartoon character.

"Captain Veneer-O is really cool, mom," Todd said. "He's really neat. He's got the power to command anything made out of wood. He can even magically make wood walls.

"Yesterday on Super Avengers, Captain Veneer-O was up against Killer Kelly. He used his super powers to catch Killer Kelly in a huge wooden box. And guess what happened. Killer Kelly used *his* super powers to bust out. But you know what happened then? Captain Veneer-O lured Killer Kelly into a forest and used his super powers to make all these trees fight Killer Kelly. Then he took him to jail. But Killer Kelly's got a plan to get out. But we gotta wait until next week to find out how he does it."

"Uh-huh." Jane only half-listened to the boy as she looked for a place to park. Eventually she found an open space reasonably close to the store and pulled the station wagon in. The pair unbuckled their seat belts and got out. Todd was in such a hurry to get to the store that he almost forgot to look before running to the doors. Then he remembered what Captain Veneer-O had once said on his show.

The superhero, dressed in body armor that resembled tree bark, looked squarely at his TV audience. "So remember kids, always look both ways before crossing a street or walking through a parking lot. Sometimes drivers can't stop fast enough, and that's when disaster happens." The screen flashed briefly to a little girl lying in an ICU with tubes and IVs connecting her to several life-support machines. "Well, that's all for today." The animated soldier saluted the audience. "See you next time, and have a Woody-Good day!"

Todd looked carefully around, making sure there were no cars rushing by before walking across the asphalt aisles. Jane walked behind

12

him, pushing a cart and brushing a bit of lint from her red, two-piece outfit while she went over her shopping list. All shoes were twenty percent off today only. It was a sale she wasn't going to miss.

The two shoppers walked into the store. Todd walked faithfully by his mother's side. He knew he shouldn't go off by himself until Mommy said it was okay. Despite his anxiousness, he kept by Jane's side as they walked past the registers, the customer service desk, and further to the left where the shoe aisles were.

Todd look up at her with hopeful eyes. "Now can I go get Captain Veneer-O?"

"Yeah," Jane said. She scanned across the rows of shoe boxes, looking for her size. "But you pick out only one toy, and come right back when you're done. I don't want to have to go looking all around the store for you."

"You promise you'll be right here when I get back?" the child asked.

"Yeah, yeah." The mother tried to determine which was the better looking of the four pairs of shoes that caught her attention. "I promise."

"Okay, I'll be right back." The boy walked quickly out of the shoe department. He used to run through the store, but his grandma taught him that good boys don't run in stores. Todd headed right to his destination, walking as fast as he could.

And then he was there. Todd was now in that revered place children and adults alike gave the same name; that time-honored Mecca of childhood. He now stood in The Toy Department.

Todd wandered past the rows of pink and white boxes that contained little girls' dolls and miniature-sized versions of the clothes on sale in the girl's and women's apparel department. He knew Captain Veneer-O wouldn't be in there. Next, he saw the games aisle. Boxes of all shapes and sorts greeted his sight as he casually walked by. Nope, Captain Veneer-O wouldn't be down that way, either. The next row of shelves had all kinds of action figures. Thinking he had struck pay dirt, the little boy walked down the lane, carefully inspecting each shelf.

Finally, Todd stood before a dozen boxed clones of Captain Veneer-O himself. His eyes focused on the box nearest him. The muscular, bold-looking plastic man stood a full six inches tall. Todd marveled at how closely the toy's wood grain uniform matched the one shown on TV. An awed "Wow!" escaped his lips as he saw the plastic, wood-styled shield at the soldier's side and the small comic book tucked neatly in the package behind the action figure. Todd reverently took the Captain Veneer-O package in his hands.

Todd started to walk away when he saw something else. It was Sergeant Sheff, Captain Veneer-O's best friend and second-in-command. This action figure was just as tall and muscular as its counterpart, but the plastic man inside sported black hair, not blond like Captain Veneer-O's, and a beard. A steel-colored plastic apron and chef's hat doubled as body armor and a helmet. An over-sized meat tenderizer was Sergeant Sheff's weapon. Todd noticed a different comic book had been put in this box. Now the boy found himself in a quandary. Mommy said he could only have one toy. So which would it be? Captain Veneer-O or Sergeant Sheff?

A thought entered Todd's mind. He looked to his jacket. Could he hide the other toy in there, like he'd seen people do in grown-up shows on TV? Todd picked up the other toy and considered the option for a moment, then thought back to another episode of Super Avengers.

Captain Veneer-O walked to the center of the TV screen, a serious look on his normally cheerful face. "Hello, kids. Captain Veneer-O here to talk to you about something serious. Stealing.

"Sometimes we want things we can't have. And sometimes we want those things so much that we think about taking them without paying for them. Kind of like what happened today when Killer Kelly tried to talk Sergeant Sheff's nephew into stealing the ZK-981." The screen did a brief flashback to the villain trying to talk a teenage boy into stealing a super-powerful car. "It doesn't matter how big or small the thing is, stealing is always wrong. I don't want you to learn the hard way like Sergeant Sheff's nephew almost did. If you get caught stealing, kids, you can be taken away from your homes and put in jail for a long, long time. Sometimes months, maybe even years." The screen flashed to a sad and scared looking youth sitting in a dark cell surrounded by several large and angry prisoners who seemed about to hurt him.

The super-soldier reappeared and spoke again. "So the next time you want something you can't have right away, and you think about taking it without paying for it, be a hero and do the honest thing. Remember, it's better to wait until you can buy something than it is to risk going to jail by stealing it.

"That's all for today, kids." Captain Veneer-O saluted the audience. "See you next time, and have a Woody-Good day!"

Todd carefully put Sergeant Sheff back on the shelf. He would be a hero like Captain Veneer-O and Sergeant Sheff. The boy proudly marched right back to the shoe department, content that he had made the right choice.

Todd walked to the women's shoe section. A look of mild confusion crossed his face when he noticed his mother wasn't there. He shrugged and walked to the men's and boy's shoes section. No Mommy. Now he began to wrack his brain, trying to think of where Mommy could be. Todd walked quickly to the women's apparel department and anxiously scanned around the various racks. Again, no Mommy.

Todd looked around and almost cried out for joy when he noticed someone in a red outfit turn a corner to go into the jewelry department. He remembered that Mommy had been wearing a red outfit. Todd chased after the cart-pushing figure as fast as he could without running. He rounded one corner to find his quarry had just turned another. Todd was persistent, however. He kept after the red-clad woman until he finally caught up with her. "I found Captain Veneer-O, mom!" He looked cheerfully at the woman's back.

A lady easily old enough to be Todd's grandmother turned around and looked down at the him. "I'm afraid I'm not your mother, little boy."

Todd's jaw dropped. He muttered a quick "sorry" and went back to the shoe department. Maybe she went back there, he thought. One more scan of the area told him she wasn't there. It also told him something that terrified him.

Todd was lost.

Todd's legs began to tremble, and he began to see everything in a different manner. Instead of being in a friendly place where Captain Veneer-O was waiting for him, the boy had gotten lost in a strange place where strangers congregated. The lights now seemed harsh and glaring, the Muzak coming in over the PA seemed loud and shrill. Todd's breathing became faster as his whole body now shook. People were milling about the store, and it dawned on the boy that there was no one around to protect him in case a stranger came up to him. He felt helpless and defenseless. Baffled as to what to do next, Todd sat down on one of the stools grown-ups used to try on shoes and started to cry.

After a few moments, someone in red walked up to him. Todd got the feeling he was being watched. He looked up, hoping for an instant that it was Mommy.

It was the old woman from the jewelry department. "Are you lost, little boy?"

Todd's mind whirled instantly to last week's episode.

"Hey kids, Captain Veneer-O here. In today's show we saw Sergeant Sheff reunited with his long-lost son. Joshua was kidnapped by the Keeper, one of Killer Kelly's henchmen." The screen flashed momentarily to a young lad about Todd's age with black hair, getting into a car with an evil looking stranger. *"We got him back, thank goodness, but most kids aren't that lucky. Now, not all strangers are bad people, but it might be too late before you find out. In the real world, most kids who are kidnapped are never seen again. Don't let this happen to you. If you're not sure about an adult you don't know, don't panic, but get away from them and find an adult you can trust and tell them about it.*

"That's all for today, kids." The wood-camouflaged super-soldier smiled and gave his customary salute. *"See you next time, and have a Woody-Good day!"*

Todd hopped off the stool and backed away toward the end of the aisle. "I don't talk to strangers, lady." He darted off, leaving the old woman bewildered and a bit confused.

Without a clue as to what to do next, Todd decided to reconnoiter in the Toy Department. He was pleased with himself for learning that word, reconnoiter. Captain Veneer-O and Sergeant Sheff used it quite a bit. The feeling of taking charge of his situation brought a comforting amount of relief to the lost boy. Todd marched back to where he had found his hero and began to think constructively. He had looked everywhere he thought Mommy might be, and she wasn't in any of those places. Now what? Captain Veneer-O had said that after being approached by a stranger, kids should find an adult they trust and tell them. But who was there to trust in this big, strange place?

"Hi, kids!" Captain Veneer-O's voice was a cheery as ever. *"Remember when Sergeant Sheff's son, Joshua, got lost in the amusement park today? He couldn't find his father or me, so he went up to someone who worked at the park and explained the problem."* The screen revealed the boy speaking to a park employee, then went back to the superhero.

"If you ever get lost or separated from your friends or family in a big place, whether it's an amusement park, a mall, or somewhere else, just stay calm. You won't solve anything by getting upset. Calmly go to a policeman, a security guard, or other employee and tell them what's wrong. Most employees wear a vest or something that marks them as an employee, kind of like a soldier's uniform lets you know he's in the army. Before you know it, you'll be back among familiar faces.

"That's all for today, kids." Again the salute. *"See you next time and have a Woody-Good day!"*

Todd smiled. Now he knew what to do. It was so simple. He would find someone who works here and tell them he's lost. Todd stepped bravely out into the main aisle and looked around. All the people who worked here wore bright red vests. They shouldn't be hard to spot.

A short, thin man came walking out from the rear of the store about then. His brown bangs almost completely covered his thick glasses. Todd eyed him for a moment. Red vest? Yep. He's an employee, the boy decided. He confidently marched up to the man.

"Can I help you?" the man asked.

"Yep," Todd said. "I'm lost and I need you to help me find my Mommy."

The man smiled. "Sure, kid. Come with me, I'll take you up front."

The pair walked briskly to the customer service desk. A chubby, dark haired young woman looking about nineteen leaned over the desk to the approaching pair. "What have we here?" She smiled at Todd.

"I believe this young man's mother is lost." The man spoke in all seriousness.

"I see," the girl said. She went along with it for the sake of the boy's feelings. "Well, we'll have to find her, won't we? Can't have any parents going off without their kids. What's your mother's name?"

"Jane Caplan."

"And what's your name?"

"Todd Caplan."

"Okay, I'll get right on it." The girl got on the PA. "Would Jane Caplan...Jane Caplan...come to the customer service desk, please? Your son is waiting for you." She turned to Todd. "It won't be long now." She held out a small wicker basket. "Want a sucker while you wait?"

"Yes, thank you." Todd perused the basket until he found a grape sucker. Todd unwrapped the candy end and threw the paper in a nearby trash can.

"Tracy," the man said, "I gotta finish stocking housewares."

"Okay. Everything's under control now, right?" The girl looked to Todd.

"Right," he said.

"Well, good luck to you, kid." The man waved to the boy as he walked away. Todd waved back.

"Thank you," the boy said.

Todd and Tracy stood there calmly for a few moments. The young woman began to worry that Todd might be getting nervous, and again went on the PA and repeated her call for Jane Caplan. "She probably just didn't hear it the first time."

"No problem."

A few more minutes passed. Another woman, this one red haired, taller and thinner, looking about thirty, and wearing a stiff-collared blue shirt, walked to the customer service desk. "I heard you call for Jane Caplan twice."

"Mary," Tracy whispered, "I've been calling for this woman the last five minutes and so far nothing. She had to have heard me."

The manager sighed, exasperated and concerned for the little boy. She was also all too familiar with lackadaisical parents. "Try again." Her voice was barely above a whisper. "If the mother doesn't respond this time, we'll have to take other measures."

Tracy nodded. They had been forced to "take other measures" twice in the six months she had been working here. The girl hoped today wouldn't be number three. In both previous circumstances, the police had successfully reunited the lost parents with their kids. But it was seeing the look of shock, fear, and grief etched upon their little faces that she couldn't stand. "Would Jane Caplan...Jane Caplan...come to the customer service desk. I repeat, would Jane Caplan...Jane Caplan...come to the customer service desk. Your son is waiting for you." Tracy put the mike down and looked at Todd. "Want another sucker?"

"No, thank you." The white stick, all that remained of his lollipop, rested in the trash can, close to its wrapper.

"What now?" Tracy asked.

Mary shook her head. "I guess we'll go ahead and-"

"There you are!" Jane sounded impatient as she strolled behind her cart to the customer service desk. "I've been looking all over this store for you."

"I went right back to the shoes, just like I promised."

"Oh." The mother's voice tightened. "Well, I got to talking with an old friend, and the next thing I know we're in the furniture department."

"But you promised to wait for me."

"All right. That's enough from you." She led him away from the desk. "Let's go."

Todd followed behind his mother, taking care to wave good-bye to Tracy and Mary. Both of them waved back. Jane looked back to see the two women giving her stern, disapproving glares. She turned back around and hustled the two of them through the checkout line. Todd obediently followed Jane out of the store and through the parking lot to the blue station wagon. Jane virtually threw their packages in the back of the vehicle, then Todd pushed the cart back to the corral. After that, the two got in the wagon and drove off.

"Well I hope you're happy," Jane said. "Now I can't ever go back in there again for all the embarrassment you caused me."

Todd held his ground. "You promised you'd wait for me."

Jane turned to face him and nearly ran a red light. "I'm your mother! I don't have to keep promises! Besides, promises to kids don't count. And I'll go anywhere in a store I want. So don't give me any more of your lip!"

The boy decided to change the subject to keep from getting into any more trouble. "Thanks for buying Captain Veneer-O for me."

"I don't know why I give in to you." She sighed hotly. "All that stupid show is good for is putting bad ideas in your head."

Todd kept silent. It seemed his best option for the time being. The boy let his gaze wander out the window. Cars and buildings whizzed by in an almost hypnotic manner. Soon, Todd's mind began to wander as well.

"Hello kids!" Captain Veneer-O faced his audience. "I want to talk to you about promises.

"When you make a promise, it's like asking someone to trust you. When you break a promise, you risk breaking the trust they place in you. And that can create bad feelings between people and destroy friendships.

"So remember not to make promises if you can't keep them. And if you do make a promise, always try your best to keep it.

"Until next time, be safe and have a Woody-Good day!"

Todd looked over at Jane. She was calm, but still pointedly ignored him. The boy quietly sighed. Maybe Mommy should start watching Captain Veneer-O, too.

Two Good Days

August 11, 1999.

The wonders of modern technology were lost upon Lester Quincy as he slowly awoke to the nerve-grating beeps of his alarm clock. Unlike similar devices he had owned in the past, the clock he awoke to now only allowed seven minutes of soul-nourishing sleep between hard slaps on the snooze button. The others had given a generous nine or ten. A trifling matter to be sure for someone wide awake and halfway through their day, but to a person determined to put off the inevitable for as long as possible, those extra minutes can seriously alter their outlook for the day. The trade-off was that the clock had a weather band in its radio. In all, Lester thought it a great deal for twenty-five bucks.

Lester shut off the alarm and sat up, reaching for his lighter and a pack of smokes. The clock read three-fourteen in the morning. He lit up his cigarette and indulged in his morning hack before getting up. By three-forty, Lester was showered, dressed, shaved, and sipping a mug of hot, black coffee while watching TV.

Lester sighed as he acknowledged the local weather forecast. While the outside world would be forced to endure a warm, sunny day with a mild breeze, he would enjoy another day in the hot, drab factory driving a forklift. Lester could envision himself riding proudly before his co-workers and hear his foreman call him on the lift's radio and say inspirational things like, "I don't give a damn how slow your truck is, I can't spare anyone to help you. Sam and Max are on vacation so you'll have to cover their jobs and do your own, too. Now get your ass in gear and get busy!"

Then Lester pictured the wonderful homecoming he would receive. His darling wife of almost two years, Betsy, might even be awake by the time he got home. Lester's mind conjured the image of his bride sitting in front of the TV in her nightgown, her curly, tumbleweed-style hair looking reminiscent of Larry Fine, while she sucked on a cigarette and slurped her coffee. He could almost sense the goosebumps on his arms when he tried to anticipate what she might say to him when he walked in.

"My horoscope said it's a bad week for me to look for a job. Piss on the bills, you'll just have to work more overtime. Why don't you spend more time at home? If you want dinner, you'll have to go to the store and get something. I forgot to do dishes, so if you want a clean plate, you'll have to wash one. Don't snap at me about the laundry! You still got a clean shirt left, and those pants'll be okay for another couple days! And no, I'm not in the mood for *that* tonight, either. So it's been five months? I went without it once for two years. As long as your hands work, you'll be fine." These were among the many things Lester was likely to hear.

And then there were Lester's step-children, twelve year old Ralph and eight year old Jason. Ralph was practically an honor student, according to Betsy. He had failed only two classes last school year instead of his usual four. And Jason, Betsy assured everyone, would surely be a mechanic or a repairman someday. Already the little darling had mastered the art of taking things apart. Now it was just a matter of teaching him how to put those things back together again. Lester belched with joy at the thought of replacing whatever the little monster chose to demolish today. He set his empty mug down and sighed.

Life was too good.

By ten after four, Lester was sitting in the factory's main cafeteria. His shift didn't start until five, but he really didn't care. He wanted to be away from the apartment as much as possible, even eating his meals at the plant whenever he could.

Breakfast usually consisted of whatever could be gotten out of the vending machines. Today it was some sort of sponge cake delicacy replete with stale icing and pebble-hard, multi-colored sprinkles on top with a can of cola. A real breakfast, however much he craved one, was out of the question. Lester needed as much cash as he could spare to pay off the astronomical electric bill he had been sent last week.

Apparently it had gotten too chilly in the apartment for Ralph, who had taken it upon himself to open his window all the way to let the cold air out. Lester had worked double shifts the last few months and had no idea that the central air had been running for eleven days straight. When confronted about the bill, Betsy only shrugged and said she also was unaware that the air conditioning never shut off until the day the motor burned up. The apartment had been sweltering since.

Lester finished his breakfast and took a pill for his ulcer before throwing the snack wrapper away. He knew he couldn't hide his potbelly, but he hated for people to watch him eat. Just as the incriminating evidence disappeared into a large yellow trash can, one of the cafeteria doors opened and Sandy Rae walked in.

Her shapely figure and boyishly cut brown hair had turned many heads, Lester's included. But what captivated him the most was her wide, wholesome smile and dark, almond-shaped eyes. The two of them had become fast friends in the three months they had known each other, and they felt comfortable just being in each other's presence.

Lately, however, the conversations had gotten more personal, and Lester began feeling tense around Sandy Rae. He had several friends at work who were women, and attractive ones at that. But Lester realized he was beginning to enjoy Sandy Rae's company a little *too* much.

21

"Hey, Lezzie." The young woman seemed to enjoy watching his expression when she used her nickname for him. "Still eating junk food for breakfast?"

Lester shrugged and smiled sheepishly. "Gotta have my sugar rush."

"Keep it up." She wagged her index finger at him. "One of these days you'll be chasing those stomach pills with insulin."

"I'm a shoo-in for it anyway," he replied. "Half my family's got it. No reason not to indulge myself before the axe falls."

"Speaking of indulging yourself." Sandy Rae tapped the table with her index finger. "When are we going to get together after work? We've been talking about it for two weeks now, and you keep stalling me."

"I'm tapped out." Lester's eyes were fixed upon the tab atop the soda can.

"I remember you telling me about the light bill." She nodded slowly. "Forget about it already, it'll be my treat." Lester frowned. Sandy's voice lowered. "Don't you want to be with me?"

His eyes locked onto hers. "More than anything else I can think of."

"It's Betsy, then." He didn't respond. "Look Les, if your marriage had any chance of surviving, I wouldn't be making the offer. But you said yourself that she's a slob, she's lazy, and she doesn't care about her own kids unless it looks like the juvenile authorities are about to be called on her." She paused, letting out a deep breath. "I know you're not the kind to go back on your vows on a whim, and I respect you for that. I really do. But there comes a time when you have to stop and think about what's right for *you*. Betsy doesn't care. I do." Her hand drifted close to his.

"Sounds like you're talking about more than dinner and a walk in the park." Lester smiled.

Sandy Rae smiled in return. "I keep a clean house, a good attitude, and a thrifty budget. What goes on between you and Betsy behind closed doors is your business, but from the way you describe her, I'll bet I can match whatever she can offer. A man can't ask for much better, you know."

Lester's smile widened. "You're such a temptress."

"I know. Look, I know it's a lot to swallow all at once. Think about it and we'll talk over lunch." She patted his hand.

"We certainly will." He gave her a thoughtful smile.

They stood up and left the table at ten till five. Sandy Rae headed toward the assembly line while Lester walked in the direction of his forklift.

It turned out to be an otherwise typical day. While Lester's body worked on autopilot, his mind acted independently as he pondered which

22

direction his life should travel. It was no big change of venue for him. Lester learned years ago that the less he thought about work, the smoother it went.

True, life with Betsy left a lot to be desired, and the life Sandy Rae proposed was quite desirable. But there were other things to consider. Lester was twenty-eight years old, and might well live at least another forty. Did he really want to spend those years with someone who honestly didn't care about anyone, even herself? The thought of leaving Betsy was nothing new; he had considered it many times. And he knew he very desperately wanted to be with Sandy Rae. But were his desires clouding his judgment? Lester could accept divorcing Betsy on the basis of a hopeless marriage. He could *not* accept simply leaving one woman for another. That made him feel shallow and cheap. Deep down inside, Lester knew the choice his conscience would dictate, the only choice he could live with.

In the end, Lester Quincy decided that too much introspection, no matter how it cleared his conscience, always seemed to screw up his life…

Lester closed the apartment door behind him. It had taken him less than ten minutes to get home. He regarded the sink full of dirty dishes with an absent expression. It was twenty till three and Betsy was still in bed. Lester would have shrugged his indifference, but considered even that a waste of energy. He filled the sink with hot, soapy water, thinking about the "shape up or ship out" speech he had planned. Lester failed to notice Ralph and Jason standing nearby until they spoke up.

"There was a man in here today." Jason's voice was solemn.

"Shut up!" Ralph hit his younger brother on the arm. "Mom said not to tell!"

The boys turn to Lester, who didn't even look at them. The man simply bowed his head and started laughing.

Yes, too much introspection.

August 11, 2000.

Lester sat at the break table, absently munching on a carrot between long swallows from the bottle of ice water he'd brought with him from home. The man took another mouthful of water, thinking about the last twelve months. His marriage had come to a bitter end, and at the same time he had lost the woman he loved. Lester swore it would not be for nothing. Something good would come from all of it.

There were times he thought he'd lose his mind, but Lester managed to quit smoking. He then transferred to the assembly line on nights so he could take exercise courses during the day. Changing his diet was another big shock to his system, but it became easier once he began to see the results of his new lifestyle. Altogether, he kept a tight schedule, if a lonely one.

Lester no sooner shoved the unwelcome thought out of his mind when the door to the break room opened. His face broke into a smile. "Sandy Rae! Didn't think I'd ever see you again. You're on nights now?"

"Just transferred last week." She looked down at the table as she took her seat across from him. Her expression brightened. "I see you're not trying to commit sugar-cide anymore. Carrots and water? Planets must be out of alignment."

"Smart ass." Lester was unable to hide his smile. "My divorce was finalized six months ago."

"Good." She sounded strangely uncomfortable. "Nobody deserves to be treated the way Betsy treated you." She paused, averting her eyes momentarily. "Look, I want to apologize for any hard feelings. I've never been one to take rejection well, but you were right. Giving your marriage one last try was the honorable thing to do. I'm sorry it ended the way it did."

"So am I." He blew the thought away with a deep breath. "Well, now that I'm single again, what do you think about picking up where we left off? We have a lot of catching up to do."

Sandy Rae smiled sadly. "Yes, we do. And I'd like to get to know you again. Especially this new you."

"But only as a friend," Lester said. He knew that look on her face. Something was up.

The woman nodded and held out her left hand, revealing an enviable wedding ring and matching gold band. "Stan and I got married three months ago."

"I see." His voice was even. "Did you two know each other long?"

"We met the day you and I had our talk," Sandy Rae said.

"Lovely." Lester's voice was flat and emotionless. "Thank you for sharing that last detail. It's not like haven't punished myself already."

"You shouldn't punish yourself at all," she countered. "You did the right thing. I should have waited for you, but I didn't. I was angry and when Stan asked me out, I thought it would be a good thing to put you behind me. He's really a decent guy, you know. You'd like him."

"You bet," he said. "He moves in and steals away a woman I loved. Sure makes me want to embrace him with open arms."

"I'm sorry you feel that way." Sandy Rae stood up. "Can we at least be friends?"

Lester frowned. It wasn't his style to be a sore loser. And he had to admit, he still cared for her. "Sure." He smiled. "I'd rather have you as a friend than not have you at all."

Sandy Rae blinked in astonishment. Stan was a wonderful husband, but she couldn't picture even him taking such a situation so easily, much less be so forgiving. "You're one of a kind, you know. Betsy was so stupid not to see what she had."

Lester laughed. "I agree. But that's her loss, and I'm in no big hurry to find a replacement. We'll talk some more on next break."

"I'd like that." Her voice was sincere. They left the break room and walked their separate ways.

Lester walked toward his job, his mind lost in reflection. He didn't have a wife anymore. Now the woman he loved was married to another man. His frown deepened.

After another moment of reflection, Lester held his head up. For all that he had lost, he had walked away with still more. Sandy Rae would always be a true friend. Lester could sleep with a clear conscience, confident that he had proven to himself and those close to him that he was indeed a respectable and honorable man. He had done right by everyone around him, including himself.

Lester Quincy smiled.

Life was good.

Thirty-Minute Century

1991.

Lilah Bloom stood before twenty-three impassive faces. It was six in the evening on a sunny, mild, Friday night in late April. Nobody wanted to be in the Creative Writing class at the St. Louis Community College's South County Branch tonight, including herself. Lilah would have preferred being at her Tealbrook Estates home, skinny-dipping with her husband in their indoor pool. Their twenty-fifth anniversary was coming up, and, outside of a few gray hairs, Hubby looked much the same as he did at twenty-six. She sighed and spoke to the college students.

"I don't want to be here, either," Bloom said. "But it's only for an hour, so let's get started."

Brandon Pierce sat, as usual, in the back of the class. His head invariably turned to look through the window behind him. It had been a long winter, and the twenty year old was happy to see another spring in bloom. The agreeable weather was a welcome change from the drab, dreary winter months.

Bloom saw his turned head and felt herself longing for the outdoors as well. An idea came to her and she decided to mix business and pleasure. "Today," the teacher said, "we're going to work on focusing our imaginations upon a specific location, but at various periods of time. Turn your desks around and face outside. Take a look at the street corner and think about how it might have looked a hundred years ago."

The entire class shuffled their desks around. Now Brandon had a prime seat. He saw the remnants of rush hour traffic scurrying like ants along the road, along the infinite stone path that bound civilization together.

"You have ten minutes to write a description of what you see." Bloom adjusted her stopwatch. "Starting...now."

Brandon's pen lay upon the notebook, seeming to move of it's own accord as he wrote.

1891.

Charles Taft looked out amongst the crowd of curious spectators. The eyes of the tall, thin, dark-haired man darted now and again to an odd, almost sleigh-like object covered by a thick burlap curtain. Taft let the gathered folk chatter a moment longer, allowing them to whet their appetites for the unknown as he absently twirled his handlebar mustache. He then cleared his throat and began to speak in a clear, resonating voice.

26

"Ladies and gentlemen," Taft said, "as the nineteenth century comes to a close, we now stand upon the threshold of a brave new era…the era of advanced technology.

"Therefore, it is my utmost pleasure to present to you the latest addition to American technological advances." He grabbed a corner of the curtain and prepared to pull it off the new invention. I proudly present to you today the horseless carriage, also known as the 'automobile'."

Taft yanked the curtain away, revealing the first car introduced to the St. Louis area. The tall man smiled proudly as the crowd went wild with cheering, applause, and sighs of awe. It was one of the proudest moments of the thirty-two year old man's life.

1991.

"All right class," Bloom said. "Time's up." The pens and pencils stopped moving. A couple students kept writing, finishing incomplete sentences. At last they, too, stopped and the room became quiet. It was then Brandon realized that he hadn't the foggiest idea when or where exactly the first car had been shown in St. Louis, but it seemed a good idea to build from, so he decided to stay with it. Bloom spoke again. "Now picture the same street corner fifty years later. Think about the social and scientific changes that have occurred in that time. Picture it as history with the fast-forward button on." She paused for a moment to reset her stopwatch. "Now mentally put time in normal play mode and start writing…now."

1941.

Charles Taft sat at the bus stop, waiting for the number nine to come along and take him home. His eyes moved to a plaque by the bench. It had been fifty years…fifty years ago today, in fact…since he had introduced the first automobile to the people of St. Louis.

His mind wandered back. As a small boy, he had seen his uncle and oldest brother go off to fight for the Confederate army. During the Reconstruction era, thousands had passed through the city on their way to the West. Some years later, he had been asked to demonstrate the city's first motor car.

Taft twirled his snowy-white mustache, still styled in the handlebar fashion, smiling as he remembered seeing moving pictures for the first time. He frowned when he thought back to the World War and how many patriotic St. Louisans of German heritage suddenly became outcasts. The grimace deepened as he thought of the second war being fought now in Europe. Taft knew the United States would end up getting involved. He didn't see how it could be avoided.

The spry eighty-two year old sighed and stood up as his bus arrived. He lingered a moment to look at the plaque with his name etched upon it. Taft had seen a great deal of St. Louis' history and, God willing, would be around to see a lot more.

1991.
"Pencils down," Bloom said. "I hope you're all being very imaginative. I'd like to pass out a lot of A's today. Now think about what could be happening on our street corner today. Again, put history in fast-forward. All of you should be able to connect with something that's happened here within the last few years. If you can't, then just make something up."

An excessively loud car passed by outside, disrupting Brandon's concentration. Some moron in a late model Camaro obviously didn't believe in either mufflers or volume control knobs for his radio. Brandon's delay didn't last long. He grinned fiendishly, thinking of an appropriate method of revenge for the nuisance outside. The young man was ready for the last chapter.

Bloom cleared her throat and reset her stopwatch. "Go," she said.

Right outside, 1991.
Friday nights always seemed to draw out the urban wildlife like moths to a light bulb. Tonight's ten-minute celebrity was a nineteen year-old in his Camaro. He was drunk and being chased by three police officers in a seventy mile-per-hour pursuit. Just as the intoxicated driver thought he might actually outdistance the cops, a fourth patrol car pulled into an intersection, heading him off. The teen swerved wildly to escape collision and capture. He lost control of his car, slamming violently into a concrete barrier. The chase was over.

An article in the next day's Post Dispatch's 'Strange But True' column read, "A high-speed chase by St. Louis county police late last night ended in a fatal crash, also destroying a local landmark.

"A plaque dedicated to Charles Taft marking the spot on Halls-Ferry road where he had introduced St. Louis' first automobile one hundred years ago today was demolished last night when a 1989 Camaro, driven by nineteen year old Ronald Taft Jr., the great-great-great grandson of Charles Taft crashed into the monument. Ronald Taft Jr. was pronounced dead at the scene. Charles Taft died in 1967, at the age of 108."

Back in the classroom, 1991.
"Okay," Bloom said. "Turn your desks around and hand your papers forward. If you're not done, don't worry. I'm only grading what you've completed. I don't have anything else for you today, so class is dismissed. Have a great weekend."

Brandon was in his car five minutes later. He wasn't really concerned about his project. The student figured Mrs. Bloom would give him at least a 'B' on his paper. Brandon pulled to the end of the parking lot and stopped at a red sign, preparing to make a right turn to get into traffic. He looked left, watching some cars pass by. His eyes moved toward the spot where his fictitious plaque had been. Brandon smiled, reflecting briefly upon how far he had traveled in thirty short minutes. An opening in traffic came, and Brandon drove off, feeling his own world had been enriched by his journey.

Where Do You Get Your Ideas From?

Donna's eyes rolled over the last paragraph of the paperback novel she held. The book was a suspense story, the plot of which revolved around a faceless assassin who seemed to always evade capture and eliminate his rivals. So engrossed was she in the tale that the 38 year old woman was barely aware of the number of pages and minutes that had gone by.

Robert, her 35 year old brother, sat at his computer desk at the other end of his living room, typing steadily as he composed the sequel to the book his sister read. Every so often, the author would sneak a glance over his shoulder at Donna, gauging his success by her expressions as she read. Robert could see she was nearing the end, and his glances came more often. By the time she'd gotten to the last page, the writer made no pretense of working; he had to see the look on her face when she finished the book. He wasn't disappointed when her face suddenly sagged. Donna re-read the last two sentences, then set the book down. She regarded him with a shocked, helpless look.

"How could you do that?" Donna asked. "How could you let him get away? He murdered those nice people and burned down that school!"

Robert shrugged and smiled at his sister's response. "As long as people want to keep reading about his atrocities, I'll keep writing books about him. But don't worry, I'm going to shed a little light on his past in the next book."

"Like what?" the older woman asked. Her voice was giddy, her eager expression matched that of a schoolgirl's.

His devious grin seemed to border on evil. "Like he's reunited with his father who abused him as a boy."

"You gotta let me read it before you send it off!" Donna practically begged.

Robert's green eyes, which were identical to his sister's, verily gleamed with unspoken delight. He'd kept his sister spellbound with his stories for more than twenty years. It was a skill he had nourished faithfully and steadily since childhood, and he had learned at a young age that his sister was something of a weather vane for his career. If she liked something he wrote, it usually sold well. Of course, he liked just being able to keep her entertained, but it was uncanny how well Donna could judge the marketplace.

"You know, sis," Robert said, "you might want to get into writing yourself. You used to write a little in high school. Why don't you start up again?"

"Oh, come on." She waved a hand at him in a dismissing manner. "What would I write about?"

"Anything that comes to mind," Robert said. "The more you practice, the better you'll get."

"But where do you get your ideas?" Donna asked.

Robert gave her a quirky grin. "I pick them up three for a buck at the dollar store."

"No, really," the brown haired woman asked. "I keep asking you and you keep shying me away. Now I want to know, how do you come up with this stuff?"

The author's expression became serious. "You really want to know? I'll tell you, if you promise me you'll try to write something."

"I promise," she said quickly.

"This is important now," Robert reminded her. "This is something that separates writers from most other people. If I tell you, you have to try to use it."

"Okay, okay," Donna said. Her head bobbed with agreement. "What's the secret?"

"First," Robert said, "it's not a secret. It's just a trait found in all types of artists, whether they're literary artists, painters, sculptors, photographers, or what have you.

"We take notice of what's around us. Like news stories, old local legends, even the little things that happen right in front of our eyes. We pick up what other people miss and call attention to it. Our creativity only comes into play when we work these things into our projects."

"So it's just a matter of taking what I see and putting it on paper with my own spin to it?" Donna asked.

Robert nodded. "In a basic sense, yes. I mean, there's a lot of tricks of the trade that we authors use in the process of cranking out stories, but those can be learned along the way. The main thing is to look around, see what's there, then imagine how you want to tell it to your audience."

Donna nodded. "I think I see what you're getting at." She looked up at the clock. "Oh geez, it's noon! I was supposed to meet Dan downtown at ten-thirty! I gotta go! Thanks for your help. I'll do like you asked."

"Good luck!" The freckled, brown-haired man called after his sister as she shut the front door behind her on her way to her car.

Donna got in her Cavalier and backed out of the driveway. She drove quickly through the maze of suburban streets of Webster Groves, heading for Interstate 44. Once on the freeway, Donna quickly navigated her way into downtown St. Louis. Her 1990 Cavalier chugged faithfully along as she hunted down a parking spot. She found one in a lot that charged five bucks for all-day parking. It wasn't as close to the Gateway Arch as she would have liked, but she was late anyway, so what difference did it make?

Donna had agreed to meet Dan on the green beneath the arch that morning. She'd made the poor guy wait a month before agreeing to go out with him, and she was the kind of person who didn't make dates without intending to keep them. Her guilty conscience urged her to walk a little faster.

Donna wasn't surprised when she reached the grassy area between the twin arch legs and didn't see her friend. She decided to hang around for a bit anyway, just in case he was trying to find a phone to call her from. Since she was wearing nothing more fancy than sandals, faded blue jeans, and a T-shirt, Donna thought nothing of plopping down on the emerald grass and gazing up into the sky. The apex of the arch seemed like a single, thin metal strip against a field of azure. It seemed amazing that the thing had remained intact for nearly forty years.

Although the Gateway Arch had been completed in 1965 and rose 630 feet in height, it had stood uncompleted for a while after its initial construction. It was originally intended to be a commemorative to the city's 200th anniversary, but missed its completion deadline by only a matter of months. In all honesty, most St. Louisans probably couldn't have cared less. They were probably happy just to see it finished.

I remember when the city used to have a summertime festival called the Veiled Prophet parade. It was a big event that drew in crowds that always numbered in the hundreds of thousands. Back in 1985, the attendance reached three-quarters of a million people. Who was it that told me about these two guys in a private airplane that tried to put on a show for the crowd? The pilot flew between the legs of the arch and did a loop-de-loop. After that, the plane went higher up in the air and the passenger parachuted out and landed on top of the arch. Everything was fine until the wind caught the chute and dragged the poor guy down one of the legs of the arch. Made a hell of a mess when he hit the concrete base, Donna remembered.

Donna looked around. No Dan. Now she felt bad. He'd probably gotten his feelings hurt because she'd failed to show. The woman looked at her watch. Ten after one. "Better head back home and call Dan," she muttered.

The woman stood up and took in a lungful of warm May riverfront air. It was really too bad she'd missed Dan, this would have been a fine moment to share with a friend. Donna shrugged. She would apologize, explain what happened, and let come what may. That was all she could do.

By the time she had resolved herself to her chosen course of action, Donna was heading back down I-44. She saw a bank on the left side of one of the roads that crossed under the interstate.

Once, back in 1992, there were a couple guys who tried to rob the place after hours. They backed their pick-up truck to an ATM standing apart from the bank and wrapped a thick towing chain around it. Both the bandits made faces into the camera, unafraid of a machine they were about to wreck. They got back into their truck and gunned the engine. The ATM was ripped completely from its foundation. The thieves stopped the truck, got out, loaded the ATM into the back of the truck, and drove off into the night.

It was estimated the next day that they had gotten away with more than $40K. But the robbers had made one small mistake. They had destroyed the video camera in the ATM, but had forgotten that the VCR it was wired to was safely inside the bank. That error cost them the ball game; both men were caught within 72 hours. The machine, or what was left of it, had been located, but the money was never recovered. Everyone just assumed the money was waiting on the first one of the pair to get his hands on it as soon as he got out on parole.

Donna passed through Crestwood, Sunset Hills, Fenton, and Valley Park. She thought of turning off on Antire Road to head for home, but decided to keep going and visit her mother in Pacific. So she stayed on the interstate.

Times Beach came up soon enough. A sad expression crossed Donna's face. Once it had been home to some of her childhood friends. Now it was literally a ghost town.

The streets of Times Beach had been left unpaved until the early 70's. The guy who got the contract to do the paving used some substandard variety of asphalt. The stuff contained a substance called dioxin. No one thought anything of it until ten years later. People in the prime of their lives were dying of cancer and other fatal ailments; the number of miscarriages, stillbirths, and children born with various deformities was too high to ignore. The problem was eventually linked to the dioxin in the pavement of their roads. Charges would have been brought against the contractor, had he still lived. Apparently he, too, had died as a result of being in constant, prolonged contact with the substance. Plans were being made to dig up the old pavement and lay down newer, non-toxic asphalt. But before anything could be done, an even greater disaster struck.

On the evening of Saturday, December 4th, 1982, one of the most violent thunderstorms in the area's history struck. Tornadoes dropped from the black skies with almost the same frequency as raindrops. Lightning sparked numerous fires and hail battered everything that hadn't been blown away. But the worst element of that particular storm was the rain. It fell in sheets, flooding all the low-lying areas. Towns up in the hills like High Ridge had been spared the brunt of that disaster, but Times Beach, being both in a valley and resting alongside a river, was completely washed out.

Eventually, the waters receded. That was when the full extent of the disaster was realized. The government wouldn't allow anyone to go back into their homes for any reason. The National Guard had been called out to ensure no one would defy the order. The dioxin had been washed downstream to plague God-knows-who-else, and the former residents of Times Beach, Missouri, were waiting on their shares of a settlement from the government. The money never came. Meanwhile, families who had no one to turn to often resorted to living in lean-to's, hunters' shacks, cars, anything they could find for shelter. Over the following ten years, many of them would die from their exposure to dioxin. The government refused to pay even the medical bills.

In 1988, the government decided to clean up what was left of Times Beach by building a huge incinerator and burning the tainted asphalt. Environmentalists across the country went berzerk at the idea of dioxin being released into the atmosphere. But again, Uncle Sam got his way. The asphalt was burned.

Donna turned off of I-44 and ended up on the main road of Pacific. She drove a couple miles and then turned off into the entrance of the trailer court her mother lived in. Donna chuckled when she remembered the reaction from the manager of the place when he first heard her call the place a trailer court. He had sharply reprimanded her and said that it was a "mobile home community." Donna hadn't been impressed by his bravado and flatly reminded him that when she was growing up they were called trailer courts and that she would continue to call them such for as long as it pleased her. The manager hadn't spoken to her since, which was just fine by her.

Donna putted past lot number 30, her mother's lot. No car. Then she remembered that it was Saturday and her mother was probably out with her pals at the bingo halls. Donna pulled in the driveway and stopped her engine. She got out and let herself in her mother's home with her copy of the house key. Donna shut the door behind her and helped herself to the fridge. After a ham sandwich and a coke, Donna left her mother a friendly note thanking her for the snack and left to head back to her home in High Ridge.

The traditional route, for most people, would be to get back on I-44, take it to highway 141, go south until reaching highway 30, then take that straight to High Ridge. Donna hated dealing with highways, especially as it was getting close to rush hour, so she took I-44 as far as Eureka, turned off, drove a mile or so, then headed down Highway W in the direction of House Springs. She turned off a few miles short of the town on Twin Rivers road and took the back way home.

This time of year, driving the hills could be a lot of fun. In the winter, driving the hills could be a death wish. The first hill Donna encountered was especially steep and had a sharp turn at its bottom. This combination had proven fatal for many unaware and careless drivers. Whenever ice storms occurred, no one with any sense at all took that stretch of road.

At least it was only dangerous part of the time, unlike old highway 21, which was dangerous all the time. The locals had named it "Blood Alley." Donna didn't even want to think how many people had died driving *that* particular road.

Donna made the bottom of the other side of the hill. A rocky crevasse on the left side of the road had been fenced over with warning signs around it. No wonder. The crevasse was actually the mouth of a deep cave.

In 1985, two teenage boys went into the cave with a couple of crude swords, thinking to go on a swords-and-sorcery style adventure. They never came out. It took three weeks for both of the bodies to be found. The first had died of a broken neck after a fall over a ledge, probably sometime during the first or second day of the ill-fated trek. The other had died of dehydration, barely two days before the rescue team had caught up with him. After the bodies were removed, the cave was sealed off and the crevasse fenced over.

Donna topped another hill to find herself at the intersection of High Ridge Boulevard. She turned left, toward the center of the town. To her left was a county library that used to be Thriftway's supermarket. An indention in the parking lot's pavement marked where once rested the foundation to a Photo Mat back in the late 70's, early 80's. On the right was an auto parts shop that used to be a bank and a trailer that had been used for more things than she could recall. Once it was a salon, before that it was a Reaben's restaurant.

Donna turned left onto Williams Creek road and hummed an old Eagles tune as she headed closer to home. She passed an old Amoco site where the trucks delivering gas to the local homes filled up. Next to that lived a guy who ran a junkyard out of his home. He'd had a tin roof that had been hit by lightning back in 1975. He'd died some years ago, and the place had been cleared out. Now a much nicer looking house sat where its predecessor had been. The thought of gas and a wrecked house reminded her something that had happened over in Murphy a couple years back.

Some doctor, she thought he was from India, had moved into a pricey subdivision. It was no big deal until the guy rented a backhoe to dig a hole for a swimming pool. The guy couldn't read English very well,

35

and so had no idea what was on the little yellow sign in his backyard. Had he been able to read English, he would have known not to dig in his backyard because of a gas main six feet below the surface. He busted the pipe open, and a rock scraping against the metal backhoe created a spark that resulted in an explosion. The man's house was destroyed, as were the houses on either side of his, and the backhoe was wrecked. Miraculously, however, no one had gotten hurt, not even the Indian doctor. He had been thrown clear and landed uninjured in the grass.

A little further, Donna turned a corner. Her side of the road had a hillside for a shoulder. The other side of the road had only a steep dropoff into the woods. A guard rail had been put up, but drunks always found ways to bust through it. How many times had the towing companies been called out to tow vehicles out of the tree tops? Donna couldn't begin to guess.

Next up on the left was a house that used to be owned by a older couple who'd been nurses during WWII. During the 50's through the early 70's they supplemented their income by performing illegal abortions in their home. Among their clientele were young, unmarried girls whose fathers had given them the choice to either abort the child or leave town, older women who were opposed to raising children late in life, and nuns who had been brought to them by the priests who had gotten them pregnant. Of course, only a few people ever knew about such goings-on, most of them the elder townsfolk. And most of them are now dead.

The old couple also had a tremendous amount of pull with the law. Years ago, the local scuttlebutt maintained that the couple had "serviced" a number of girls the sheriff had slept with, underage girls who had looked older than their real age. Naturally, having that kind of dirt on someone like the sheriff lent them a hell of a lot of influence. Influence the couple had never been afraid to use as they saw fit.

On the right was a house owned by a widower who had been suspected of molesting his son. Oddly enough, the house next to his had been home to a family of three in which the mother had molested *her* son. The father, who was some kind of appearance-freak, vehemently denied any truth to the accusations. With the law in the area being what it was in the 80's, nothing was ever done about either situation, and no adult spent so much as an hour in jail.

A quarter mile later, on the right hand side of the road, sat the former Carol-Jan apartments. The place had been cleaned up for some time, but for about twenty years it was a haven for drug dealers, prostitutes, fencing operations, you name it. The cops had gotten into gunfights with some of the scum that used to live there at one point or

36

another. Then, quite suddenly, the police stopped responding to calls concerning the place. No one could prove it, but local talk hinted that the cops had been paid to leave the place alone.

Donna passed the apartment complex. A quarter mile later, she turned left into her driveway. She turned off the ignition and walked to her mailbox. No mail. Donna unlocked her front door and walked into her house. She looked at her answering machine in the living room. It was flashing wildly, indicating she had messages. Donna cringed, thinking Dan had left her a piece of his mind. She tapped a button to hear her just-desserts.

"Hi, Donna." It was her mother. "I'm going out with Phyllis, Joanne, and Alvetta to that new indoor flea market, the one out in Sullivan. So if you call or come by and you don't see me, don't worry. Bye."

Donna waited for the next message.

"Hey Donna, this is Dan." Here it comes, she thought. "I'm really sorry, but we had to rush my dad to the hospital about four this morning. It was his heart. We don't know how bad it is, but we're at St. John's right now. I'll call later. I hope you're not mad. I was looking forward to today. Some other time, I hope. Well, talk to you later. Bye."

Donna let out a sigh of relief. She was off the hook, but she felt badly for Dan. Donna's father had died of a heart attack nine years earlier, so she could sympathize with how he felt. She didn't know if she would admit to being late for their meeting, but at least things were okay now between the two of them.

Donna walked to her computer desk. A tinge of dread made its way to the forefront of her thoughts. She stared blankly at the monitor as the PC booted up.

Nothing came to mind.

Donna summoned the word processing program to the screen. An empty white field greeted her eyes.

Nothing came to mind.

"We pick up what other people miss and call attention to it," Robert had said.

That was fine, but what did she know that might interest someone else? What had she ever picked up on that could be turned into a story of some kind?

Nothing came to mind.

Once upon a time... Donna deleted it.

It was a dark and stormy night... Donna shuddered as she virtually punched the delete key.

The cat ate my homework. Donna erased it.

"I promised I'd try," the woman said aloud to nobody. "But nothing's coming up. Maybe if I'd thought about my writing on the way home instead of letting my mind wander over all those old stories..."

Old stories...
Stories...
A smile exploded onto her pleasant face. Donna's eyes seemed to light up as her fingers danced upon the keyboard. Now she knew where writers got their stories, and they weren't three-for-a-buck at the dollar store.

A Frenchman's Night Out

Ah, it was the night that forever changed my life, my friend! But here we sit at our table with a wheel of cheese, warm bread, fine wine, and the whole evening before us. Shall I trouble you with my tale, yes? It does my heart well to have a friend such as you.

To begin, it was a Friday night most warm. I was in the plaza by the street, walking toward the theatre when I saw this beautiful woman walking in my direction. Because of the shadows I could not see but her left side, but it was enough for me. Her dress, it was black, but oh her curves and her walk were *magnifique*! Her hair, it was dark and cut short, but most feminine. And her eyes! Brown they were and shaped like almonds. Our eyes met, and it was as if she had expected me.

I started toward her, for surely her most beautiful eyes were calling to me. But some people, oh they were most rude, they came out of the theatre. I could not see past them! But when they were gone, so was she.

I hoped we might meet again, but I would not waste such a perfect evening. So, I bought my ticket and went into the theatre. It was such a good film! Two lovers, they meet at the *Asphalt a Montmartre*. Both of them, they are married to people they do not love. But this one day every year, they come to be together for a day. It is a reminder that love is patience as well as passion. Ah, but they are forced to part, though they vow to meet again next year. It is perhaps my favourite film.

I was leaving the theatre lobby with the others when I felt a light breeze, like someone blowing on the back of my neck. I turned around and I saw her silhouette vanish into the crowd. My friend, if only I could tell you how my heart leapt! I wanted, I did, to search for her. But I knew I would not find her. Instead, she would find me. This I knew.

It was but a short walk to the café. I was so anxious, I could not have even bread with my wine. My friend, Pierre, he tended the bar. I told him what had happened. He laughed and said I was a hopeless romantic. Surely she was but having fun and she knew she could get away with it. But I did not agree. This I told Pierre. With this, there was no chance, but fate. Truly this was meant to happen.

Pierre laughed. But he was not laughing later when he approached me and told of a request for my company at a table. I looked to where he was pointing. And there she was! The object of my desire beckoned to me! I wanted to run to her, but I did not want to look like a fool. So I walked to her- how do they say?- smooth. I introduced myself. Her name is Monique. I sat down at her table. Together we shared some of Pierre's finest wine. We talked, but I did not hear the words. I heard only the voice of an angel. And her eyes! Her eyes, and the touch of her hand upon mine, holds me like no chain could!

I had no idea whatever I said, but she laughed. Monique, she said she has teased me to test my resolve. Perhaps I interest her as much as she interests me, what else could I think?

She need say no words. Her eyes, her hand then upon my leg. It was time to leave for more quiet accommodations. I leave Pierre his francs. Monique and I walked with her arm in my arm. We went to the garage where my car is parked. The light, it was dim while I searched for my keys. I found them, and I unlocked her door first.

Ah, but this is the sad bit, my friend. Before I can open the door for her, she has a stiletto. It is pressed against my neck! All this, so she could rob me!

Monique, she took my keys. And then she took my watch. I say, "Here, take all that you will. Take all that I own! But do not leave me in this misery! Have mercy upon my broken heart, fairest one!"

Monique, she leaned forward. She kissed me while she took the wallet from my suit coat! Never has a single kiss delighted me so! So soft but full of passion. Ah, but it was over too soon!

Yes, my friend. She did take my car, and my watch, and my wallet. But she did also take my heart. And that, my friend, can never be replaced.

I go back to that plaza sometimes to find her. But not for my things. They are only things. I go because my heart tells me. I do not know if I shall ever find her again. But as I say before, love is patience as well as passion.

Champions of the Dead

I
The Small Hero

A small gust of wind erupted into a swirl, turning the leaves scattered before the gates of the iron-fenced, thirty-acre cemetery into a tiny tornado. The dry leaves flew furiously for a brief moment, then settled back to the gravel. The last rain to fall here fell early last week. No more was expected for several days.

The Eternal Life cemetery, like so many other graveyards, sported relatively few trees. Most of these were evergreens, and those planted in neatly planned clusters in the older section of the cemetery. But here and there stood birch and elm trees. Leafless and gray in the full moonlight, the trees seemed as lifeless as those who resided here under the earth. Except when the wind blew. Then they took on a semblance of semi-life. To the melancholy, the trees seemed to mourn those no longer among the living. Other eyes might have seen them as presenting an ominous warning to those who would intrude here, or perhaps a challenge to those with the courage to stand bold.

Or perhaps they were simply trees whose uppermost branches swayed in the cool nighttime breeze.

The full moon in the cloudless sky illuminated the steps of four nocturnal visitors as they jogged through the entrance to the cemetery. The gates swung open at their touch, eliminating the need to risk injury jumping over the spearlike tips adorning the top ends of the vertical bars in the fence. The young men kept their chatter and mischievous giggles as quiet as possible while they went about their business. No one lived very close to the place, but this was Halloween and the cops were sure to drive by at least a couple times throughout the night. And, as the old saying goes, better safe than sorry.

Rodney Hagen was not laughing. An inner fire seemed to burn deep within the tall, burly twenty year old. Dark haired, dark-eyed, and dark-tempered, the young man swung the sledgehammer he shouldered with iron-strong hands. The chains hanging from his leather jacket clinked in rhythm to the hammer strikes. First one headstone, then a second, crumbled into gravel. While the other three vandals were content to tip over some grave markers and spray-paint others, the leader of the quartet would only be satisfied by the stones' destruction.

Hagen, whose life was filled with angry outbursts from others, most notably his parents, decided to unleash some of his own inner rage on the stone markers, his sledgehammer an extension of that rage. Although the six foot two Hagen wasn't aggressive enough toward others to be counted a bully, the young man was seldom pleasant to deal with. Even his friends knew better than to tease him very much.

Perry Laughner was the clown of the bunch. Seventeen mischievous years old and as merry as Rodney was serious, the five foot eight trouble-maker practiced his artistic talents, or lack of, upon the larger headstones. Exaggerated drawings of human genitalia adorned some graves and scrawled swear words decorated others, all courtesy of the can of spray paint Perry kept tucked in a pocket of his denim jacket. Blond haired and bearing green, pixie-like eyes, the youth thought the whole ordeal as nothing more than a wonderful party.

Laughner took nothing and no one seriously. He knew well enough not to anger Rodney, but to the rest of the world he was a joke-telling prankster, the kind of kid who got hours of laughter and personal enjoyment out of wrecking portable toilets and throwing bags of shit at the front doors of people who pissed his friends off. Laughner never received a neutral opinion from anyone; either they loved him or they hated him.

Troy Houser, also seventeen, was in some ways opposite of both Perry and Rodney. Houser's sweaty brown hair wrapped around his mousy ears. Despite the night's chill, he wore only a thin wind breaker. His blue eyes darted here and there. He didn't like being here and wished they could all go home soon. The boy wouldn't have even come, but he didn't want to be left out of his friends' doings, even if he didn't approve of them. He nervously helped his other friend push over a rather heavy marker. It fell to the ground with a dull thud. Rodney was beside them in the blink of an eye. His sledge hit home again and again, rending the century-old stone into rubble.

Houser, in the estimation of those who knew him even casually, was a good kid. The young man's non-threatening, lean, five foot five frame, as well as his agreeable and easygoing countenance, made it easy for people to warm up to him. Out of the three youths Houser ran with tonight, Perry was his closest friend. Rodney's brusque manner and zeal for wanton destruction somewhat intimidated Houser. Since he posed no threat to Rodney's position of leader, Rodney had no problems with Houser.

Edward Calmers was the true oddity of the quartet. Two months away from his seventeenth birthday, he was slightly taller than Houser, but his shaved head accentuated his dark blue eyes and generally droopy facial features almost to the point of being a caricature of humanity. He was also the most emotionally removed from the whole ordeal. In his mind, this was one more night in a long stream of nights. The main difference was, on this particular night, he was breaking the law and vandalizing gravestones. Other than that, it was no big deal. The youth seemed almost as resigned and lifeless as those whose markers he was trashing. Anyone looking closely enough at him might well have thought him quite at home in the dismal surroundings with his odd appearance and black, ankle-length trenchcoat.

42

Calmers had a certain fascination with death that made the invitation to come to the cemetery irresistible. The transition from this world to the next had held him in awe for as long as he could remember, and to such an extent that he no longer feared death. Some of his friends thought this made him fearless. It didn't. It simply helped Calmers acquire a fatalistic outlook on life. Calmers had joined this motley group on the outside chance something interesting would happen and either validate his apathy toward life or give him some new bit of enlightenment.

"Are we about done?" Troy asked. "It's getting late, and our folks are going to wonder where we are."

"Oh, don't be such a baby," Perry said. "It ain't nobody's bedtime yet. Come on, give me a hand with this one."

"This one belongs to a Bethany 'Betty' Golladay." Rodney spoke offhandedly, pointing with his hammer to a rose-colored marker before him. "Died in 1953. Well Betty, this one's for you!" A powerful swing ended with a loud crack and a chunk coming off the marker. Three more hits rendered it into so many pebbles.

"Are you gonna bust up every one of these things here?" Edward asked. "Troy's got a point. Sooner or later, someone's gonna show up. Besides, that hammer's kind of loud."

"Right!" Troy was thankful that someone was finally listening to reason.

"Yeah, I guess we've had enough fun for the night." Perry was reluctant to concede the point. "I'm about out of paint, anyway."

"Just one more." Rodney ran over to a marker that sat far apart from the others. The stone was black, shaped like an obelisk, and almost invisible even in the bright moonlight. It was mostly hidden by the foliage that had grown over and around it. Had he not already known it was there, Rodney would have missed it entirely. The vandal didn't even attempt to remove the vines and weeds that entangled the marker. His first swing broke a chip off the side. A second knocked the tip off. A third put a large crack through the middle of it.

An especially cold gust of wind blew furiously through the graveyard just then. The four vandals looked to each other. Something was out of place with this burst of freezing air. It was far, far too cold for even this time of year. Then the screaming began. High-pitched and ear-piercing, it seemed carried upon the unnatural blast of wind. The voice and the frigid air it rode upon vanished as quickly as it had come. The vandals were thankful the temperature returned to its moderately tolerable level, but then there came another shift in the night air, something sensed rather than felt. No one said anything, words weren't needed to express the thought that ran through their minds.

They weren't alone.

"Hey misser!" A child's voice called from behind a pile of rubble that up until a few minutes earlier had been a four foot tall headstone.

The four youths spun around to face their discoverer. It was only a black-haired boy of about six, wearing pants, suspenders, a plaid shirt, shoes, and a cap that seemed like things out of an old movie. Troy almost wet himself at the sound of the kid's voice. Perry and Edward weren't overly concerned by the child's sudden appearance, although they wondered how the kid could stand in thirty-nine degree weather without a jacket of some kind and not be shivering. Rodney took charge of the situation by being as intimidating and threatening as possible. "Hey kid, what're you doing here?" The biggest vandal virtually growled at the child. "Don't you know it's dangerous to be out here at night?"

"S-sorry s-sir," the little boy said. "I was just wonnering how come you guys knocked over my rock."

"Your what?" Troy asked. Had he had heard the boy right?

"My rock, you knock d'it over," the boy said. He pointed to the broken hunk of stone that lay beside him. "This one here. I mean, it ussa stand up straight. But you knock d'it down. How come?"

"Go on, answer the boy." A stern voice came from behind the obelisk. The stranger stepped close to Rodney. Everyone turned to see a tall, thin, clean-shaven man, standing roughly six foot four, clad in a black shroud. His wavy hair was a medium shade of brown and lay straight back, his features sharp and angular. No one could see his eyes clearly enough to tell what color they were. Unlike the boy, who had no particular smell, the tall man exuded an odor reminiscent of scorched earth and sulfur. Combined with his pallid complexion, the tall man cut a fearsome appearance. "The little punk got here before I did, but he deserves his question answered anyway."

"None of your fuckin' business!" Rodney wasn't impressed.

The dark man grinned evilly. "I say it is." He threw a hand out. The gates to the cemetery slammed shut. The young men heard the locks click. That was enough for Troy, who screamed and ran for the fence. The wrought iron barrier's spired tips grew and turned over upon themselves, prohibiting anyone from climbing over. Now even Perry and Edward seemed anxious and worried.

"Let us out." Rodney's voice was calm, but there was a lethality in his tone that clearly revealed his fearlessness. He shouldered his weapon easily, ready and eager to put it to use.

The shrouded figure's broad grin became wider. "Force me." The hammer swung in, aimed at the man's head. Without losing his smile, the dark figure effortlessly caught the weapon's handle, close to its head. Rodney grimaced. It felt as if he'd hit a steel wall. Rodney started to throw a hard punch with his left hand when the man's other hand grabbed his wrist. The vandal felt a terrible cold envelope his arm. The

44

chill of death, far colder than the hardest, thickest ice, penetrated the young man's arm through to the bone. A short, pained grunt escaped the vandal's lips, but his resolve remained firm. The shrouded man's other hand plucked the hammer away from the younger man and threw it aside, then locked onto Rodney's neck. Rodney was able to see into the man's crimson eyes and swooned as he peered into their dark depths. He felt something taking part of his energy away. It was an inexplicable sensation, almost as though his body was somehow slowing down, becoming less efficient, less energetic. The vandal stopped struggling, and shrouded man let him drop to the ground.

"Dude, your hair's white along the temples," Edward said. A trace of genuine fear laced the morbid young man's voice.

The dark figure stared triumphantly at his defeated opponent. "Now that we have determined who's in charge here, let me make some things clear. First, the boy and I, and some others you will meet in due time, were chosen to come here and discuss your poor choice of recreational activities. I'd rather not say by whom as He and I are not on the greatest of terms. Second, everyone you will meet tonight has been dead for many years and will never return to life, so I advise you not to try to develop any friendships here unless you're fond of disappointments. Third, we were specifically chosen to come here tonight because it was decided that we stand the best chances of getting through to you moral and physical weaklings. Lastly, of all the things you will see this night, only those of us who have returned from the grave may be touched." He grinned eagerly. "And, as you have seen, we can touch you in return. Everything else will be strictly illusions created to get our point across.

"Now, are you going to answer the boy's question?" the malevolent spirit asked. "Or do I have to peel another two decades off your intended lifespan?"

"I don't know, okay!" Rodney said. He slowly stood up. "I was mad today, and we all came out here to have some fun and tear up stuff. No big deal."

"It's a big deal to us," the shrouded man said. "And it's a big deal to the people who come out here to visit. Go on, look at the boy. Look at him and see what it was you were having fun with."

The youths turned to face the sad looking little boy, standing by his headstone. The words, "Bonifacio 'Bo' Garcia, born March 6, 1941," were all that were visible in the moonlight. Suddenly, it was no longer night. The intruders blinked furiously as they gazed up into a warm springtime sky that was now blue and nearly cloudless. The four vandals looked down from the bright, early afternoon sky as their eyes adjusted to the light to see themselves standing on a dirt road close to a wooden bridge spanning across a quickly flowing stream. It vaguely resembled a paved overpass they knew of on the south end of town. Trees in full bloom stood upon either side of the road, forming a natural tunnel on both sides of the bridge. Only the opposite bank upstream from the bridge was relatively treeless. The dark man was there as well, his countenance as foreboding as before. The boy walked down the lane from where the others stood. He carried a crude fishing pole in one hand and a small wicker creel in the other. The boy chose a suitable spot and sat down upon an edge of the bridge, facing upstream. He seemed totally oblivious to the onlookers.

"Hey, what the fuck?" Rodney's voice sounded more scared than intimidating.

"Control your language, you're not impressing anyone," the ghostly man advised. "You are watching the boy's last moments. Like the old Dickens' classic, all of you are powerless to interfere. None but I can see or hear you, so trying to help, if you're so inclined, will be useless. Now stand quiet and observe."

"If no one else can hear or see us," Edward asked, "what's the point?"

The shrouded man instructed them calmly. "Watch."

Saturday, June 14, 1947.

Bo sat upon the edge of the wooden bridge, looking into the water below. He'd been here an hour and hadn't even a slight nibble at his bait to show for the effort. Soon, he was sure, he'd catch a whopper of a fish and take it home to Poppa. Wouldn't Poppa be proud of him, he thought. A big fat catfish would really be nice, the boy fantasized. Poppa would help him clean the fish and they'd have a big dinner with Momma and brother Gregory.

An absent smile formed upon the boy's face. The grin faded when he saw three older boys running down the edge of the creek below. All of them were shirtless, shoeless, dirty, pock-marked with chigger and mosquito bites, and wore ragged pants. It looked like none of them had washed their hair in ages, so from the scalp up they bore the same greasy shade of brown hair. One of them, the tallest one, swung a cloth sack to and fro. Bo could hear the distressed wail of a cat coming from inside the crude bag.

"C'mon!" The smallest of the trio jumped around the other two wildly. "Throw it in! Let's watch it drown!"

"Go on, Donny!" The second truant youth was as jubilant as the younger one. "Give it a good toss!"

"Allrighty then." The largest of the boys, looking about twelve, swung the bag back and forth toward the water, ignoring the plaintive cries of the captive animal. "One for the money, two for the show, three to make ready, and four to...GO!!!"

Bo watched, horrified, as the cat shrieked, the animal possibly sensing its fate, before the bound sack splashed into the water. The whole scene reminded Bo of something that happened on the radio last night. The bad guys had a girl tied up, tied up like the mouth of the sack was tied, and it was up to the Lone Ranger to rescue her. Well, he might not be a big hero like the Lone Ranger, but he had to do something. Seeing the air bubbles coming up from the sinking bag spurred the boy into action. Bo dropped his fishing pole and, without hesitation, jumped into the creek. Immediately he realized his mistake.

Bo didn't know how to swim.

"Will you get a load of him." The middle boy pointed to Bo, noticing him for the first time as the little boy leaped into the water. The other two boys stood by quietly and watched. Bo bobbed to the surface of the water. The little boy thrashed about in a panic.

"Help!" Bo's mind was in a frenzy. Why were they just standing there? "Help me! I can't swim! I'm dwowning!"

The strength ebbed from Bo's little arms, and despite his tremendous effort, he slipped under again. The boys on the bank watched with keen interest, waiting for the would-be hero to come up again. Bo didn't surface. A minute passed. Then three. It began to dawn on them that something was wrong and that the little boy wasn't going to come up to the surface again. Not ever. They walked along the bank casually, looking into the stream. The current wasn't strong enough to pose a threat to an adult swimmer, but Bo was neither an adult nor a swimmer, and he was swept downstream. The older boys looked to each other.

"Last one in's a rotten egg!" The oldest boy jumped into the shallows and started splashing thigh-high water at his fellows. "Somebody save me! I'm dwowning! Help!" The two younger boys laughed and jumped in, splashing about merrily, all of them pretending to share Bo's fate and mocking his imperfect speech.

Tuesday, June 17, 1947.

The three boys, dressed in their Sunday suits and neatly combed (though still unwashed) hair, looked almost civilized as they stood before the small pine box. There was nothing the undertaker could do to make Bo presentable, considering the swelling and bloating that had occurred in the two days he had spent at the bottom of the creek. The boys looked to each other knowingly.

Felicia, Bo's mother, held a handkerchief to her face. She could barely walk by herself and had to be led to her younger son's closed casket. Her husband, Dominic, escorted her in silence. He looked far older than his thirty-eight years, his grief giving him a wizened appearance. Gregory sat in the front pew with his head in his hands. The ten year old sobbed despite the pain in his sides. Even that could not lessen his mournful heaves.

The young trio walked quietly past the casket, as did the rest of the townspeople who attended the solemn event, and came to stand by the sheriff. The tall, stout man with a thick mustache and gleaming brass badge quietly shook each of their hands, one by one.

"Its always a shame to lose a young one." The middle-aged lawman spoke softly. "I know it must be hard on you boys, especially. Seeing him fall into that creek and jumping in to try to save him...but you can't blame yourselves. You did what you could and I know if that boy could speak he'd be saying thank you for trying. You three know that, don't you?"

"Yeah. We know, don't we?" The oldest boy turn to his two friends, both of them nodded and mumbled their agreement. The sheriff patted them on their shoulders and let them go about their way.

The boys left the building. They walked behind the chapel and looked around. Seeing no one else, the oldest one spoke.

"I'm dwowning! Somebody save me!" He jumped around wildly, flailing his arms in a parody of a swimming motion, drawing laughs from the other two, who began to emulate their hero.

II
Will You Love Me Forever?

The sunlight faded, then darkened to the moonlit night the vandals had been used to. The chapel was gone. The coffin, mourners, and evil children faded away with it. Now there were only headstones, some broken and others defaced, and trees swaying listlessly in the cool, dry breeze. The vandals shivered as they readjusted to the chill of the late October night. They saw Bo standing once more by the remains of his headstone.

"So they got away with it," Rodney said. He shrugged. "I mean, it's too bad about the kid and all, but what's that got to do with us? We didn't throw any goddamn cat in a creek or tell some dumb ass kid to jump in after it." He looked squarely at the little boy, who simply hung his head. Not even a flicker of emotion shown upon the young man's face, even when the boy's bottom lip began to stick out and quiver.

The little boy turned to Troy. "Don't he know? I dint want to die. I just wanned to be like the Lone Ranger and save that kitty-cat. I wanned to grow up and be big and strong like my Poppa. But I couldn't swim and those bad boys wouldn't help me and I came here 'nstead."

Perry and Edward watched the scene with thoughtful expressions. Troy wept quietly, but openly. He didn't give a damn at that moment who saw him. The other vandals regarded Troy curiously. Even Rodney's hardened face softened. They had never seen their friend cry before.

"You do not yet understand as your friend does!" The shrouded man aimed his anger at the other three vandals. "He came here with you and went along with your foolishness out of loyalty, despite the urges of his better judgment.

"And here you are, thinking yourselves so unique, so special to the world. Just like them." He gestured to a young couple who appeared a few yards to his left. A tall, lanky, blond haired young man looking about their age and dressed in blue overalls sat at the base of an old, dead tree, rubbing the back of his head. The young man seemed lost in thought, as though not so much feeling pain as remembering it. Standing a few feet away from him was a thin woman in her early twenties with long, braided, dark hair. Her dress was plain and its style dated back to around the first World War. An expression of sadness marred her somewhat attractive features. Her hands rubbed at her midsection, in much the same manner as the young man rubbed his head. They looked away from each other, but it seemed they shared a mutual sadness. "The foolishness of youth. You think yours is the only generation to ever be young and feel immortal? Is that situation reserved especially for you? Think again. They were young and foolish, too, allowing themselves, as young fools often do, to fall in love."

Perry walked over to the couple. Both of them were too preoccupied with their own thoughts to give him the slightest regard. The living youth looked around the ground where their headstones should have been. A heap of white stone that had been two separate headstones lay strewn about. The names "Anna Marie" and "Johnathan" were the only names that could be seen. One had been born in 1897, the other born in 1898. No other information could be discerned from the chalk-like rubble. "What were their last names?" Perry asked.

"Don't you see them?" The host's sneer was unmistakable. "They should be right there on the headstones. Not there now? I suppose you'll never know, then. What's the matter? They're dead, shouldn't they be forgotten as well? You four must think so, you've just permanently erased their last names from the world. Those stones were the only testimony to their existences."

"I don't want to see this." Troy looked away.

"But you will!" The dark robed man's snarl pulled Troy's gaze to him. "You followed them in here, just like he followed her, and so it will be that you will share the punishment of your fellows! Watch! Learn!"

Again the sky brightened, but now it was later in the day. Perhaps late afternoon. The air was warm again. The vandals and their host stood no longer in the graveyard, but in a grassy stretch of land between a white, two-story farmhouse and an unpainted barn of similar height. There were no telephone poles within sight of the farmhouse or the expanse of land around it. The road running along one edge of the farm was dirt, packed hard mostly by the horses and wagons that

49

frequently passed by. The tracks of some ancient automobile could be discerned in the baked mud.

The observers stood a dozen yards away from a bonfire. The young couple from the cemetery laughed and square-danced with at least twenty or so other people. Some of revelers resembled her, others looked similar to him. The two families seemed quite familiar with each other, and no one took issue with the couple walking off by themselves, hand in hand toward the barn. Some of the children threw casual taunts, but no one tried to stop or follow them as they walked away.

"She is the fool." The shrouded man's voice was soft and expectant as he spoke to the vandals. He sounded eager to witness their demise, hers in particular. "Her folly, coupled with his, will bring them both down. But we will focus mostly upon her."

The four youths said nothing and watched as the couple entered the barn.

Sunday, April 11, 1915.

Whoops and joyful hollers erupted as much from the adults as the children as they danced near the bonfire. One of the older men, a blond-haired chap looking about fifty, spun a lively tune from his fiddle as the assembled friends and family joined in the revelry. It was Sunday, the commanded day of rest for the God-fearing folk, and nothing, in their minds, was as restful as a good shin-dig.

Anna Marie had heard the gossip that passed around. Usually a man picked out a wife who was younger than he, and some thought their situation a little odd. She was eighteen, nearly a year and a half older than Johnathan, who would be seventeen in June. But the two seemed to get along so well that no one really kicked up much of a fuss about it. She wouldn't have cared if they did. He was hers, and she was his. Nothing else really mattered as far as the young woman was concerned.

Anna Marie sat in the hay loft, her legs hanging from the knees down over the edge. She looked out the open loft door a few feet to her right and listened quietly with her beau. She swung her feet in the air. "Uncle Jeb plays his fiddle pretty good."

Johnathan nodded. He sat to her left, his feet dangled close to hers. "Yep. He does."

Anna Marie turned to look at him, her expression amused. Johnathan's scraggly whiskers might someday be a full beard, but now she thought they made him look silly. His pale blue eyes looked off in the distance. She reached behind him and rubbed his back with her left hand.

"I love you, you know." Her voice was matter-of-fact.

He turned and smiled at her. "I love you, too."

"Will you love me forever?" Her voice was plain but confident.

"Of course I will." He was surprised she would asked such a question. Surely she should know that by now.

"Well a person wouldn't know it by the way you never hold my hand or hug me or anything." She pouted mockingly.

"I did too hold your hand," Johnathan argued. "New Year's Eve, I held your hand. Kissed you on the cheek, too."

Her voice was soft. "You never let me kiss you back. I mean, if we're getting married you gotta at least give me a real kiss and let me kiss you back."

"I didn't think we were supposed to do that until after we got married," he said. His voice sounded ominous. "The Parson said so."

"Well, we're getting married, ain't we?"

"Yeah."

"You ain't gonna change your mind are you?"

"No. Never."

"Then what's wrong with it?"

"I don't know."

"I know." She stood up and took his hand, helping him to his feet. "It'll be dark over here. No one will catch us."

Johnathan was clearly nervous, but now in a different way than before. He loved Anna Marie with all his heart, there was no doubt about it, and he wanted nothing more than to kiss her full on the mouth and let her do the same to him. But he had been raised to believe that only sinners do that before marrying. Still, he thought, she might have a point. They were getting married as soon as he turned eighteen and would be kissing each other every day after that, not to doubt. What could it hurt if they started early? It wouldn't make him stop loving her. He let her pull him to a dimly lit corner of the loft.

They sat beside each other on a small pile of hay. Anna Marie giggled at his nervousness as she moved her face close to his, brushing their lips together. His breath became heavy as she did it again, enticing him to take charge like a good husband should. She felt a wave of pleasure overcome her as he took her in his lean arms and pressed his lips against hers. The kiss was passionate, but not rough. By the way he rubbed her back and led her through the kiss, she knew he had wanted this as badly as she.

Soon, too soon by her estimation, he slowly drew back and shifted to lean against a bale of hay. He shook his head and blew a deep breath. "Wow." He smiled broadly.

"I knew you'd like it if I got you to do it. You okay?"

He nodded. "I'm just a little dizzy."

She giggled. "You want to kiss me again?"

He silently leaned forward and took her again in his arms. There was no humor in this next kiss, only the blossoming of a newly born sensation within them both. Neither of them knew what it really was or

51

how powerful it would become, and neither of them cared. The word 'passion' wasn't one they used in everyday talk, but they would have agreed that the very sound of the word was as beautiful as it felt.

Her nails scraped gently across the back of his neck as one of his hands moved around to the front of her plain dress, moving up from her waist to its intended goal. She gasped as a wave of excitement, the likes of which she had never known before, caused her to throw her head back in response. When he began kissing her neck, she felt an electrical surge of energy race throughout her entire being.

It was wrong, she knew. Only sinners did this, he had been told. But neither passion nor desire heeds to such high ideals. Now it consumed them both. Johnathan undid his overalls while Anna Marie pulled up her dress and removed her undergarments. Nothing else in all the world seemed to exist beyond the two of them. They were two halves joining as one. In that single instant, she felt a slight pain that slowly eased. She was vaguely aware of his loud shudder as he shared a similar experience.

All the years of righteous teaching; all the hours of sermonizing, broke apart and melted like ice upon a warm lake. Nothing that felt so wondrous could be so wrong, she believed. The kisses, the hands upon her naked breasts, the ecstasy of being taken, were all as parts of a long, single, glorious moment. Her grunts were nearly as loud and animalistic as his as their lovemaking reached its climax.

Anna Marie was barely aware of her hands putting her bloomers back on and straightening her dress or of sitting up. Johnathan dressed himself and, also barely conscious of his movements, sat next to her in the relative darkness. Neither of them spoke for what felt like an eternity. Far from tense, however, the silence was comforting as they both thought privately of what had just happened.

"We'll get to do that all the time after we're married." Her voice reflected her desire.

He grinned slyly. "Just you wait until our wedding night." His mock threat brought a smile to her pretty face.

She laughed. "Be worth waiting for."

They sat there, holding hands in the hay loft for a while longer. Finally, they went outside and rejoined the partygoers. One of the younger children teased them about probably kissing while they were gone. The adults laughed at the notion. The young couple also laughed and joined the square-dancing. No one needed to know anything, they decided. The special look they shared throughout the day and into the evening spoke volumes.

Saturday, October 9, 1915.

The Pope Hartford slowly ground to a halt. Jeb and his brother, Anna Marie's father, Luke, got out of the car first. The young woman eagerly hopped out of the vehicle and looked around. The hustle and bustle of the town proper appealed to all three of them.

"How long are we staying?" she asked.

Luke shrugged. "A while. Why?"

"I'd really like to go to the cinematic," she said. "May I please, father?"

Luke reached inside a pocket. He handed her two dimes. "Jeb and I got some things to get, then we're heading for the saloon. When you're ready come get us."

"I will. Thank you." She walked across the dirt street to the wooden sidewalk that would lead her to the house of moving pictures.

"I hope that Johnathan knows what he's getting into," Luke said. He and Jeb headed toward the general store. Both men laughed.

"Before you know it, she'll have one of them moving picture machines in their house." Jeb clapped his brother on the shoulder as they headed along their way.

Anna Marie stopped at the entrance to the movie house. She handed one of her shiny new dimes to an elderly gentleman who bid her a pleasant show. The young woman walked into the cramped theatre lobby. A young boy, looking roughly thirteen or so, stood behind a counter that resembled a tavern's bar. Anna Marie handed her second dime to the boy. After a cheerful greeting, the lad reached under the bar and produced a cool bottle of brown liquid. He dropped the coin into a cigar box kept under the counter top and handed her seven cents change. The young woman took the nickel and two pennies and slipped them inside her purse.

Anna Marie removed the bottle's cork and swallowed a sip of the fizzing brown drink and walked into the theatre proper. Planks rested atop orange crates for those sitting in the back rows. Closer to the front were three rows of seats that had once been church pews. An old piano and a stool with a battered cushion rested in the far right corner, far enough away from the screen to keep it from blocking the view.

Anna Marie sat in the row furthest back, knowing that sometimes the people who came in to see the show were as interesting as the moving pictures themselves were. Two women, women of some means, judging by their dress, sat down in the row just in front of Anna Marie. More people filed in. Most of them were farmer folk, like herself, and some of them were townspeople who loved witnessing this modern miracle again and again. Lastly came the old man who had collected the admissions. He took his seat at the piano while the lights turned off. The film machine turned on a few moments later, probably operated by the drink boy, she guessed.

The film began to roll. The old man, who had played in saloons frequented by the gunslinger types many years ago, played the bulky instrument in response to the mood depicted by the moving images on the white-painted wooden wall. Most of the audience laughed as the world's funniest man, Charlie Chaplin, displayed his newest antics on film. The old man's music, played in high, fast-paced notes, accented the humorous pratfalls of the Tramp's escapades.

Anna Marie noted with some interest that the two refined ladies before her were lighting up cigarettes and carrying on a casual conversation. She watched them intently as women of any good repute didn't smoke. That was when it dawned on her why they sat in the back of the room. No one would pay them any mind, and their smoke would blend in with the fumes coming from the cigars and pipes smoked by the men in the front. The young woman admired their inventiveness as well as their daring.

Next onscreen was the real reason why Anna Marie came to the cinematic. 'The Perils of Pauline' was her favorite show. The piano played low-range notes at an increasing pace, slowly building up to a crescendo. In the last episode, Pauline was tied up inside a room at the top of a burning building. Now it was time to find out how she got out of the jam.

Sure enough, her hero came to the rescue. In the last episode, he was too busy fighting the villain to save Pauline. Now the fight was over, the hero had won, and he bravely scurried up a burning staircase. The piano's notes became even higher and shorter as it neared its crescendo. The handsome hero untied Pauline and tied the ropes that had bound her to a support beam that hadn't yet caught fire and used them to effect an escape out a window to safety. The piano player pounded a series of notes that echoed the hero's triumph. Anna Marie clapped and cheered the heroic task with the rest of the audience.

But the villain eventually returned and again managed to steal Pauline away. The music again reflected the urgency of the situation. This time she was tied to a set of train tracks. Hard pounds on the mid-range keys. The audience took hardly a breath as a powerful locomotive came zooming toward the hapless woman. More hard key pounds, this time half an octave higher.

Groans of disappointment erupted as the short film ended. Everyone would have to wait until the next chapter was released, and that might well be another month, maybe two. The lights came back on and the old man got up from his stool and closed the cover of the piano keys. He bowed proudly as most of the patrons applauded his performance.

Certainly Pauline was a goner, Anna Marie concluded when she left the cinematic. No one could survive being run over by a train, and there was no way her hero could get to her in time. He was tied up on a conveyor belt in a saw mill, getting ready to be sliced in half. She shook her head. Anna Marie would come back to see the next film, just to pay her respects to her hero and heroine, if nothing else. At least her own hero was back home waiting for her. She smiled fondly.

By late afternoon, Anna Marie was home and strolling with her intended a few hundred yards away from her house by a wooded patch of land. Luke and Jeb were sitting behind the house talking. Elvetta and Ruby, Anna Marie's mother and aunt, were in the house, probably knitting.

"Did you have a good time with your father and uncle?" Johnathan walked with his hands in the pockets of his overalls. They walked alongside a shallow trench that had once been a creek bed. Now the water was gone and grass grew where minnows once swam.

"Oh, it was wonderful." She sounded ecstatic. "Pauline made it out of the burning building."

"Did she, now?" He wore an amused smile.

"Yep. Her hero climbed up a burning building and saved her," she said. The young woman looked at her beau with wondering eyes. "Would you do that for me?"

"Sure." Johnathan kicked a small rock by his foot.

"Would you climb that tree for me?" Anna Marie pointed to a dead tree by the edge of the old creek bed. Lightning had struck it two years ago and the tree never recovered.

"I'm not climbing any old tree."

"Oh, come on." She nudged his shoulder. "Would you do it for me? All I'm asking is for you to climb one little tree. You can come right back down. I just want to see you do it. Please?"

"Oh alright." Johnathan threw up his hands in defeat and walked toward the old tree. He turned around and gave her a pleading look.

"Go on, I dare you."

Johnathan shook his head and pulled himself up one branch, then a second. Anna Marie smiled as she watched him scale the tree. Her expression revealed shock, then horror. She heard a 'crack' as one of the rotting limbs snapped. There was nothing nearby for the young man to hold on to. Johnathan's head hit an exposed tree root on the ground below. The young woman heard a second 'crack.'

Anna Marie was at his side in an instant. She cradled his broken head ever so gently, ignoring the blood that coated her arms and lap and begged him to speak. When it became clear to her that he would never speak again, the young woman laid him down carefully and ran to the farmhouse, screaming incoherently. It was all her fault, she was certain. She had just as good as killed the man she loved more than life itself. There would be no more walks together, no long life with lots of children, no more cuddles in the hayloft. It was all gone, gone forever. They would put her in jail, she thought. It would be just as well, she believed; that's what she deserved.

Anna Marie was barely aware of strong hands holding her, shouting words at her. It was all her fault. She felt someone making her swallow some horrible tasting concoction. She had killed Johnathan. Someone made her lie down on a bed and urged her to calm down and rest easy. She didn't deserve to live.

Then there was darkness.

Wednesday, October 13, 1915.

Rain spattered against Anna Marie's sullen, pallid face as she walked down the muddy lane with the other mourners behind the motor truck that held the pine box Johnathan lay in. Her expression, dulled by the many home remedies she had been given, distantly reflected her utmost grief. She heard the Parson give his speech, but failed to acknowledge any of the words. Anna Marie felt neither the rain nor the chill. She watched them remove the coffin from the truck. All the many times they had shared together flashed before her eyes as they lowered her love into the cold, muddy ground.

There would be no more talk of marriage, no more secret smiles. There wouldn't be anything left of Johnathan after today. They hadn't conceived.

Anna Marie wanted to stay longer, wanted to stay by his side a while more, but Luke's strong, gentle arms quietly led her away. Only when she heard the first sounds of dirt being shoveled onto Johnathan's coffin did she cry again. This time her tears were silent and without irrational motion. Only now did she realize how much she missed him. Only now did she realize how much she had taken him for granted.

Only now did she realize how deeply she had loved him.

Sunday, February 23, 1919.

Anna Marie looked up from her writing desk. A cold winter rain hit against the window pane of the small cottage she lived in, turning to ice. The young school marm got up and drew the inside shutters closed. The leaden din of the rain and the chill in the air reminded her of the day they had buried Johnathan. Predictably, she preferred to cloister herself on such days.

Normally she would have went to church today, but the weather convinced her to stay home. And, she admitted privately, she felt a great sense of disappointment in the church when Johnathan died. It was so utterly senseless. How could God allow it? The young man had been as God-fearing as they came, so why did he have to die?

Anna Marie cleansed the thought from her mind. Those questions would probably never be answered. She had to prepare lessons for tomorrow, anyhow. There was no time for indulging in such tomfoolery.

A sharp pain in her mid-section brought her from her sorrows. The twenty-two year old woman would be glad when tomorrow came around. Doc Frye would be in and she would find out what this pain was all about. It had bothered her now for a few days, but Anna Marie decided to wait it out, thinking it only a stomach ache. It had gotten much worse since then.

The woman walked to the potbelly stove in the kitchen and stoked up the flames to chase away the chill. Another blast of pain, this time not easing right away, put Anna Marie on her knees, retching. A sickly green bile spilled out onto the creaking wooden floorboards.

There would be no waiting until tomorrow, she decided. This was serious. She had to get to Doc Frye's house right away. Anna Marie wiped her face clean, put on her coat and turned toward the door.

A final wave of agony put her on her knees again. Anna Marie leaned forward, her teeth clenched. She fought to stifle a scream. The woman meant to put her forehead on the floor. If she could catch her breath, she might at least be able to crawl outside and try for a neighbor's house.

Anna Marie's breath never came to her.

III
Devotion

Anna Marie collapsed lifeless to the floor. The heat from the fire faded, then died out altogether. The cottage turned as cold as the weather outside.

Now both lovers were gone.

The host's visage was that of smug triumph as Anna Marie, then her home, faded away, leaving only a clearing by an icy, muddy lane. The lane became a paved road, the clearing an open field close to town. The air warmed slightly as the sky darkened. Clouds gave way to the moon and its infinite celestial companions, all of them floating in endless, timeless orbit, remaining constant while circling a world of unceasing change. The ground was dry once more, the trees in the distance became headstones. Some standing, some not. The long-dead lovers reappeared in their previous spots, Johnathan sitting at the tree and Anna Marie standing nearby. As before, neither looked at the other, both seemed lost in their thoughts.

"They're thinking about what should have been," Perry said. It seemed obvious to him. The thought brought a wistful tone to his normally jovial voice.

The vandals paused to consider the previous scene. True, both Johnathan and Anna Marie were both gone, but something else seemed missing, something intangible but nonetheless present.

"You felt their bond." The evil host spoke in an even voice. "The love between them was almost a presence of its own. Now it, like them, is only a forgotten memory. Everyone who knew them has also long departed from the world of the living." He shrugged. "But to you I'm sure they're just two more dead people. Who gives a damn, right?"

"So what happened to her?" Perry spoke quietly.

"Burst appendix." The shrouded man shrugged again. "Who cares? All that matters is that he gave in to her once and lost his virginity. He gave in to her a second time and lost his life.

"Her first act of stupidity could have led to an early pregnancy which would have been, in that day and age, a terrible scandal and disgrace. Her second act of stupidity, putting him up to that idiotic dare, cost her the love of her life. Her third big error was sheer ignorance. She might well have lived many more years if she had gone to a doctor sooner.

"Now they are both dead, and nobody alive today remembers them. Another forgotten footnote in the annals of history. But I am sure this is all pointless rhetoric to you four."

"You're dead, just like they are." Troy tried vainly to stop sniffling. "How can you stand there and insult them and their lives?"

The shadowy man leveled a malicious glare at the youth. "You are alive, just like they once were. How can you insult their lives by desecrating their graves?"

"I'm sorry." The young man spoke softly. "Really sorry."

Edward looked to Rodney. He was about to speak when Perry felt something touch his shoulder and promptly screamed. They turned around to see a plain-looking woman standing calmly behind them.

The woman was short, barely five feet tall with wavy brown hair and bright blue eyes. She looked a bit thin, somewhat small breasted, and about forty years old. Out of all the strange and tragic individuals they had met so far tonight, this one looked the most pleasant. Her genuinely friendly smile lent her a housewife-ish kind of beauty, attractiveness accented by maturity. She looked to the youngest of the truants and aimed her grin at him.

Edward's face sagged a bit. Secretly, he had always favored older women, and he found himself captivated by this one, despite their unorthodox introduction. To think of her being cold and dead, and he being somewhat responsible for the wrecking of her tombstone, left him feeling confused by the angry swirl of emotions fighting within him.

"Hello, fellows." Her friendly voice sounded far from what they would have expected from a dead person.

"W-who are you?" Troy dared to ask.

"I'm Betty." She held a hand out. "Betty Golladay. Nice to meet you."

"Nice to meet you, too." Troy held back, too afraid to shake her hand.

She showed no offense, and offered her hand to anyone who seemed at all interested in making her acquaintance. Edward timidly took the offered hand. He was surprised at it's softness and gentle touch. Now it was he who had to fight to hold back his emotions.

"What's wrong?" She sounded truly concerned.

The shrouded man said nothing. He watched the scene intently.

Edward's voice came out a whisper. "I'm sorry."

"Sorry? About what?" Her face registered genuine confusion. Edward couldn't speak past the lump in his throat. He simply nodded toward the broken heap of reddish granite that had once been her tombstone. Betty walked to the destroyed monument. "You broke it."

Edward managed a choked-up, "yes."

Betty stood there, eyeing the shattered stone for a long moment. Still the dark host said nothing. He stood silently, concentrating intently upon the changing environment. After a long moment, she turned away, toward the vandals. Now they all stood in the backyard of an aging house the youths recognized as one that still stood in the northeast part of town. A hot afternoon sun beat down upon them all mercilessly, making it hard for the four vandals to breathe. Slowly, they acclimated themselves to the muggy air. Betty seemed not to notice any of them as she struggled to mow the tall grass. The young men gave the contraption she wrestled with a curious glare. It looked similar to a lawnmower, but there was no motor, only two wheels and a half dozen curved and twisted metal blades set in a cylindrical fashion. Sweat began to pour from Betty's face as she went about her work, now oblivious to the young men and their sinister host.

Friday, July 10, 1953.

The thermometer attached to the side of the old, white house read one hundred four degrees. Betty shook her head with disgust as she gave the temperature gauge a withering glare. She hauled the lawnmower into the backyard from the garage and prepared to cut the foot high grass. A chair in front of an electric fan and a glass of iced tea sounded like heaven to her, but there would be time enough for that tonight when she got home. She got paid to work, not lay around. Besides, she told herself, the sooner its done, the sooner I can get back to the kids.

Her concern grew as she thought of her oldest, Roger. The sickly twelve year old had broken his left arm a month ago when he tripped going down a flight of stairs. Roger was never one to complain, and had even lied about the pain so as not to upset his mother. But she knew, as most mothers do, when their children are in pain. Betty pushed the rusted instrument harder, trying not to think about the mounting doctor bills. Doctor Clive was an understanding man and hadn't pressured her about forking over what she owed him, but she hated to test the man's patience.

Catrina, or "Katty" as everyone called her, was totally the opposite of her older brother. The eleven year old was tough as nails and could wrestle down most boys her age. Betty was extremely grateful that God had blessed her with that one. Katty, in addition to inheriting her mother's kindly disposition, was as hard a worker as her mother and did her best to pitch in with the family's expenses. In fact, Katty had been hired to cut the grass. But Betty, not wanting her daughter to risk getting sick in this ungodly heat, had sent Katty home to do the chores that Betty herself normally did. The mother dutifully took the grass-cutting job on herself.

Then there was Albert, her youngest. The ten year old was identical to his father, and Betty had bore the boy a special love because of that. Not that she didn't love her other children, for surely she did, but Albert had a special place in her heart. She also felt sorry for him because the boy had never seen his father, Mitchell. Mitchell had gone off to war and never came back. He had been on a battleship that went down somewhere in the Pacific. Betty took his death especially hard; the man never knew he had fathered a third child.

Betty looked at the progress she had made. She had cut a swath of grass the entire width of the backyard, but only three feet back from the house. At least another forty feet remained. The woman looked up at the sky. Not a rain cloud, or any other kind of cloud, blemished the hazy sky. There was no breeze, and the humidity made the air stifling and hard to breathe. The back door of the house opened and a wrinkled old woman of about eighty poked her head out.

"Dearie, won't you come in out of that terrible heat for a spell and relax?" The old woman's voice and smile were pleasant. "I've made some nice, cold lemonade. You can come in and rest up if you'd like."

"Thank you for the offer, Missus Blake." Betty's words came between panting breaths. "But I really shouldn't. I'll be done before long. I just want to finish up here and get back home. I need to see to my oldest."

The old woman's eyebrows raised, revealing her surprise. "Well, I suppose. But mind you, you'll do yourself in working so hard in this devilish heat. Mark my words, dearie. You'll do better for your children by taking care of yourself."

"I'll be fine." Betty puffed a couple breaths and continued working. The old woman shook her head and disappeared into her house. The tired woman forced the unwilling device through a dozen more swipes across the width of the backyard. Betty sped up her pace so she could get under the shade of an apple tree that stood in the middle of the lot a little sooner.

Instead of feeling cooler, Betty simply felt less overwhelmed by the heat as she stood beneath the low hanging limbs. But without the sun beating down upon her, she felt her situation improved nonetheless. She stopped pushing the cantankerous gadget to lean against the tree's trunk.

One breath, two breaths, three breaths…the air came into her wheezing lungs a little easier with each intake.

"Dearie, I hate to sound like a crotchety old fuddy-duddy," the old woman called from the shaded coolness of her laundry room window. "But I simply hate to see you doing this to yourself. Won't you please come in out of that hot sun and sit a spell with me? You'll feel better and I'd like the company. Please?"

"I'll be just fine," Betty replied. "I've got it half done. The other half won't take long. Not long at all."

"Heaven help you and your children." The spindly woman shook her head as she lamented. "Mark my words, girl. You'll end up wearing a wooden overcoat if you don't take better care of yourself." Old lady Blake shook a chastising index finger at the younger woman and retreated further into the house.

Betty shook her head. Missus Blake's offer sounded very tempting, but she really wanted to get back and see to her oldest. On a rational level, Betty was sure he was fine, but the mothering instincts within her ordered her back to work so she could get home sooner. She wished she didn't need the money so badly, but work was hard to come by. True, they all ate well, but paying the mortgage and doctor bills were totally different matters altogether. Now more than ever she missed and needed Mitchell. But he was gone and she couldn't afford to dwell upon his memory. Her children needed her too much to allow that.

Betty irritably grabbed the handle of the old mower and began pushing. She came to a sudden stop. Looking down, she saw a partially rotten apple caught between the blades. Betty reached down and gently pulled the sour fruit free. She felt something stab one of her fingers. Betty let out a short scream and dropped the fruit. Bees started flying out of a hole in the rotted part of the apple. Betty swatted at them as they buzzed about her head, backing away as she did so.

The woman looked around, all of a sudden wondering why she was in someone else's yard. Betty's head began to swim, her thoughts grew clouded. Something was wrong. She had to get to a hospital, she was allergic to bee-stings. Where were the kids? Betty started toward the house…the children had to be fed soon. Mitchell was dead, Betty had to break the news to the children.

Betty didn't feel the pain when she hit the ground face first. She didn't feel anything. There was only darkness and a distant, vague sense of urgency.

Betty awoke slowly. She had no idea how long she'd been asleep, but figured it had to have been a while since it was dark. Her back ached. It figures, she thought. Sleeping on the old woman's hard couch would give anyone a back ache. Thank goodness she was nice enough to let her to come in and rest.

Betty began to stretch. She had felt the padding on her left side, but why was the couch padded on the right side as well? Betty started to sit up and promptly hit her head on something hard. She started to raise her arms, but discovered that whatever was over her head was over her arms as well. Betty maneuvered her hands and feet and realized something heavy was on top of the couch, boxing her in.

Then the horrible truth dawned on her. They had buried her! She was still alive and inside her own coffin! Betty screamed in panic and began to scratch and frantically beat against the lid of her coffin. She twisted around, shouting her denial, trying to find some way to free herself. The total darkness magnified her terror. Betty tried scratching at the cushions at her sides to no avail. Again and again, she resumed trying to beat on the coffin's lid. She had to get out! She had to get back to her children! What would they do without her?

Betty realized that there would be no escape, no returning to her children. She began to cry. Why her? She loved her children, she worked her fingers to the bone to support the four of them. What had she done to deserve this? If only she could see them again. She never had a chance to say good-bye or "I love you" one last time.

Her sobs were broken by gasps for air. Grief turned to blind panic as Betty threw herself as hard as she could against the coffin's lid. She ignored the pain, ripping and tearing her fingernails against the hard wooden slab just above her face. Betty wanted to scream, needed to voice her terror. She barely managed a frightened whisper. Her head began to hurt. Sweat ran into her eyes, burning them terribly. Betty desperately tried to gasp a final prayer. Nothing. She strained her lungs in a futile attempt to pull in air that no longer existed. Tears ran down her cheeks again as the end drew near. Her poor children!

What would happen to them now? Spots burst before her eyes as her oxygen-starved brain began to shut down. Why hadn't her love been enough to prevent this fate? Her chest was in agony, the pain in her head was almost enough to drive her insane. Who would take care of Roger?

Betty, despite her utmost resistance, closed her eyes and went to sleep.

IV
The Dark One

The ineffable darkness gave way to moonlight. Although the vandals could still breathe, they hadn't been able to see Betty. Instead, they heard her gasps for air and sensed the pain and terror Betty endured at the time of her death. The feeling passed as her eyes closed. The vandals could again see their breath as the air they breathed dipped to the thirty-nine degrees of the cemetery's surface.

Betty once again stood among the vandals. She stared at the broken headstone with a mixture of anger, grief, and fear. The young men felt uncomfortable, not knowing what kind of reaction to expect from the ghost.

"It's just as well." Betty kicked at a piece of rose-colored rubble. "They had no right putting me in the ground! None! Why didn't they wait? Why? I wasn't dead! I woke up, but they had already given up on me! Why?" The short woman began to cry again. "I was a good mother...I needed to get out of there and get back to my children...but I couldn't! I couldn't get out of that box! Why? Why did they leave me in there?" She leaned against Edward, who slowly put his arm around her.

Had he not known better, he would have sworn there was a living, breathing woman leaning against him. The shudder of her shoulders, her sniffles, the softness of her flesh beneath the dress...it was too real yet completely unreal for the young man. Edward didn't know whether to feel sadness for the woman's tragedy, anger and regret for their destructive antics, desire for her plain beauty, or fearfulness for being so close to a walking, talking person who had been dead for so many years. "I don't know." He leaned his face closer to her ear. "At least you're not in there now."

"But I *was* in there!" She wailed. "I couldn't breathe and my fingers hurt, but I had to get out and get back to my children! Don't you understand?"

"I want to," the young man replied. Betty said nothing. She continued to lean against him, weeping quietly.

The evil host now stood behind Edward and lay a cold hand upon the vandal's other shoulder. It smelled of sulfur and decaying meat. "Do you still romanticize the transition from life to death? Were you lost in wonderment when the boy drowned? Did the young farmer's injury remind you of some slapstick comedy? Did you find yourself excited when the young woman bent over in her death throes? Can you find anything other than tragedy in witnessing the suffocation of the woman beside you? Could you look into her eyes and explain how her death fascinates you?"

Edward looked into Betty's eyes. There was no more room for neutrality in his heart. At that moment, the young man wanted nothing more in all the world than to hold and comfort the woman beside him. Edward felt the hot sting of tears. He started to speak when Betty pressed two fingers to his lips.

"Don't." Her voice reflected more concern for him than for herself. "Something good has to come from this. My time is over. I don't want you to spend yours dwelling on me. I didn't want to leave the world like I did, but I've gone to a better place. And I know all three of my children turned out just fine. And don't you go on dreaming about death, either. When it's time, you'll find out what it's like. Just remember that death is forever, but life is only for a while. Enjoy it while you have it."

Edward nodded and bowed his head. "I'm sorry things can't be different."

Betty smiled sadly. "I know you won't forget me, so I won't even ask you. But I want your word, if you care about me even just a little bit, that when you find the right girl, you won't hold back. You'll give her all that you have inside of you to give. Can you promise me that?"

Edward stilled his quivering lip. "I promise."

"Thank you." Betty smiled. She gently withdrew from him and stood away, closer to the malevolent spirit.

Rodney turned to the shrouded man. "So what about you? You're not so old. How did you end up here?"

"I would tell you." The dark figure talked slowly. "But if I had any breath, I would just be wasting it on the effort. Besides, why should you care? You came here to have fun and wreck things, remember? You have accomplished the latter, but tell me, O Violent One, have you had much fun tonight? Have you enjoyed watching people die? Do any of you still believe fun can be had by destroying the only remaining testimonies to these people's lives? Consider also this: all of you are still young, but someday each one of you will find a place for yourselves right here. How then will you feel when a group of idiots similar to yourselves comes along and smashes the only reminders that any of you have ever lived? Well?"

"I care." Perry spoke softly. No trace of his earlier humor remained; he was as solemn as his fellows.

"Me too." Troy nodded his head.

"I care." Edward said it as much to Betty as to his dark host.

"Yeah," Rodney said. His tone had lost its surliness, even sounding sympathetic. "I'll listen. Tell me about yourself. Which one was yours?"

"That one." The shrouded form pointed to the black obelisk.

Rodney walked over to it. He noticed his eyes weren't quite as sharp as they normally were, but he could make out the lettering in the full moonlight. "'Malachai Ian MacGriffith. Born March 23, 1923. Died September 14, 1967,'" the man read aloud.

"There is more at the base, if you care to read it," Malachai said. His tone sounded more grim than before.

"'As dark as the heart that once beat here,'" Rodney read, "'this stone stands, a reminder to all who would lend death to their fellow man in the name of science.'"

"Y-you killed someone?" Troy asked. Now he wondered if he would ever be allowed to leave this terrible, and terribly sad, place.

Malachai nodded wordlessly. There was no hint of sadness or regret in those dark, soulless eyes. Only pain and hatred resided in his expression. "And now my tale," he said quietly.

The young men stood silently, mesmerized by the change again in their surroundings. The mild air smelled of springtime. They were surrounded by more than a hundred people, all dressed in robes, wearing graduation caps, and seated in wooden chairs facing a makeshift stage in the middle of a football field. A heavyset, bald man made his way to the stage, which bore a single microphone. Though the instrument was archaic in design, it looked relatively new. The sun hung low in the clear sky, heralding the coming twilight. A younger version of the shrouded host sat with his arms folded before his chest, an angry glare on his youthful face.

Wednesday, June 3, 1942.

The dark blue gown made Malachai feel as if he were wearing a funeral shroud. He stood among a hundred other people wearing the same garb, perhaps none of them realizing that they all looked like so many walking stiffs. Something in the back of his mind told him he ought to feel happy, even elated, at being here today. It was the same voice that didn't seem to get the hint that ambition, not pointless optimism, led to achievement and success.

The assemblage watched as a short and pudgy, bald and bespectacled man in a suit older than all of the students and some of the teachers climbed three steps to reach the floor of a makeshift stage set upon the school's football field. It was Elmer Gislow, the school superintendent. The aging educator approached a microphone standing front and center. Gislow cleared his throat and spoke into the device.

"Good evening, ladies and gentlemen. First of all, I want to congratulate each and every one of you for being able to come here tonight." The headmaster spoke in a voice Malachai couldn't hear. The tall, brown haired young man watched the man's lips intently, soaking in every word. "It is my sincerest hopes that in the days and years ahead, each and every one of you will use the knowledge you've gained here to help make the world a better place. When this war is over, a war we *will* win," cheers and whistles filled the early evening air, "it will take many hands to rebuild this world into a place better than it was before. And when I look out amongst the young men and women here tonight, I know for a reassuring fact that the world is in good hands." The gathered students and their families clapped and cheered again.

Yeah, get on with it, Malachai silently huffed. The duffer could be agonizingly long-winded, the high school senior thought to himself.

"Leading this class into that brighter future," the educator continued, "is a young man whose brilliance, tenacity, and determination shines as a beacon for others to follow."

Any place is better than this, Malachai thought.

"So let's have a big round of applause…"

Kiss my ass, Gislow.

"…for the graduating class of 1942…"

I wish I had a gun right now.

"…class valedictorian…"

I hope you rot in hell.

"Malachai Ian MacGriffith!"

Malachai's parents clapped heartily as their only child faked a smile, walked forward, and humbly climbed the steps to the stage. The lead graduate accepted his diploma in one hand, and shook the headmaster's hand with the other. Applause from his classmates was scattered and half-hearted. The valedictorian seemed just as happy without his classmates' enthusiasm. Malachai noticed the glare of the overhead lights reflecting off the man's bald head and almost burst out laughing. He managed to limit his reaction to a smile that the short man took as a gesture of friendship.

The graduate barely resisted the urge to punch the chief educator right there in front of everyone. This entire ceremony, to Malachai's mind, was nothing more than a waste of time. Despite all the speeches touting the limitless potential of the young people amassed here, most of them would end up living mediocre lives toiling away at menial jobs. They would live without any inclination to better themselves, yet prod their children into trying to conquer the world. Those children, in turn, would end up just as miserably average as their parents. And this fat bastard, Gislow, was instrumental in perpetuating this cycle of false hopes and broken promises.

Malachai had gone through his first eight years of education at a private school for the handicapped, his hearing lost to scarlet fever when he was two. Even then his mind grasped at everything they could teach. At the end of his eighth grade year, he had wanted to go to a normal high school. He was certain he could do just as well as anyone else. His parents had hesitated, but they ultimately allowed it. On an academic level, Malachai was akin to a giant among dwarves. Socially, however, it had always been the other way around.

And now Gislow was making him into a spectacle once more. One last chance to put him on the spot because he was different from everyone else. Malachai wished the old man would just leave him alone. He had tried to beg out of this dreaded task, but the superintendent had insisted. Malachai was the smartest student in the school. The young man's parents also encouraged him to make his graduation speech. Malachai knew they meant well, but he wished they would have stayed out of it. So here he was.

"Congratulations, Malachai." Mister Gislow's voice was warm and sincere.

Cocksucker.

"Thank you, mister Gislow." Malachai's voice sounded no different from any hearing person's.

"If you please." The older man motioned invitingly to the microphone. "Won't you say a few words to your classmates? You've been such an inspirational student here, Mister MacGriffith. We would love to hear your acceptance speech."

"Certainly." Malachai walked to the mike. He stood there for a moment, surveying the crowd before him. He had both his speeches prepared; the speech he would give with his voice, and the speech he would give with his heart. Satisfied that all was ready, he began.

"Fellow classmates of Manchester High School graduating class of 1942, it has been a true honor to have studied among you these last four years." All these years I have walked among you, feeling like a stranger in a strange land. I look like I could be one of you. But I am not one of you.

"Truly, it has been a blessing and a privilege to have been a member of this student body. My father has often told me that the hardest challenges bring the greatest rewards. You could say that that axiom was proven true tonight on this night of nights, but I would disagree. I would say it has been proven every day that we left this school building with the knowledge that we have expanded our own worlds, even if only by small degrees." I have pushed myself to my limits and beyond, physically and academically, just to have any chance at all of surviving in your world; a world of radios, records, laughter and singing. A world of sound, in which I have no place.

"As I look out among you tonight, I see the future leaders of America's proud tomorrow. I see doctors and lawyers, engineers and financiers. I see also the firemen and policemen, the factory workers and soldiers, the backbone of our great society. We are tomorrow's leaders, and I am proud to stand among you." You girls laugh at me, you guys make jokes about my deafness. The coach wouldn't let me run track because I couldn't hear the starter's pistol. God damn every last one of you.

"It has been said that achievement is the measure of a true man. I say that achievement is measured differently for each of us. I believe that achievement should be measured by the difference between what a man begins as and what he becomes. Therefore, say not to your fellow man that his profession is inferior and that he is a lesser man than you. For it is not how high we climb, but how far we have come that defines true success." No matter how hard I try, no matter how many mountains I climb, I'll always be different from you, and I hate you, all of you, for it. You have the one thing I would give anything to possess, and you take it for granted. I'm smarter than you, all of you, but in your minds I'll never be equal to even the least of you.

"In closing, I want to thank all of you, my classmates as well as the faculty, who have made my time here a joy and a privilege. So let us go now to do our best to win this war and create that brave, new tomorrow Mister Gislow spoke of." I don't give a damn for either the Japs or the Nazis, but I'd love to see them win for no better reason than to see you all in chains, starting with this fat prick standing next to me.

Malachai proudly stepped down from the stage to a solid round of applause. To the graduate, it looked like they were all performing an odd sort of two-handed wave. I curse them and they love me for it, Malachai thought with a private smile. He waved to his parents as he rejoined his classmates. The young man continued to smile even as he sat among his peers. It crossed his mind that while he went on to medical school, some of these bastards would get shot full of holes thousands of miles from home. It was a heart warming thought for the young man.

Friday, December 20, 1957.

Malachai sat in a chair that could generously be described as uncomfortable. Or it could have been the fact that he now sat before the Board of Directors that made him uneasy. These ten men would announce the course of his career within the next thirty seconds or so. It was enough to make Malachai want to vomit. Medical school, the further education in medical science, the years working on projects of lesser importance, the dreams of seeing this day come to pass for the last fifteen years, it all hinged on what the young doctor considered a proverbial flip of a coin.

The spokesman for the board, Doctor Stephen Raymond, a handsome, white-haired man with a square jaw and powerful build casually looked over a ream of papers while the other nine men sat quietly. Some of them looked thoughtfully at Malachai while others were clearly as bored as he was nervous.

Finally, Raymond looked up at Malachai. He remained silent for a moment, gauging the young scientist's reaction to the unexpected delay. Malachai matched his gaze with one of his own. The two men entered a silent contest of wills as each man mentally commanded the other to break eye contact first. The other board members began to fidget about nervously, all of them wondering what was going on.

Raymond blinked first, satisfied with the younger man's tenacity. "This Board is in a quandary, Doctor MacGriffith. Your educational records are exemplary, and we're convinced you have the skills necessary to lead the research group you've put together.

"But, quite frankly, we think your proposal has very little realistic chance of producing the desired results. And, lest we forget, the Parke-Davis research project was a decided failure. As much as we would like to grant you funding for your project, we're inclined to reject your proposal. However, if there is anything you would like to say that that might convince us otherwise, now would be the time to say it."

Malachai stood, hoping the elevation difference between himself and the seated men would give him an advantage. He carefully controlled his facial expressions, hiding his anxiety and fear of rejection beneath a mask of confidence. Slowly, he convinced himself of that confidence. He cleared his throat and began to speak.

"Gentlemen of the Board," Malachai said. "It is with the utmost pleasure that I accept your compliments as well as your faith in my abilities. But if I may, I would like to diffuse any misunderstanding regarding my projects, past and present.

"First of all, I would like to remind this Board that although the research project at Parke-Davis has been deemed a failure, there have been a number of success cases.

"When my team developed phencyclidines, or PCP for short, we believed at the time that we had discovered the perfect anesthetic. The drug numbed the central nervous system even as it mildly stimulated the heart. This made it possible to perform surgeries on patients who could not have otherwise survived being anesthetized. And it *was* a success for a number of patients. True, some recipients reported feelings of weightlessness and other similar reactions, but thirty percent of the people who were given this drug reported no side-effects whatsoever. Thus, PCP was not the total failure that many of its critics have called it. Had the funding not been cut at the first sign of trouble, my team could have corrected the problem and PCP would still be in use in hospitals today. Even now, PCP is in use by veterinarians as a favored animal tranquilizer. So the claims that the Parke-Davis research project was a total failure are not only exaggerated, but completely false.

"In regards to my current project proposal, I think this Board is being hasty in its decision. What I am proposing isn't just a medical breakthrough, but a technological one as well. Through the use of plastics, we believe we can reconstruct the bones in the middle ear, thus restoring hearing to many who would otherwise remain deaf. We are also trying to develop ways in which the main auditory nerve can be restored."

"And what sort of progress has your team made toward that end?" A balding man named Rudy Goldstein regarded the young doctor skeptically. Goldstein's thick glasses sat perched upon the end of his hawk-like nose as he stared at the man he addressed. He obviously had no love for this upstart, his checkered qualifications, nor his outlandish claims. The young poppinjay might as well announce his intentions to sail to the moon for all the believability his claims carried.

"We are still exploring the possibilities," Malachai admitted. "But we have made progress toward a possible transplant procedure of the cochlea. All of the research done to date is in the packet I have submitted."

Raymond looked around to his peers, trading hushed comments with them. Two of them shrugged their indifference, Goldstein threw up his hands in disgust, but the majority seemed interested. Raymond faced Malachai again. "I know you have a personal stake in this, doctor. In a way, that makes me hesitant toward backing your research. Wild promises ending in failure could prove disastrous, financially for us, professionally and emotionally for you. But considering your qualifications, references, and past successes, however limited, this Board has concluded that the funding for your research should be approved." He sighed. "I'm not sold on the idea of repairing the main auditory nerve as I don't believe it can be done, but the other proposals merit attention. Therefore, we're going to create a budget in an amount to be determined within the next thirty days. You'll be contacted after the first of the year when the next meeting is scheduled.

"Congratulations, doctor. I hope your research is successful, for personal reasons as well as professional."

The ten seated men stood up together and began to file out of the room. One by one, Malachai shook hands with them, thanking the men and bidding them farewell. Goldstein's handshake lacked all sincerity. Malachai couldn't care less. He had gotten his approval and that was all that mattered. The young doctor walked to a stairwell and descended toward the ground floor. He was too keyed up for the elevator.

All the years of being different, separated from the rest of the world, rushed to the forefront of his mind. Malachai had pursued a career in medicine with the distant hope that someday this day might come. Now he had his chance, he had gotten his funding. Someday he would make his experiments work.

Someday he would hear again.

Monday, August 16, 1965.

Malachai gave the hallway he stood in a melancholy glare. He hadn't seen the inside of this building in more than twenty years. He had hoped when he left this place that he would never again see its interior. But here he was, back in his old high school, now as a teacher rather than a student. He hefted a stack of books and papers as he walked into a classroom. It was empty, but within a week there would be students attending classes here.

It was simply a means to an end, Malachai reminded himself. The former scientist had come across some old folders detailing medical experiments conducted by the Nazi's during the war. Some of them had greatly helped Malachai and his team in making some of the breakthroughs they had aimed for. The plastic ear bone replacements had worked, the only side-effect being a chemical property within the plastic itself that caused infections. Had Goldstein not shut them down, Malachai and his assistants were certain they could correct the problem.

Goldstein. The name stuck in Malachai's throat like a glob of sour bile. Goldstein had never liked or trusted him. And when the old Jew learned about the folders, he was as happy as he was enraged. As Goldstein saw it, it was a continuation of the Holocaust, but it was also the ammunition he needed to discredit Malachai and cancel his generous funding. But the researcher's woes didn't end there. Goldstein had pressed on until at last Malachai's medical license was stripped from him.

After being defrocked, Malachai moved back to the house his parents had owned a few miles outside of town. They had both died some years earlier, and the former scientist had to renovate the place just to make it livable again. In the process of fixing the place up, he had turned the basement into a crude but serviceable laboratory. Goldstein might have taken his funding and his license away, but Malachai still had his parents' considerable amount of money and he still had the old folders. He would just have to work out of his house and conduct his experiments by himself. But if he could prove his theories beyond a shadow of a doubt, perhaps he could persuade enough of his former rivals to defy Goldstein and overturn their ruling. Success would be his redemption. Nothing else would get their attention, and nothing- absolutely nothing-else mattered, Malachai believed.

Now the research was expanding to a point where he could no longer afford his work solely on the money his parents had left him, so he had applied for a job at his old alma mater. Soon he would be teaching science and math courses to support himself while the family fortune paid for the high-powered microscopes, X-ray machines, and contracts to various plastics manufacturers. He hoped that within two years he would be at the same point he had been when Goldstein bullied and cajoled his peers into standing against him. Another year after that, who knows? It was a distant hope, but enough to keep him from giving up.

A fringe benefit of his new job, one that made him welcome this bittersweet opportunity, was unlimited access to the school's lab. Now the school system would indirectly fund some of his research. The scientist smiled.

Monday, September 26, 1966.

Malachai wiped his sweaty hands on a dry towel. He shook them, trying to work out the jitters that came over him. The cat lay still on the table before him. He didn't use much anesthetic, hopefully just enough to put the animal out for the duration of the surgery. Money was getting dear and Malachai didn't want to waste any more supplies than was absolutely necessary. The scientist stroked the cat's striped side as he looked at the small cart beside him.

Everything was ready. It was time to remove the animal's hearing organs. Once this was done, Malachai would have the precise dimensions of each individual part of the cat's inner ears. These dimensions would then be given to the plastics contractor who would, hopefully, fashion some artificial hearing organs to be replaced inside the animal's aural canal.

The scientist adjusted the intense overhead light and slipped on a pair of specially crafted glasses that would enable him to see well enough to perform his delicate work. Malachai took a couple deep breaths to calm himself, then set to the task. He held open the cat's ear with two fingers of one hand, and began performing the first incision.

The animal awoke with an ear-piercing shriek and jumped off the table. Malachai, taken totally by surprise, fell backwards off his stool. He regained his composure and stood up. The animal, more afraid than hurt, wailed again as it huddled in a corner of the basement laboratory. Malachai smiled as he looked at the small beast. He dropped his scalpel and laughed until tears of joy fell down his cheeks.

He had heard the cat's screams.

Malachai had no idea how long he had just stood there, staring at that beautiful animal, marveling at this discovery. When the immediate joy of the moment subsided, the former doctor realized that his hearing had not miraculously been restored to him. Rather, he had been able to hear high-pitched screams all along. He just hadn't heard one until now. Sure, Malachai had been around cats before, he had seen plenty of them in his science classes, but this was the first time he'd actually heard one wail.

The phenomenon of some hearing-impaired people being able to hear certain sounds and not others wasn't new to Malachai. He had assumed long ago that he was totally deaf. Now that Malachai knew he wasn't, the question of what other sounds could he hear surfaced. Could he, perhaps, hear a human's scream? Could he, perhaps, kill two birds with one stone by continuing his work with a human subject?

Could he, perhaps, cross the line none of his peers had the courage to breach?

Saturday, January 14, 1967.

Malachai's narrow, beady, green eyes locked onto the wide open, nervously darting blue eyes of his least favorite student, Wally Atkinson. The eighteen year old gave his mentor his undivided attention. This was a first, the teacher noted wryly to himself. Malachai let the youth wait a bit longer. He had savored this moment on both professional and personal levels for some time. No reason to rush things, the older man believed. He cleared his throat before speaking.

"Suppose I told you that this unorthodox meeting was set up because of your failure to pay proper attention in my class." Malachai couldn't resist teasing the young man.

"I swear, I won't slack off again!" The terror was evident in Wally's face and voice.

Malachai chuckled. "No, Mister Atkinson, I assure you, this has nothing to do with your lack of scholastic enthusiasm."

"Is this about me making fun of you behind your back?" the boy asked. "I'm sorry! I really mean it!"

Again the short, bitter laugh. "I would be doing this anyway, Mister Atkinson. However, your dismal academic performance, coupled with your insensitive jibes, merely convinced me to select you for this project. You see, my funds are dwindling and I can no longer afford my contract with the plastics manufacturer I do business with. So I'm forced to borrow some of your body parts instead of having them artificially constructed." Malachai held up a tiny scalpel. "The various pieces of your middle and inner ear are vital to my research. Of course, I will not be using any sort of anesthetic. Your screams will give me something to listen to while I work. It is also why your head has been completely secured to the table I built especially for this purpose. After all, I can't work if you start squirming and turning your head around. And I have to have something suitable to restrain you upon, don't I?"

"Please don't! Don't do it!"

Malachai scoffed. "And let you go? To forego my research in favor of prison? I think not. Besides, you'd just end up in some dead-end job, living the all-American dream of hopeless mediocrity. Believe me, I'm doing you a favor.

"But, as compensation for the extreme discomfort I'm about to put you through, I promise to kill you quickly and painlessly when we're finished."

"No! Oh, God please!" Wally said. "Don't do it!"

"I can't hear you." The researcher's voice was light and mild as he inserted his instrument into the young man's left ear. "I'm afraid you'll have to speak up."

Wally tried to hold back a shout when he felt the first incision. Malachai concentrated mightily, as much upon his carving as his listening. His perseverance was rewarded when he picked up on the young man's agonized shrieks. It was almost too low for the scientist to hear, but hear it he did, even if just barely.

Malachai smiled, even deigning to hum along as he probed and cut deeper into Wally's head. Another victory for science, the surgeon noted triumphantly. A warm feeling washed over him. His research was taking a huge step forward.

Truly this was a beautiful day.

Sunday, February 26, 1967.

"You don't know how sorry I am about your boyfriend." Malachai spoke to seventeen year old Jody Heltzel. His tone was solemn, if not sincere, as he looked intently at the tall, red-haired young woman. Jody stood a full six feet tall with hair that spilled down to the middle of her back. Her appearance was one of incongruity, a well-muscled body with large breasts and an attractive face. Malachai could easily understand Wally's attraction to her. "Poor Wallace. Losing one so young and full of life is always a tragedy. But then, life seems naught but full of tragedies." He stroked the side of the girl's face with a soft hand. "Consider yourself: a beautiful young woman whose life has been turned upside down by the loss of her boyfriend. And if that weren't enough, the young man was lost to a mysterious disappearance. Tragic."

Malachai picked up a scalpel from a table and wiped it down with a paper towel moistened with disinfectant. He turned back and regarded Jody curiously. "How did you ever figure out that I had something to do with Wallace's demise?"

"I didn't know anything! I swear! I told you my car broke down a mile up the road!" The girl struggled against the leather straps that held her fast. "Please! Let me go! I won't tell anyone! I promise! I just want to go home!"

Malachai regarded her with an I-know-better-than-that expression. "You know I'm not going to believe you. About the not telling anyone part, that is. And even if I were so foolish, I certainly couldn't release you until my work on you is complete. Not to mention that you haven't screamed for me yet." He shook his head. "I have no idea what the youth of today is coming to. So foolish and rude.

"Now that you're here, I'm going to give you one final lesson. You were a good student, so hopefully you'll grasp my reasoning for this whole ordeal you're going through.

"Inside a person's ear are a great many tiny hairs. Certain sounds cause certain hairs to vibrate. These vibrations are transmitted to the brain and then translated into recognizable sounds. When these hairs are damaged, they cease to function. That is why some people can hear some sounds and are totally oblivious to others.

"Such is the case with myself. I lost my hearing to scarlet fever when I was very young. For more than forty years I had thought myself totally deaf. But recently I discovered that I can indeed hear certain sounds. For instance, I can hear screams, but only if they're high-pitched and produced at a suitable volume level.

"Your boyfriend, for example, was a good screamer, but he was a bit low-pitched. I'm hoping you'll produce better results. Hearing you scream when I remove the bones within your middle and inner ears and implant those of your boyfriend's is a welcome bonus. Of course, the main purpose here is to find out if one person's middle and inner ears will function inside another person. It would mean a big step toward restoring my own hearing…in a roundabout way."

"But I thought you were a doctor!" The girl held back her fearful tears. "How can you do this?"

"It's too long a story to go into, but suffice to say that I came to the conclusion years ago that in the field of medical research, the ends justify the means. Speaking of doctors, hold on." Malachai picked up a contraption that looked like a cross between a tiny flashlight and a stethoscope. He flicked a small switch on the device, then placed the stethoscope end to the girl's chest. Malachai watched the light blink in time with her heartbeats. He scowled and shut the thing off before laying it aside. "You have a heart murmur. Damn."

The scientist considered her for a long moment. "I can't afford risking a cardiac-related episode by exposing you to a great degree of trauma. So there won't be any screaming for you. Still, I might be able to save the day yet."

Malachai turned around and walked to a small wall cabinet. He withdrew a large glass vial and a hypodermic. The scientist extracted enough serum to nearly fill the syringe. Malachai returned to his patient and gently injected the liquid into a vein in her arm.

"What are you doing?" Jody was too terrified to raise her voice above a whisper.

"A little anesthetic," Malachai said. His tone was assuring. "In fact, I invented this myself some years ago. Those idiots at Parke-Davis never gave me the credit I was due, but then that always seems to be the case. There." He withdrew the needle, then dabbed at the tiny wound with a bit of cotton. "We'll just give it a moment to put you under." He turned around and replaced the syringe inside the cabinet. "Now we won't have to worry about triggering a heart attack when I start cutting." Malachai turned around and picked up the scalpel he had cleaned off. He stopped and stared in confusion at Jody's enraged expression. What the hell was going on, he wondered. She should have been put out by now.

Malachai's confusion became total shock when Jody snapped out of the leather bonds. He moved to restrain her. She grabbed his arms and threw him over the table he kept his instruments laid out on. Malachai scurried backwards and stood up, the scalpel still in his grasp. Jody continued to advance. The scientist cut a long gash down her right arm. She ignored it and threw him hard against the back wall. Malachai dropped the blade and tried to shield himself from the fists as strong as battering rams that pummeled him.

For the first time in his memory, Malachai was truly afraid. What had gone wrong? This had never happened before! He would ponder the mystery later. Right now he had to win this fight.

Malachai squatted down and rolled away from his attacker. He overturned tables and chairs to slow Jody down. She plowed through his feeble barricades as she chased after him. The girl batted away the objects her captor threw at her with similar ease. Malachai grabbed the syringe from the cabinet and filled its chamber with air. He steadied himself, then lunged at Jody as she flung herself upon him. They collided with a loud 'thud.' Malachai pumped the huge air bubble into her as she grabbed him by the neck. The scientist fervently hoped he would live long enough for the air bubble to hit her brain. Malachai tried to pry her hands away from his neck while trying to see past the spots exploding before his eyes.

Jody's body jerked suddenly. Malachai slipped free and leaned against a wall. The air bubble had reached her brain. The flow of blood forced the air bubble to rupture a vessel in the girl's brain. Jody fell to the floor, dead from the stroke her captor induced. Malachai collapsed beside her.

She had very nearly won, Malachai realized. The thought scared him. Had she went for the stairs instead of trying to kill him, Malachai knew he couldn't have stopped her. The scientist lay there a moment, rallying his strength. This had never happened before with anyone under the influence of phencyclidines! Worse, his lab was a complete wreck. Malachai sat up and looked around. It would take some time to repair the damage.

The doctor got up and further examined the wreckage. To his glee, none of the tissues and organs appeared damaged. Malachai looked to dead Jody. At least he could extract the parts he needed from her. But now he would need a third subject. He shook his head. Malachai needed to fix his lab and recover from the terrible beating he had taken. When all was in order, *then* he would find a third subject. Again the scientist shook his head.

Today had not been a good day for science.

Thursday, September 14, 1967.

Malachai walked away from the lake, and the corpse he had just dumped there, making his way toward his car. The sun would be up soon, he noted. He picked up his pace. There were classes to teach, a daily routine to follow, a life to lead. The blond fifteen year old soprano soloist's petite body lay at the water's bottom, her body having rejected the body parts implanted within her. Not even her melodious screams had persuaded him to spare her life. Malachai had beaten her restrained body to death with his bare hands.

Malachai got into his car and pulled away from the local fishing hole, totally unaware of the eyes that watched his grim task and subsequent departure. The fisherman, sitting in a rowboat and concealed under a low-hanging tree branch, waited until the school teacher left, then rowed to where the body had been dumped. After searching the general area, the middle-aged man found the body and hauled it to shore. His eyes widened with grief and shock when he recognized the young girl.

His eyes narrowed dangerously when he remembered the identity of the man who had brought her here.

Malachai sat on the couch in his living room, mulling over a cup of black coffee. What now? He had hidden this last body as he had the others. He hoped that, like the others, the body would be suitably decomposed before being discovered, preventing anyone from finding out what had been done to them. But that wasn't enough. What would he do now with his work failed? He would go on with his job, surely, but what else was there? Malachai was a scientist first and foremost. What else was there for him? Were there no more mountains for him to climb? Had this road really come to a dead end, or did there still exist a way to prove his theories correct?

Malachai's thoughts were shaken from him when he saw the silhouettes of two men bounding up his front porch. He didn't question their presence, he simply dropped his coffee and ran to the back door. Malachai reached for the knob as the door burst open and two more men in plain shirts and jeans lumbered in. The scientist backpedaled and raced down the stairs to his lab. His only hope lay in getting to the gun he had stowed away there since the incident with Jody. Malachai opened a cabinet and grabbed the weapon as strong arms seized him. The school teacher tried to turn around to fire the gun when more arms kept his weapon pointed safely away. Malachai managed to squeeze off a shot that flew harmlessly to the side before a younger man's hands wrenched the weapon out of his grasp.

Then the beating began. All eight fists slammed into his chest, face, and stomach until Malachai collapsed in pain. Then they began kicking him, breaking two of his ribs before he was hauled to his feet.

"Why?" A middle-aged man who looked a great deal like the girl dumped in the lake shook the murderer. "Why Linda?"

"I needed to know." Malachai hissed through clenched teeth. "I had to see if the experiment would work." He hung his head in final, ignominious defeat. "It didn't. Her body wouldn't accept the tissue I transplanted into her from the others."

"You mean the other two kids who disappeared?" This next man might have been an uncle. Malachai nodded.

"Look at this!" A young man of about twenty, perhaps the girl's brother, held up a ledger he had briefly thumbed through.

The fourth man, a seemingly unrelated man of about thirty with dark hair, took the book and glanced through it. His eyes got wider the more he read. He shook the book accusingly in the scientist's face. "You been chopping these kids up for some sick experiment?"

Malachai stood his ground. There was nothing left to lose. He looked at the book-holding man defiantly. "You take your hearing for granted, all of you! And what are you? You're common rabble! What purpose do any of you serve besides being beasts of burden? I had it all! I came from a rich family, I was strong in mind and body. Except for my hearing. And because of that, I had to fight twice as hard to get ahead in your world! And everywhere I went I was an outcast for a flaw I had no control over.

"So when I saw my chance to continue my work, I took it. And what would those damn kids have amounted to, anyway? Would they have made the contributions to science that I have? Would any of them have ever risen above the level of trailer trash?" Malachai lowered his gaze. His anger was spent, now there was only emptiness.

"I heard enough." The father's voice seemed to growl. He and the uncle proceeded to strap Malachai to the table he had placed his human test subjects upon. "Get his books and what-nots."

"Gonna turn him over to the cops?" the son asked.

"I got something better in mind." The other three men gathered the ledgers and papers Malachai had accumulated over the years. The father lumped these in a heap by the table the doomed man lay upon. The uncle, son, and family friend left, allowing the man a moment alone with Malachai. The son returned a minute later with a can of gasoline. The father's face was expressionless as he took the can and doused the paper, the walls, and everything else flammable with the liquid. They ignored the curses Malachai hurled as the girl's father soaked the disgraced scientist with the remainder of the gasoline.

The two men walked to the stairs, making some parting comments the former doctor couldn't hear. The father allowed his son to strike the match that fell upon the heap.

Malachai couldn't hear the whoosh of the flames erupting from the sodden mass, but he could see the blaze spreading. He coughed violently as smoke filled his eyes and lungs in the cramped confines of the basement lab. Then he felt the flames ignite his pants and shirt. Heat beyond anything he had ever experienced set every nerve in his body wild with agony. The stench of burning flesh filled his nostrils, making him want to retch. His ears began to thrum as the very last sounds he would ever hear began to register.

The sounds of his own screams.

And then there was only the silent crackling of the flames.

Epilogue

The popping and sizzling of the fiery blaze waned and faded out completely. The burning images of Malachai and his laboratory vanished in a fog of thick, stinking, black smoke. It hung about them for a long moment, then slowly, mercifully, dissipated in the autumn breeze. Now the vandals were back in the cemetery. Malachai stood by them again, his arms folded, his visage no less grim and unforgiving than before.

"And now the screams, the shadows, and the flames are my only companions," the shrouded man said.

"But you can hear now?" Rodney was perplexed.

"Hearing is a thing of the mortal world," Malachai responded. "Suffice to say that I am aware of what is being said, much like a dead blind person would be aware of their surroundings now.

"The point to all of this is that I had more than anyone else I knew of, more than a lot of people ever attain in their entire lives. But I became angry and bitter because I had been denied the one thing everyone else had. Even when I had compensated for my disability and succeeded far beyond everyone else's expectations, I let my anger and hatred turn into an obsession. And you saw what became of that obsession.

"My place in the afterlife is set and cannot be changed. Yours is yet to be determined, however. Think carefully about the courses your lives are taking now. Of all the things that motivate you to action, why choose anger? I had the power to change people's lives, even save lives, but I threw it away in a futile chase after the demons I allowed to haunt me. Now those demons dominate my very being.

"When you leave here, you will return to your lives. After you're gone, I will return to the flames and the screams. Consider if you want to share my fate, or forge one more peaceful, like the boy's."

The four youths turned to see the boy, suddenly bloated and water-logged, vanish from sight. Despite Bo's tragic demise, the living young men felt sensations of endless freedom momentarily overcome them as the boy returned to the afterlife. For a brief instant, they envied the child for his final destination.

"Regardless," Malachai continued, "perhaps you will take greater care to prolong your lives than they did."

The former vandals saw Johnathan's head crack open and Anna Marie's face contort in profound agony as they, too, disappeared. Their momentary pains gave way to a brief glimpse of the divine serenity of their eternal reward as they left.

Betty Golladay looked at Edward and gave him a fond smile and a silent farewell wave. Her face then turned blue and contorted in as much terror and grief as pain, again looking as though she was trying to draw in air that would not come. The woman passed completely from the world, revealing to them for a moment the boundless peace and joy that the living were never meant to know.

"Our time here nears its end, as does yours," Malachai said. "Here we will part ways. Pray, for your sakes, we never meet again."

Troy's face shown sadness and regret. "You don't seem so evil. I mean, your teaching us a lesson means you're sorry for what you did when you were alive, right? Won't this change the kind of afterlife you have to go back to?"

Malachai looked at the youth intensely. "I had my chance and I ruined it! Nothing I do here can change that, idiot boy! Even if I were to remain here among the living and cleanse every evil from the world, I would still fry in everlasting Hell for my crimes against God and humanity! Remorse? Penitence? Bah! We were sent here to remind the four of you that the bodies resting here were once as alive as you are and should be granted some respect. The others came here willingly, but I couldn't have cared less. I think perhaps it was for that very reason I was chosen to lead this motley group of souls. In any case, those who were chosen to come were deemed the most likely to get our point across."

"We get the point," Perry said. The other three youths nodded and agreed.

Malachai nodded, his eyes narrowing. "Don't forget what you've learned tonight. Wait."

Malachai's spectral image vanished, only to reappear before Rodney. The shrouded man lay a pale, thin hand against the youth's chest. Rodney froze in place, unable to move his body below the neck. Instead of feeling the unearthly cold of Malachai's ghostly touch, Rodney screamed in unbridled agony as a searing heat emanated from the undead hand to his chest, and from there to every end of his body. It felt as though his very blood was on fire.

But for all the unspeakable pain he endured, Rodney didn't feel his flesh actually burn. The change felt purely internal. The young man felt himself grow stronger, more energetic, even younger.

"The fires of youth burn within you again." Malachai removed his pale, thin hand. "I give you back now the twenty years that were taken away, but your hair will remain streaked with gray. Consider it a reminder in case you're tempted to downplay this night as some bizarre dream.

"Your youth comes at a price. Release your anger and live the life of a better man, and your debt will be paid. Or you can continue down the path you now tread, in which case you will find yourself sharing the same afterlife that I now endure, with one exception. Your soul will be *mine* to torment as I am the one you are now indebted to, and you will find I will not be a merciful master!

"So go now, all of you, and never forget this night."

"We won't." Troy's voice was sincere.

"Remember that the dead do not forget," Malachai said. "To us, a century is the same as a day. Time means nothing. Bear that in mind, O Violent One. I look forward to our next meeting!" Malachai smiled predatorily at them, his teeth glinting.

The shrouded host's smile became a grimace of agony as his skin bubbled, charred, and cracked as if by some unseen blaze. Malachai Ian MacGriffith loosed a hellish shriek before vanishing with a sudden gust of gale force wind that almost knocked the four young men over.

And then he was gone.

They were alone again.

The boys looked around. The spots in the grass Malachai had stood upon were burnt, the ground itself scorched and stinking of sulfur and burnt flesh in those places. The spired wrought iron fence bent and slid back into its former, unthreatening shape. Several clicks ticking around them told the youths that the gates had unlocked. They looked up to see the sky turning from violet to lavender as the dawn slowly approached. Looking around, they saw no other apparitions standing by to block their way, only many blocks of black, gray, white, and rose-colored stone. Some of which had been broken, tipped over, or defaced with paint.

Solemnly, they walked out of the cemetery. Their paces were slow, almost plodding, as they made their way to the road. A pair of headlights shone in the distance. They looked to each other. If they were quick, they would be able to hide before the car arrived. Rodney looked to the others, who, in turn, looked to him for leadership. The young man could make out the red and blue light coverings atop a police car. There was still time to hide. But was that the way a better man acted?

"I look forward to our next meeting!" Malachai had said to Rodney.

Rodney stepped out into the road and flagged the police car down.

Red Light District

"For God's sake, go through the light!" Bea lay uncomfortably in a birthing position in the backseat of the 1946 sedan. "This kid's coming, and I can't wait until we get to the hospital! Hurry up!"

"If I go through the light, we're all dead." Frank eyed the series of trucks passing through the intersection in front of him.

"I'll get you for this!" Bea's voice dissolving into a scream, which became a duet after a shrieking grunt.

And so it was that Carmine Arthur Redman was born on the night of Valentine's Day, 1947.

Bea slowed the '46 sedan to a halt before the red light, looking fondly at her thirteen month old son. "Won't my little Carmine be happy to see Grandma Mary again?"

"Ma-maw!" Carmine shouted as he clapped his hands joyfully.

"Oh my God!" Bea put a hand to her mouth. "You just said your first word!"

The light turned green, and Bea sped to her mother's home to spread the news.

Frank sighed as the '46 sedan ground to a halt at the stop light. The seven year old car still ran like a dream. Absently drumming his fingers on the steering wheel, the man awaited the green light. His thoughts were disrupted by the squealing of brakes coming from behind him, followed by a jarring impact.

"They guy nailed me from behind while I was sitting at the light," Frank said to a cop sometime later. Carmine approached them.

"Anyone with you?" the cop asked.

"Just my son, Carmine." The father pointing a thumb toward the boy.

"You hurt, son?" the cop asked the child.

"I lost my first tooth." Carmine held up the bloodied piece of enamel for the officer to see.

The policeman grimaced and turned to Frank. "Get in your car, sir. When the light turns green, I'd advise you to get to a hospital and have that neck looked at. You okay to drive?"

"Yep."

The officer waved for them to go, giving Carmine an annoyed look before going to speak to the other driver.

Cathy looked beautiful in her prom dress, Carmine decided as he stole a glance at his date. He silently wished he could have driven her to the prom in something flashier than the old '46 sedan his father had given him as his graduation present. It looked like hell, but the old jalopy still ran good for being almost twenty years old.

"Don't worry." Cathy's voice was relaxing. She always seemed to know what was on his mind. "I don't care what kind of car you drive. It's the driver I love."

In that instant, Carmine felt the gleeful surge of love and joy course through his body, sending his mind into a state nearly free of mortal cares and worries. After blinking his eyes, Carmine threw on the brakes, having nearly run a red light. They lurched forward, both giggling as they righted themselves. Carmine turned to his heart's desire and pressed his lips to hers.

When the kiss ended, his first real kiss, Carmine sped past the now-green light, every ounce of testosterone in his body aching for the redhead seated next to him.

"Class of '65 rules!" He waved to a neighbor.

"Dad says he can get me an office job where he works," Carmine said. The prom was over and he was driving his date. "Eighty dollars a week as a sales representative. He said in a couple years I could make floor supervisor. Who knows where it could go from there? Yeah, the future looks pretty bright. But I'd like to share that future with someone. Someone special."

"Did you have anyone particular in mind?" Cathy feigned ignorance. Her not-so-ignorant smile made her heart's love grin.

Carmine absently stopped at a railroad crossing, only marginally aware of the lowered and red-flashing arm and the passing train it guarded. "Cathy Preston, will you marry me?" he asked.

"Yes." Her smile was as wide as his. "Of course I'll marry you."

Carmine kissed her again, longer and more passionately this time than last. When it ended, Cathy's knowing gaze shifted slightly in the direction of the backseat. Carmine put the old sedan in park. No other vehicles were around. The train was pretty long and seemed in no hurry to move on. The young couple adjourned to the backseat.

"I told you to lose this lemon!" Cathy tried desperately not to scream.

"It's classic," Carmine said. "Twenty-five years old this year. Just think what it'll be worth someday."

"Right now this car ain't worth a damn thing to me! What are you doing?"

"I'm stopping for the red light."

A blood-curdling scream erupted. Carmine turned to the backseat just in time to see his son push his way into the world. "Hold on, baby. I'll get you to the hospital." He floored the pedal, racing through the green light.

"Its too late, you dummy." She groaned. "The kid's already here..."

Carmine pulled up to the white line, giving the red light an evil glare. Out of the blue, he slapped his thirteen year old son's hand away from the radio knob. "We're not listening to that punk rock junk in *this* car," he said. "And not that hard metal garbage, either."

"You mean heavy metal, dad," young Allan said.

Whatever." Carmine turned the radio on. "I didn't restore this car just so you could turn it into a mobile bang box."

"Boom box," Allan replied.

"The business report should be on." Carmine ignored his son. "Let's see if I'm sending you off to college or off to work to feed your mother and I in our old age."

"...And in other business news, Chrysler shareholders are celebrating another record-shattering year as revenues and stock values soar..." the announcer said.

"Yes!" Carmine thrust a fist up. "I knew that stock'd pay off!"

"So am I going to Harvard or Yale?" Allan asked.

"Community college for you, smart alec." Carmine gave his son a playful shake.

Father and son laughed as they drove through a light turned green.

"I can't believe you still drive this old egg-beater," Allan said to Carmine. "Every day, back and forth, home to office, office to home. How old is this relic, anyway?"

"It's fifty years old." Carmine ignored the feeling of lightheadedness and tried to forget about the chat he'd had with his doctor earlier in the week. "How's Joan and the baby?"

"Great," Allan said. "Had a hell of a time getting to the hospital. I ran four red lights on the way."

"Never once in my life have I ever run a red light," Carmine said. "And I've been driving for over thirty years." He turned to the strong, healthy young man seated next to him. "Driving like that's going to ruin your record."

"The cop said it was okay, what with Joan about to deliver and all," Allan said. He noticed his father was pulling up to a red light. "Go ahead, dad. Run it. You'll feel better. No one's around. Who's gonna know? Run the light."

"Shut up." Carmine rubbed his suddenly throbbing head. "I am *not* running the light."

"Oh come on," Allan said. "What's the matter? Getting old already?"

Carmine only half-heard his son. His mind wandered. What did that dumb doctor say about stress and his diet? He couldn't remember. He only heard Allan's last words.

"...*getting old already?*"

Carmine's reply was a harsh gurgle. One eye drifted out of alignment from the other. He slumped forward, thinking only of the red light, his guide to the afterlife...

The light turned green, and the 1946 sedan's engine sputtered and died. It ambled lifelessly forward.

Forward past the light.

The Prisoner Unaware

The soft glow of light drew Phillip's gaze toward its source. To his utter shock and amazement, the man saw the ghostlike image of a fellow in his mid-sixties, clad in Scottish garb and bearing a lantern in his right hand. The spectral form wore a kindly smile and silently motioned for Phillip to follow. With nowhere else to run and two killers after him, he followed.

Phillip never lost sight of the silent, transparent form as he jogged through the darkness of the fog-enshrouded night. After what seemed an eternity of minutes, he found himself at the door of an old lighthouse. The place looked as though no one had lived in it for at least fifty years. Even so, the door's latch opened easily. Phillip never questioned his good fortune nor considered the risks as he went inside the old lighthouse. He closed the door quietly and locked it with the thick bolt latch.

Now able to breathe a sigh of relief, Phillip pulled a small flashlight from his pocket and turned it on. He saw a rusty lantern which closely resembled the one the old Scotsman had held. The man thought it wise to conserve the flashlight's batteries and tried to light the lantern. It had been many years since he'd used such a device, but eventually he got its flame burning once more. He was beginning to wonder about the old gent who had doubtlessly saved his life when he saw a dusty picture frame. The portrait itself could not be seen past the thick layer of dust that had settled upon it. Phillip gently brushed the picture clean and was not surprised when he saw the image of the old man who had helped him, though the portrait revealed a somewhat younger version of the spectral figure. At the bottom of the oaken frame was a small brass plate engraved with illegible lettering. Phillip blew the dust off the brass and read the inscription, "Silas MacGregor, born September 14, 1883. Died November 19, 1947."

Phillip nodded his head, smiling at the thought of the old man still guiding innocent travelers so many years after his death...

Allen sat before the PC's monitor, his entire being focused upon the screen, typing as though the words were being pulled out of him by some magnetic force. This was the thrill of his writing. This was the level of consciousness he attained when creating words from nothing but his own thoughts. To Allen Hume, this was where he felt truly alive.

But eventually his hands and head began to ache. Allen wanted to continue, but he knew it was pointless. The pain would make him lose his focus, his concentration, and it would ultimately mar the quality of his work. That was intolerable. Allen saved his work to disk, shut off the computer, and stood up. After a long, healthy stretch, the tall, thin, dark-haired man went to the medicine cabinet in his bathroom and swallowed a couple aspirin with a small cup of water.

He left the room and walked outside. The mild spring air was invigorating, and the view of the woods from his front yard was both relaxing and inspirational. The mid-morning sun cast its light at an angle that set Allen's thoughts off and running. Forgetting his aches, the thirty-five year old man headed back inside his house to grab his camera. Allen dashed outside before the moment was lost. The tall, lanky man focused his lens upon an old cedar tree. The sunlight at its present angle gave the tree a commanding air, as though it had been made to rule the other trees, all standing poised to pay homage to their liege...

Allen clicked away from this perspective and that, saving as much of the cedar tree's grandiose onto film as possible. After nine exposures, the roll was finished. Allen nodded and smiled, satisfied with his work and put the camera away.

The ringing of the phone brought Allen's mind back to conventional reality. He reluctantly picked up the receiver. "Hello?" He flipped a lock of his long, stringy black hair from his face.

"Good morning, mister Hume." The voice on the other end of the line sounded cheerful. "This is Leonard Fredericks from Bradner Publishing. I was wondering if you could spare a few minutes."

"Sure," Allen replied plainly.

"Good," the cheery voice responded. "We were wondering if you would be interested in doing a tour to promote your newest book. The critics' review is a real love letter. You might even have a shot at an award or two."

"I guess so." Allen's voice sounded as flat as a Kansas golf course.

"Great!" Fredericks was jubilant. "Meet me in my Chicago office Monday morning and we'll go over the details."

"Okay." The tall man's voice was mild as he hung up the phone.

After returning to his own world, Allen went out to his garage. No tools or autos cluttered the small building, only various keyboards and microphones rested upon the worktables. He reached for a stack of discs, flipping through them until he found one that appealed to him. Allen turned on one of the synthesizers and pushed a button, opening a small hatch. He put the silver disc inside and started playing different tracks. Each track played the same tune with various instruments.

Allen exchanged the current CD for a blank one. He cleared his throat and hit 'record.' The man's baritone voice sang the words to the song he had created, his rich vocals lending a lilting quality to the composition. After a couple minutes, Allen shut everything down. He would put the song together later, his mind went over which instruments should get the most emphasis, at what point the vocals would begin and end, and so on.

Allen was only marginally cognizant of having left his house when he pulled into the parking lot of a local department store. He walked in and headed straight to the electronics department, veering only to keep from being hit by other people's shopping carts or walking into racks of merchandise. He looked around to find some recordable CDs but seemed unable to locate them.

"May I help you?" A young female salesperson, a chunky blond woman of about twenty-five, approached him.

Allen paused. His mind seemed in a nervous twist as he searched for the words. "I...uh...I need some CDs."

"Okay," she said patiently. "Rock and roll, country, R and B, or what?"

"Blank," Allen blurted. He silently cursed himself. He probably sounded rude. Perhaps now she won't like him. Resigning himself to the fact that he had just made yet another social blunder, he sighed and decided to go through with it. "I need some blank CDs. For recording. Audio recording."

"Oh, I see." Her voice sounded courteous and unoffended. "They're over here." The young woman led him to a shelf and reached for some recordable CDs. "How many do you need?"

"Two boxes," Allen answered. "No, wait. Uh...make it four."

"Here you go." She handed him four boxes of blank compact discs. "Would you like to pay for that back here or pay up front?"

Allen paused. Although he would rather have paid for the discs where he was at, he worried that if he walked past the front registers without stopping someone might think he was shoplifting. And, he reminded himself, there were some other things he wanted to look at. "Up front," he murmured.

"Okay," she smiled at him. "Have a nice day."

Allen returned the gesture with a nod, genuinely touched that she had thought enough of him to bid him a pleasant day. He could feel his face turning red, and he walked quickly out of the electronics department. Allen remembered her pretty smile and wondered if perhaps he should have tried to strike up an actual conversation with her. Then he recalled his earlier blunder and let it go. She probably would have been revolted by the attempt. *Just like a lot of other women had been*, he reminded himself.

Allen paced toward the office supply aisle when he came upon a group of shoppers talking and ignoring him as they blocked his way. He turned to walk down another aisle, hoping to avoid them, when he came upon a young mother and her children. The two elder children, looking about five and three, respectively, were begging the mother for a toy or some such thing. The mother, in turn, ignored their pleas as she fussed with a crying child too young to walk with its siblings.

That was when everything seemed to hit Allen at once. The crowds, everyone talking, pushing, untouchable young women of graceful beauty, old people blocking aisles with their carts as they checked their depleted funds with sorrowful expressions, children crying their incessant wails like shrieks of the damned...the entire scene seemed surreal. Allen began to feel as though he were in an oven. The air grew hot and stifling as the seconds ticked by mercilessly slow. No one seemed to want to give anyone else some breathing room. Frustrated and afraid he would pass out, thus being totally vulnerable to this collection of rude, grasping people, Allen pushed past a crowd of idle shoppers and made his way to the check-out lines. He found the shortest line and quickly walked to it. Three people stood in line ahead of him.

"Kind of crowded today. I'm Frank." A tall, stout man of about forty stood behind him. Allen nodded, rubbing his eyes with a shaking hand. "Got a headache, fella?"

"Sort of," Allen admitted.

"Well, I'll help you out," the man said. He called out to the cashier. "Line's getting kind of long, you know! We got a guy with a headache back here! Let's speed it up!" He patted Allen on the shoulder. "That always gets them going." He looked back to the register to see one shopper finish her business and leave. The next one walked to the cashier. The big man saw an old couple putting clothes on the counter. "Aw, geez! Do you really have to pay for that with a credit card? Do you know how long that takes?"

The elderly couple looked at Allen and the rude man with shocked expressions. Allen felt their stares drilling into him, felt the choking, stifling air, felt Frank's smothering presence. Allen wanted to vomit, but managed to hold it in. That would only attract more unwanted attention.

"Yeah, I'm talking to you two!" Frank pointed to the old people. "I wish you'd hurry up. Christmas is only eight months away!" He guffawed and landed another hard clap on Allen's shoulder. "That was a good one, wasn't it?"

Allen nodded for no better reason than to keep his body moving, thus reminding himself that he was not asleep and in the throes of some nightmare. At last the elderly couple scuttled away. A young woman with a toddler paid for a case of soda with cash.

"That's more like it." Frank's voice was surly. "Okay, pal. It's your turn."

Allen put his CDs on the counter and produced a checkbook. Frank let out a plaintive wail. "Aw, come on, man! I thought you were all right! Don't take too long!"

Allen scribbled the necessary information on the check, grabbed his receipt and his bag, and hurried out of the store. The mild springtime air hit him like a welcome wave of relief. Everything was still spinning, and the traffic made the parking lot feel almost as cramped as the store, but at least now Allen could breathe. He made his way to his car and quickly got in. Allen rubbed his eyes again, taking deep breaths until his hands stopped shaking and his head stopped spinning. He put his key in the ignition and his car, his chariot to freedom, roared to life. Allen was home in less than ten minutes.

After putting the CDs away, Allen poured himself a small glass of sour mash, anxious to put the public ordeal behind him. He wasn't much of a drinker, but in small amounts it helped him relax. With his nerves calm again, he went from his kitchen to the living room and stared at an easel before him. The likeness of the old ghost from the lighthouse story stared back at him, smiling as kindly on canvas as in writing. Allen put on a full-sized, paint-splotched smock that had hung on the hall tree and gathered his paints.

Once more, Allen reigned supreme in his own world. Once more, Allen had witnessed and survived the terrible evils of society. Once more, Allen had willingly returned to the cage he himself had built, a cage he had no idea even existed...

Severed Chains

Peter Faunce, age 26.

Peter pulled his car into the parking lot of some plaza he was sure he had never been to before. Oblivious to the rain, he casually walked from his car into a mom-n-pop type record store named "Sound'n Off." He strode in, barely noticing the contrast between the cold, damp air outside and the warm air inside the shop, and paid only marginally more attention to the slender, dark-haired young woman passing in front of him.

"Hi." He spoke only out of politeness.

"Hi." She responded without even looking at him.

As was his habit when frequenting music stores, Peter went immediately to the "Y" section of the pop/rock aisle. As he flipped through the now-archaic twelve inch vinyl discs, an alarm seemed to go off inside his head. The more he thought about it, the more he was certain that perhaps he had been here before.

Peter looked around. The arrangement of the fold-up tables the boxes of records rested upon, the cash register, the large windows, all of it in some strange way felt as familiar as home to him. Then the woman. Kneeling before a box of records under a table by the window, Peter realized that out of everything in this room, she was the one with whom he was the most familiar. They had never crossed paths until just then, but he felt as if he'd known her for years.

The young man's heart pounded as he recognized the whole scene from dreams he'd had over the last decade. Dreams he had never forgotten, but never expected to see become reality. As if pulled by something greater than himself, Peter walked up to the squatting young woman. She turned and looked up at him with a smile.

"Need some help?" she asked.

"You wouldn't happen to have anything by YELLO, would you?"

She shook her head. "No."

"I see," he said. "By the way, my name's Peter."

She stood up. "I'm Simone."

They shook hands. "Are you familiar with YELLO?" Peter asked.

Simone shrugged. "They put out some interesting stuff about ten years ago. Most of their CDs have to be ordered from Europe. That's all I really know."

He nodded. "How about that new group from Washington D.C.? Tricky Dick and the Watergate Five?"

She gave him an incredulous look. "Never heard of them. Are they any good?"

Peter shrugged. "I don't know. They burned all the tapes."

She laughed. "Well if I ever come across them someday, Mister Seventies," Simone went along with the joke, "I'll give them a listen."

"Mm-hmm. How about over dinner tonight?" Peter offered.

"I'd like that very much." She accepted the invitation with a smile.

Her smile. It was all Peter could think about as he drove home a while later, still oblivious to the rainy March weather.

Peter Faunce, age 28.

Simone walked into the living room where Peter sat. "It's your agent." She handed the cordless phone to him. "I think she's got a buyer for your book."

Peter eagerly took the phone and, after five minutes of yeses and uh-huhs, was all smiles as he hung up the phone. "The book's sold, and the publisher's got some friends at Fox studios who think they might be able to turn it into a movie."

Simone wrapped Peter up in a big hug. "Honey, that's great! I'm so proud of you!"

Peter kissed his new wife passionately, her ardor surpassing his. They had made a pact before taking their vows. They would wait until Peter had sold his first book before starting a family, the idea being that neither of them wanted to bring children into the world until both of them had solid careers. Peter had lived up to his end of the bargain, now Simone was eager to live up to hers. She took his hand and led him to the couch. He offered no resistance whatsoever.

Peter Faunce, age 34.

The November air was crisp that Saturday morning, thanks in no small part to a cold front that had passed through the area a few days earlier. Snow would soon cover the leaf-strewn ground, the weatherman predicted.

Not that any of it registered in Peter's mind at the moment. He was walking through the sculpture park, staring into Simone's eyes. Her chestnut hair flown in the breeze, and she seemed as content as her devoted husband.

Their reverie was momentarily set aside by the running approach of their three children, Dorothy, Wesley, and Louise, ages five, four, and three, respectively. The couple's eyes met again, and they smiled.

Life didn't get any better than this.

Peter Faunce, age 25.

Peter awoke to the beeping of his alarm clock. Five-forty in the morning. In less than an hour, the daily grind would begin again...the fifteen minute drive to work, a few jovial (if crude and dirty) jokes shared with friendly co-workers, clock in, work, break, work, lunch, work, break, work some more, then the last few eternal minutes until three-thirty. Clock out, go home, and find something meaningful to do until ten. Then sleep.

That had been his schedule, more or less, for the last two years, but Peter, driving toward the cabinet factory, knew there would come a time when his eight hour shift would be replaced by six hours a day of his choosing in front of a keyboard typing. Always typing, always creating, doing what he loved best.

It was just after the first break did Peter ask himself the question that had haunted him the last several years, ever since he came to realize the possible penalties for knowing so much.

What good is life when you know in advance how it all turns out?

The day passed easily, as if working was something done as absently as one listens to background music. No real solutions came to mind, just more thoughts probing the implications of his question.

A friend he was working with, a short, balding man of twenty-two, asked him during break why he had been so quiet all day. Peter told him in confidential (and effete) tones that he was trying to decide what color drapes would matches his wallpaper. It wasn't the best joke he'd told, but it was a good enough smoke screen to aim the conversation in another direction.

It wasn't that Peter didn't want to discuss his problem with anyone, but who would believe him? He had shared his secret with a few people over the years, but they usually gave him a blank stare for a moment, then made excuses to walk away. They always avoided him afterwards. It had been three years since he had confided in anyone about his dreams and, though he desperately wished there was someone out there he could talk to about it, he knew that if there was an answer to be found, he would have to be the one to discover it. Besides, people though he was nutty enough as it was, what with the way he always talked about characters from various stories he had written.

Driving home, eating dinner, and playing video games were among the things Peter did without really thinking. The thinking part of his mind was absorbed with other thoughts. Sleep was hard to come by that night as Peter's thoughts were filled with anticipation and dread for the future. But eventually slumber claimed him.

Peter Faunce, age 36.

The bedroom door closed behind Peter. He was safe, for now. Simone and the kids would be gone for an hour or two. Now, here, in private, Peter felt better. Not good, not by a long shot, but not as bad as being surrounded by everyone. Finally he had the space he needed.

Peter balled up his fists, his teeth clenched. Snarling with helpless rage, he slammed his fists down hard on the dresser. Again he hit the piece of wooden furniture.

Nothing had changed! his mind screamed at him. The books he had written, the honors he'd been paid, the admiration of his readers, all of it had been no more than nails in the coffin he felt trapped in. Peter felt as though his life consisted now, and would always consist, of simply walking a path that had been completely laid out for him. All the vows he'd made years ago to change his future had come to nothing. Worse, his words seemed to have twisted into a cacophony of voices that now mocked him, cursing him, for his weakness. How could he, a man not known for possessing a great deal of inner strength, hope to alter the course of the mightiest river in existence, the river of Time?

Peter fell to his knees. Once, years ago, he had the chance to alter his destiny. He could have simply walked out of that store the day he met Simone. He could have left and never returned. True, he'd probably have never found fame or fortune akin to what was now his, but he would have been free.

Freedom. The word burned in Peter's mind and heart like a searing cattle brand. It was something he would never again have in his life. Only when that thought fully registered in his mind did Peter break down, sobbing hysterically. He wasn't even aware of how hard he'd slammed his head on the floor until the darkness seized him...

Peter Faunce, age 38.

"Remember when we first started dating?" Peter asked Simone, trying with his utmost effort to not sound frantic. "Remember when I told you that I thought there would be trouble in the future because of those dreams I have? Dreams about the future?"

Simone rolled her eyes. "Are you going to start that again?" she asked, not bothering to look at him. She continued to put clothes in her suitcase.

"You took my hand and told me we would deal with it together," he reminded her. "That's what you said! You said you'd stay with me..." Peter took a deep breath, working past the sob building in his throat. He leveled his voice and his gaze at his wife, hoping to get through to her. "I need you so much right now. More than ever before."

Simone put her coat on and ushered the children toward the door. "No," she corrected, "you need a doctor right now. And I need a life with a real husband, not the shell of one."

"Wait, please." Peter gently held her back. He swallowed and took a deep breath, trying to compose himself. How could she sympathize with him if she didn't even fully understand what it was that was driving him insane? She stopped and allowed him to speak. "Listen to me, and try to understand. Try to picture how you would feel if you

94

knew right now how the rest of your life would turn out. Everything. What would happen at this point and that. There wouldn't be anything new in store for you, ever. You'd lose hope, and before long you'd start to feel yourself unravel. I know, because that's what happening to me! I can't hold it together like this, Simone. Please don't leave me. I love you, and I love the children. Don't make me go through this without you. Please, help me."

Simone paused. Peter let her go, though his gaze seemed to hold her fast. He knew she would leave, he had seen it happen exactly like this in his dreams. Simone would leave and take the children. Her pause gave him a flicker of hope. If she stayed with him and helped him through this, things would change; the cycle would be broken. If Simone did the unexpected and stayed, Peter was certain he would be free to lead a new life, get his head back together, get back into writing. If only...

"You're unraveled all right." Simone shook her head. "But not for the reasons you think. I'm leaving you, Peter. You'll hear from my attorney."

And then Simone and the children left.

Nothing had changed.

Peter Faunce, age 42.

Another weekend with the kids had come and gone. Peter watched the children as the very shiny, very new, and very expensive car pulled into the driveway. He silently appraised the professional-looking man who got out and opened the passenger side door and let Simone out.

The man was in his early forties, Peter guessed, though he possessed the build and vigor of a man half his age. Not a single gray marred his neatly styled raven-black hair.

"Daddy!" Louise squealed, running to the stranger. She wrapped her arms around his neck as he bent to hold her.

"Peter, this is Charles." Simone gestured to this new person whom he now loathed.

Peter flicked a lock of white hair from his face and politely shook the man's hand, all the while fighting the urge to punch Charles in the eye with his free hand.

"Hello." The refined man's voice sounded genuinely friendly.

Peter countered with a flat, unwelcoming voice. "And good-bye."

Charles' face sagged a bit at the insult, though he was far too well-bred to lower himself to the level of trading base insults with others. He turned to Simone. "The children and I will wait for you in the car, darling."

"I won't be long." She flashed Charles a loving smile.

"Daddy?" Peter asked when Charles was out of earshot.

"In a few months," Simone said. "I didn't want to upset you with it."

"I suppose an unexpected wedding invitation mailed to me the day before the event would have been more appropriate." His voice came out almost a hiss. "Besides, the kids already have a father!"

"The kids have a psychopath!" All pretense of civility had disappeared. "What else do you call a man who holds to lies about knowing the future? If you knew about all of this sixteen years ago, why did you ask men to marry you?"

"Because I lov-loved you," Peter shot back.

"You don't know what that means!" Simone narrowed her eyes at him.

"It means I was faithful to you!" he replied. "It means I tried to make our marriage work. I didn't bail out when I first started to lose my head. You left me! You left me when I needed you the most! And you took my kids away from me! My kids! To live with that Dapper-Dan looking son of a bitch you're parading around with!"

"You're insane." She shook her head disdainfully. "You've lost your mind. I'm going back to my attorney. I don't want your support. I'm canceling your visitation rights."

Peter shouted at her as she marched back to the car. "Fine! You might as well! All they did was mope around and talk about how much they missed you and that Super-Prick you're screwing! Wesley even asked me why I wasn't 'in a straightjacket like all the other crazy people.' Why did you turn them against me?"

The door closed and the car sped off before Peter had finished his question. He tried to wave good-bye to the kids, but all three of them had their heads turned away from him as they left.

And then they were gone…

Gone…

Peter walked to his front door, pausing a moment to gaze at his reflection in a window. Though only forty-two, he looked at least ten years older. His once thick, dark brown hair was gray, white in some spots, and starting to thin. He had had a pot belly in his youth, but had slimmed down considerably after Simone had come into his life. Now he was bloated and his face seemed to sag. Only his eyes remained as a testimony to the handsome man he'd been just ten years earlier.

All gone…

Peter Faunce, age 25.

Peter awoke with a start. After shutting off the alarm, he clawed his way to the light switch and flipped it on. When he looked into the mirror, he breathed a sigh of relief. Peter was greeted by his stocky, yet wolfishly handsome, twenty-five year old face.

His smile faded when he realized the time frame he was working within. He would be twenty-six in two months. Another month or so after that would put him into March. Peter put together everything from his dreams, for perhaps the ten-thousandth time, and he realized that if he meant to escape the prison he was doomed to live in for the rest of his life, he had to act soon. Time was running out. He had to find a way to sever the invisible chains that would drag him into a future of great fortune and far greater consequences. It was either that or resign himself to a life of hopelessness, despair, and, inevitably, insanity.

As he had done the day before, Peter seemed to work at his job on auto-pilot while he wracked his brain for an answer. He knew that it would all start with that day in the record shop, the day he would meet Simone. That would be the turning point.

The young man was so absorbed in his thoughts that he had barely acknowledged that lunch had come and gone by the time his shift ended. Peter, with only a few absent good-byes to his friends, said nothing else as he walked out of the plant and through the parking lot. He got in his car and took off. Peter didn't go home right away. He usually did his best thinking while behind the wheel. Peter took the shortest route out of city limits, past the suburbs, and into the country. While he drove the relatively isolated roads, he continued to ponder his options.

Peter was no fool, he knew his limitations. If he were to come face-to-face with his future wife, he knew would find it difficult to simply walk away from this woman whom he did indeed love. And if he did, he knew he might break down in a moment of weakness and go to find her again, perhaps putting himself back on that path he feared to tread.

With that notion, Peter knew there was nothing he could do to lessen her desirability to him. So he had to find a way to lessen his appeal to her. A good basis for a solution, but what could he do? Peter wanted to go on with his life, yet he wanted to deter Simone from wanting him, wanting his children.

Then it hit him.

Children. That was the key. Peter knew that his future wife wanted kids the worst way, that much was evident in the way she had fought (or would fight?) in his dreams to get them away from him. If he couldn't give her kids, she wouldn't stay with him. And then he would be free. After she was long gone from his life, Peter could find someone else, perhaps, and have the vasectomy reversed. Or he could stay free and single.

Those thoughts delighted him, though Peter was troubled by the high cost of his freedom. Dorothy, Wesley, and Louise. The children haven't even been born, hadn't even been conceived, yet their smiling faces seemed so very crystal clear in Peter's mind as he drove home that afternoon. Their laughter in his mind brought tears to the young man's eyes as he realized he was contemplating denying them their very existence.

His mind flashed back a handful of years to the time when his cousin, Dorothy, had died. She had died at the age of sixteen of ruptured blood vessels in her brain. She had been more like a sister to him than a cousin, and her death had wounded him deeply. Peter would, therefore, name his first daughter in the memory of his beloved cousin.

Now Peter was considering ending the lives of three children even more dear to his heart than his cousin Dorothy had been. Unlike his cousin, however, there would be no tombstone, no photographs, no testimony at all to their existence. Nothing except memories of three lives that would never be.

Which course would serve the greater good, Peter wondered. Save himself, or allow three children to enter the world who would eventually be taught to throw his love back in his face?

Peter saw the telephone pole in the distance. He was on an open road some twenty miles outside of town. Peter gunned the engine, passing the speed limit, passing fifty-five, passing sixty-five. The crash would end his torment, taking the decision out of his hands for good. With the pole less than a hundred feet away, Peter's car roared past seventy-five. It was so easy...

Too easy. Peter guided the car fully back onto the road, allowing it to coast down to forty-five. No, he would make the choice himself. He wouldn't let anything take that away from him again. Ever. Peter would make his own decisions from now on, for better or worse.

Having made that assertion to himself, falling asleep that night was much easier. Peter felt confident that he was in charge of his life, at least for the time being...

Peter Faunce, age 44.

She was very attractive, her thick mane of blond hair fell past her shoulders. Peter had been entranced by her deep, sea-green eyes. Alice was barely twenty, and her energy made Peter feel almost young again which, for a man of forty-four, was a welcome change.

There were no illusions between Alice and Peter, though. He was a middle-aged man desperately trying to recover even a fraction of what he had lost. She was a college student who took immense pride in playing weekend wife to an established name in the literary field, though Peter hadn't written anything in seven years.

Peter's divorce nearly wiped him out and, with the loss of spirit, came the loss of the desire to write. Somehow, without a reason to write, the task seemed enormous. And Peter was too tired to keep pace. In the end, he went back to work for the cabinet factory he had labored at twenty years earlier.

A nurse stuck her head into the waiting room. "Doctor Ross will see you now, Mister Faunce,"

Peter got up and walked into an examination room. The doctor, a husky chap five years his junior motioned for him to sit on a table, which he did.

"Well doc," Peter asked, "what's the news?"

Ross raised his eyebrows as if to shrug off any bad luck for having to give a patient news he didn't want to hear. "Not very good, to be honest with you," he began. "You have high blood pressure and you're diabetic. Either one of those could have been the reason why you passed out at work this morning.

"You need to slow down and take off that weight. A man your age with your height and build should only weigh one-eighty-five. You're two-fifty-four, that's almost seventy pounds overweight."

"I gotta work, doc," Peter said evenly.

"You've been my patient and my friend for eight years," Ross said. "And my advice, as both, is for you to get back into writing. This workaday stuff is okay for some people, but you can do better than that, I know. Listen." He moved closer, warming up to his subject. "Write another book. Even if it's trash, your name alone will sell it. Tell your foreman to go to hell, and give that good looking blond out there in the lobby a reason to think you're a hero. Do it for her, and yourself."

Peter nodded, sighing. Ross was right, as usual. He hated the way he was living. Maybe he should make a real effort to start over again.

"If you don't," Ross warned. "I can tell you right now that things will only get worse. A lot worse."

Peter stood up. "Point taken," he said. "I'll give it another try."

"You do that." The doctor smiled as his patient left the room.

Peter and Alice settled the bill and left the building. He slid his hand into hers, her touch making the years melt away from his weary heart. She smiled knowingly at him.

"I know what that means," Alice said. "I'm buying lunch. Pizza or burgers?"

"A salad," Peter said. "Then we need to talk over what my next book will be about."

Her eyes popped wide open. "Are you serious?" she asked. When Peter talked literature, it was always in the past tense. Never did the subject of anything new come up unless she suggested it.

Peter nodded. "But before I actually write it, I want you moved in with me, if you want this to continue."

She gasped. "Do you mean it?" Peter nodded again. She hugged him and kissed him so passionately that Peter wondered if they would ever get around to lunch anytime before midnight. Then he realized that he didn't care. He had a second chance to make things right for them both.

Peter Faunce, age 51.

Peter stared at the divorce papers he held in his right hand. The left one wasn't strong enough yet to perform that task. He would have cried, as he had the day he first received the papers, but there were no more tears inside him. All that remained was a solemn grief and despair that filled only a small part of the empty void within him.

Simone was forever gone, living with Charles. Peter was glad he had blackened the man's eyes four years ago when he tried to visit the kids for Thanksgiving. That thought brought a hint of a smile to his face. It was washed away when he remembered that Alice, too, was gone, having left him a year ago to live with his agent.

In a way, Alice's departure hurt worse than Simone's. It had taken a lot of courage to try again, to let go of Simone and allow himself to fall in love again. And it had all been for nothing.

A nurse walked into his room and spoke in a businesslike voice. "Time for your therapy, Mister Faunce."

"Why bother?" His voice came hard to him.

"We want you on your feet and out of here." The woman wheeled him out of his room. "You need to recover from your stroke so you can paint again."

"I write," he growled.

"Whatever." She pushed him a little faster in an effort to get him off her hands that much sooner.

"I used to write," he mumbled.

"Oh, I heard your birthday was last week." Her insincere cheerfulness irritated Peter. "Happy sixty-third."

"I'm fifty-one."

She didn't respond.

Peter Faunce, age 58.

Peter stared at the ceiling. He would have put his hands behind his head and sighed his boredom, but now neither of his arms responded to his command. Peter settled for a tired grunt.

He had turned fifty-eight two months ago. Wesley had been by the home a week before the big day and reluctantly asked his father what he wanted for his birthday, thinking the request would be mundane, such as a new razor or a book to read.

"Look, son." Peter voice had gotten thicker from all the medications he had to take. "I'm not doing so good. The doctors say I'm hanging on by sheer willpower and nothing else. If you really want to do your old dad a favor, just have your mom and sisters and the grandkids by to see me, just once. I'd like to at least see what might have been before I cash in my chips. Even a picture of you all together would do. Please, son?"

"I don't know." Wesley sounded grim. "That's a pretty tall order. I don't think they'll go for it."

"Son, please," Peter said. "I know I lost my temper with your...with Charles that one day. But I'd never hurt you or anyone else in my family. I'll never walk again, anyway. And I've never seen my grandchildren! The oldest one is what? Eleven? Twelve? Is everyone that ashamed of me?"

Wesley gave the sobbing old man a vile glare. "In a word, yes," he said. "No one ever forgot how you lost your mind years ago. Or forgave, either. We had to move out of state so no one would know we were related to a lunatic. Me, mom, my sisters, we had to give everything up because of you and your insanity!"

"Then why did you come here?" Peter tried to ignore the feeling of light-headedness that was coming upon him. "I love you, son, even if you don't love me, and I love your sisters and their kids, even though I've never seen the little ones. And I still love your mother. I never stopped loving you all, even when I cracked up. Why can't you see that?" He rubbed his temples with his right hand. He had to hold it together, he told himself.

Wesley gave Peter a cold glare. "I came here to see if you were being paid back for all the embarrassment you caused us all over the years." The younger man eyed his father's bedridden form, paralysis having claimed the lower half of his body, as well as most the left side of his upper body. He nodded with satisfaction. "You have what you deserve."

"You don't even know what I was going through then-"

"And I don't care." The young man turned to leave.

"You were too young to remember a lot of it," Peter said. He had to make the boy understand soon, he knew. Now the whole room was spinning. "Let me explain-"

Peter was silenced when the door closed. Literally.

Peter now stared at the sun outside, wondering how things had gone so wrong. Not that it mattered now. There was no time to begin again. He would just lay in bed and count the hours until someone would come in and change him.

That thought reminded him that it was eleven at night. Yet the sun had become brighter. Now it was drawing nearer.

Unable to smile, Peter merely closed his eyes and knew no more.

Peter Faunce, age 25.

Peter opened his eyes. It was dark. Only when he took in a deep pull of air did he realize he was still alive. The glow-in-the-dark numbers

101

on his clock had lost their luminescence hours ago. After pushing a light button on the back of the clock, he learned that the time was two-forty-five in the morning.

Laying back, Peter thought about his dreams. To die in his late fifties wasn't something he really wanted, he would at least like to hit seventy before kicking off. And to die an invalid, shunned by those he had loved, disgusted him. It was completely intolerable.

Calm and assured he was not about to die, Peter closed his eyes, his choice made. There would be no backing out. He was strong enough to abide by his decision, he knew. In the morning he would find a urologist and arrange for the vasectomy. No doubt about it. Tomorrow...

Sleep found Peter again. This time there were no dreams, just an image of two chains snapping flickered through his mind, but otherwise there was only an unknown darkness.

Edgar Henry's Final Lap

Edgar Henry put a loving, wrinkled hand upon the fender of his car. Car and driver both were ancient, but Edgar always saw to it that the car weathered the ravages of time better than he. Both had been through a lot together.

The 1957 Chevy was in as good of shape as it had been the day it ran its last race. Edgar Henry, number 16, had come in second in the 1967 Indy 500. Most of the other drivers had driven newer vehicles, but Edgar wouldn't be swayed from driving his beloved Chevy. With a little tweaking, it ran as well as any so-called 'modern' race cars. It had blown away most of its competitors during the time trials.

On the day of the big race, everything went off without a hitch. The Chevy roared like a lion as it zoomed past all but the lead driver. It was razor close, which made it all the more heartbreaking when number 16 lost to the winner.

Edgar Henry would have to settle for that.

The 84 year old man got in the car and revved up the engine. It still roared. But then he remembered he wasn't a race car driver anymore, and hadn't been one since that day 40 years ago. He sighed, then backed out of his driveway.

Edgar drove slowly through the streets of Indianapolis, heading toward Interstate 65. It was an odd sight. There he was, an old man driving a restored race car that belonged in a museum. Edgar putt-putted away at a whopping 20 miles per hour in a 35 zone. He could have gone a lot faster, especially after all the other "tweaking" he had done to it even after retiring, but he was in no big hurry. As many people gawked as honked.

After the '67 500, Edgar decided to get out of racing for a while. He opened up a mom-and-pop type diner. His friend and former mechanic, Arnie Wexler, opened up a pizza place a few blocks away. Both of them promised to get back in to racing "one of these days." But that day never came around.

Things went well until early 1983. That was when the big restaurant franchises began expanding into their neighborhood. They offered both men a generous buyout, this including the buildings and equipment. Edgar took the offer and retired.

Arnie decided not to cave in and fought them to the last. Predictably, he was bankrupt within three years. Four months later, he suffered a massive stroke. Arnie wasted away in a nursing home and died in 1996.

It broke Edgar's heart to see his best friend suffer and die. That same year, Edgar's wife Cassie (everyone called her Coozie because of her speech impediment) passed away. She had suffered from stomach cancer, and though Edgar missed her terribly, he was relieved to see her suffer no more.

Now Edgar concentrated on maintaining bonds with the other members of his family. His three kids had fanned out after growing up. His older son Paul had become an accountant in Seattle. His younger son Martin was a nurse at a hospital in Boston. His daughter Cassie was a doctor in Houston.

Edgar passed the Crawfordsville exit, heading north on I-65. His closest relative was his granddaughter Judy, a lawyer in Chicago. Edgar was going to spend the three-day weekend with Judy and her friend, Andrea. The two of them grew up together, and even went through law school together. In truth, Edgar (and everyone else in the family) looked upon Andrea as one of the family, but he could never understand why, even after they were both established in their careers, they never got their own places and settled down to start their own families. Then on Labor day a couple years back, Edgar had walked in their kitchen unexpectedly and caught them kissing. He pretended not to see anything, but after that he never brought up the subject of boyfriends or husbands again. At least they're happy together, he figured.

A honk brought him back to reality. Edgar looked to his left and saw some young punk, barely 50 by the looks of him, smiling and waving at him. The punk was driving what looked like a 1956 Ford.

"I used to eat those things for breakfast." Edgar muttered to himself as he nodded politely to the punk beside him.

The punk revved his engine and lurched forward a bit, challenging him. Edgar sneered. "You don't want any of this." He issued his warning, though the other man couldn't hear him. The punk challenged him again, this time with an even bigger grin on his face. "I'll whip you like I was your daddy!" Edgar wagged an index finger at the other man. When the punk's reply was laughter, Edgar's face and bald head reddened angrily. "You asked for it! Come on, baby! We're going to town!"

Edgar and his engine roared and flew forward. It seemed to the aging driver that the car was shouting its approval of at last being in another race. The punk looked on in shock as Edgar gave him the finger and zipped ahead of him. Edgar laughed as his competitor fought to regain ground. There was no way in hell he was going to let this race go to his opponent, not like that last one. Edgar felt positively young again. He was really racing again, just like in the good old days.

Just like in the good old days...

"What the hell kind of track is this?" Edgar mumbled. "Only two lanes? Hah! That'll just make it easier for me!"

Edgar gunned his engine. The punk had been left far behind. More cars were ahead of him. Moving his wheel as gracefully as he had done in his youth, Edgar weaved in and out of the competition. All they could do was stare in shock, though a few honked. They didn't stand a chance against number 16. The '57 Chevy was unbeatable, Edgar knew. He'd lost once, but that was due to his own carelessness. Today he was in his prime, today he'd claim his rightful victory!

Edgar laughed aloud. The competition was squeezing into a single lane, leaving one open for him. Edgar wasn't one to pass up an opportunity. If they all wanted to lose, he would be happy to accommodate them. The Chevy raced into the empty lane. Edgar thought he felt something brush up against his car, something orange flitted on the edge of his peripheral vision. It was gone in an instant. The race car driver paid it no mind and continued on.

Edgar saw another driver on his left side. The man was motioning for him to pull over. "Yeah, you'd like that, wouldn't you?" Edgar urged his car even faster. The other driver caught up with him again, now his car was doing strange things. "I don't care how many lights you've got or how much noise you make, I'm not losing this goddamned race!"

Edgar gunned the engine. It blew past the other car as if it were standing still. He had to give the other guy credit, he was persistent. He didn't stand a chance, but he was persistent. Something up ahead caught Edgar's attention. "I'm almost there!"

He could see back in the distance more drivers, all of them driving the same kind of goofy car. Lights flickered red and blue in his rear view mirror, reminding Edgar of the flash of camera bulbs. "They must think I'm the winner already!" He steeled his jaw and pressed on. Edgar stopped looking at the speedometer after he'd passed 140. He could almost hear the cheers of the crowd. The finish line was just ahead.

"And the winner is…" Edgar flew through what must have been the tape they sometimes put across the finish line to help determine the winner. "Number 16, Edgar Henry!"

Edgar let out a cry of triumph! This was the moment! This was the moment he'd waited for! To win, at last to win! The old driver felt for a moment like he was floating on air, then darkness enfolded him, much like someone sleeping will dream and then return to the depths of slumber. A warm, joyous feeling overcame Edgar as he ended his final lap.

"What do you make of it?" Officer Tamme asked.

Officer Reynolds shook his head. "The old guy was going like a bat out of hell through traffic. Then he hit an orange barrel and went into a lane that was closed for construction. I tried like hell to get him to pull over, but he was in this race car-"

"Yeah, I saw it in the distance," Tamme and his friend watched a tow truck haul the smashed remains of number 16 out of the deep ravine it had flown into. "Thing's an antique."

105

"Yeah, well that antique blew the shit out of every squad car on the road," Reynolds continued. "I was going 145, and I couldn't begin to catch up to him. I called for backup, but it didn't do any good. He smashed through an orange and white barricade and flew into that ravine."

"Who was he?" Tamme asked.

"Edgar Henry," Reynolds turned his head away when he saw what was left of the old driver in the car. "Used to be a race car driver once upon a time. Retired restaurant owner. We think he had Alzheimer's, but the granddaughter in Chicago said she was unaware of it. She was expecting him to spend the weekend with her."

"*That's* Edgar Henry?" Tamme looked at the body being removed from the wreckage.

Reynolds nodded. "Know him?"

"I was just a little fella," the cop said. "But I remember he damn near won the 500 back in the 60's. I heard he'd gotten out of racing. Always wondered what happened to him."

"Take a look," officer Reynolds said.

Both men watched as Edgar Henry was put on a stretcher by two women from the coroner's office and carried away. Number 16 was placed on a flatbed, heading no doubt for a junkyard. Officer Tamme was saddened to see the end of an era. Car and driver were now both dead and would soon be buried.

Edgar Henry, number 16, had won his final lap.

The Black Pariah:
"Predators"

This story contains scenes of sexual deviancy and gratuitous violence. Naturally, it's one of my favorites. Those who might be offended by this material are encouraged to go on to the next story. Everyone else...read on and enjoy!!!

-The Author-

May 6th.

The eyes of the predator scanned the partially wooded landscape. The world was full of victims. All that was required was to find the right one. There was a craving to feed, a hunger without end.

A man walked along a paved path through the park, less than ten feet from the predator. He looked about thirty, with a medium shade of brown hair. His height and weight were average. And best of all, he was alone on this fair, if somewhat humid, evening.

The predator left the security of the shadows and silently approached the target. Hands gripping a crowbar raised, then came down hard. The first blow struck a tendon between the victim's neck and shoulder. A second blow shattered the collarbone. A third broke two ribs.

The victim was gagged and dragged into the bushes. He was barely aware of his pants being removed and himself being laid face down in the dirt...

May 8th.

Terrence "Terry" Fitzpatrick looked down at the corpse a jogger had found laying in a small clearing amid a cluster of bushes. This wasn't just another mugging gone bad or an act of revenge against the deceased. He had been beaten with a length of pipe or possibly a crowbar from the looks of the wounds. But not fatally beaten. The perpetrator (or "perp" in cop-ese) wanted the victim alive to feel the pain and humiliation of being raped. Judging from the lack of bodily fluids or visible foreign pubic hair, it seemed as though the perp had shaved himself and used a condom. Fitzpatrick muttered some choice expletives. The lack of incriminating evidence meant that whoever had done this knew what they were doing and that they would likely do it again. And again.

Fitzpatrick scribbled the details in his notepad hurriedly. The tall cop, who possessed a profile similar to Ben Affleck, watched the guys from the coroner's office arrive for the body. He had no desire to hold them up. The faster they could take the body away, the sooner they might dig up some vital evidence. "The perp put away the blunt instrument, finished his turn with the victim, then slit his throat. He used a large blade, possibly a butcher's knife." Fitzpatrick crossed his t's as he spoke to a lieutenant standing beside him.

107

"It's enough to make you think it's an unfriendly world out there," the lieutenant said. Being somewhat short and round-faced, even if in a pleasing manner, made him look less like a fellow law officer and more like a vaudeville, slapstick style sidekick.

The detective ignored the stab at humor and slapped his pad across the palm of his free hand. "It's enough to make me think, by God, that we've got a second stiff in four weeks who's been murdered in the same fashion. Beaten, sodomized, then killed. And not a goddamn shred of evidence to be found."

"Maybe that in itself is a clue." The lieutenant ran a hand through his dark hair.

"Now what the hell is that supposed to mean?" Fitzpatrick's blue eyes narrowed. "If we can't find any evidence, we don't have any clues, and the goddamn investigation goes nowhere." He sighed. "Sorry. I know you're trying to help. But this thing is wearing me out." The cop straightened his tie and ran a carefully trimmed fingernail across his hairline to straighten any stray black hairs. Fitzpatrick's raven black suit and silk white shirt, complete with a striped blue and gray tie and gold-plated stickpin, along with his sixty-dollar haircut, gave him less the look of a law officer and more the appearance of a primping mid-level executive trying to impress his higher-ups. "Let's see what else might be laying around here. After that, you can watch the captain hit the roof. I better call April and tell her I'm going to be late for dinner." The detective pulled his cell phone out of a pocket.

"You and this April gal getting close, eh?" the lieutenant, Barney Styvik asked.

"We would be if I didn't have to keep breaking our dates." Fitzpatrick started pressing numbers. "But she's pretty understanding about it."

"A new tie for to show off to your girl, eh?" Styvik said.

"Appearances are everything." The detective's reminder came with a stern edge.

May 17th. 12:45 p.m.

To the casual observer, he was simply a grizzled man of average height, looking in his fifties, wearing a trench coat and carrying a ragged-looking suitcase. His ankles shown from beneath his coat. He might have been a street person or perhaps only a poor old man making his way across town. Deiter Isaac Esconti had appeared to casual observers to be a great many things over the years. Today he was a bum carrying a suitcase and looking as if to go nowhere in particular. Tomorrow he would look like someone else. Even his employers had no idea who he truly looked like. At times that was an inconvenience, but it was far preferable to keep everyone at a distance and feel safe than it was to risk a friend betraying him. Anonymity is an assassin's best friend, and

Esconti was a master at blending in wherever he went.

The number on the ramshackle apartment building matched the number given to him by his employers. 1613 South Norfolk avenue, apartment 3-F. Esconti tugged at his fake gray beard with a palsied, age-spotted hand and muttered absently to himself as he entered the five-story building and ambled up the rickety steps.

Esconti saw no one else in the third floor hallway. He stood directly in front of the door to 3-F. The resident was out of his home and would likely be gone for at least an hour, maybe two. Esconti set his suitcase down and removed two small picks from a coat pocket. These he slid into the locks on the door. Within ten seconds, the door lock and the deadbolt had been unlocked. Esconti replaced his picks and carried his suitcase inside the apartment. He took a last look to check for witnesses. None. Esconti closed the door behind him.

The apartment was dingy and sparsely furnished. The wall across from the door looked as though the last one to paint it had chosen turquoise, but the color had faded considerably over the years. The prodigious amount of dust in the place added to its dismal appearance. Well, Esconti thought to himself, perhaps the next tenant will take better care of their home.

Esconti set his suitcase down on a coffee table and popped it open. The first thing he withdrew was a small black box similar to a flute case. This Esconti set a careful distance away. Next, the disguised man withdrew a crossbow, an electric screwdriver, and some screws. Esconti placed the butt of the crossbow against the wall opposite the door and measured where the apartment occupant's mid-section would be. The butt of the weapon had a wide, flat metal base bolted to it that allowed the user to mount it to something solid. Esconti carefully attached the weapon to the wall, then walked back to the coffee table.

Esconti withdrew a large spring from his suitcase. Each end ended in a loop, allowing it to be hooked to whatever the user chose. Esconti attached one end to a loop-screw he set into a wall to one side of the room, then opened the front door to the apartment and attached the other end to the door, using a second loop-screw. It took a fair bit of strength to close the door, but the disguised man managed it. He made certain to relock both locks.

Esconti screwed a thick loop-ended screw into the door, five feet from the floor and eight inches inside the frame. He then put another loop-screw into the wall at an equal height and a foot outside the frame. The intruder put a third loop-screw into the opposite wall directly across from the second. A fourth was put into the wooden portion of the crossbow's stock, four inches back from the trigger. Esconti withdrew a length of thin rope from his suitcase and tied one end to the loop-screw in the door, threaded it through the hole in the screw in the wall closest to him, then the loop-screw in the far wall, the screw in the crossbow's stock, and tied the other end to the weapon's trigger. To safeguard against failure, the disguised man allowed a reasonable amount of slack in the rope.

This done, Esconti went back to the crossbow and set it ready for use. Then he retrieved the black case and carefully opened it. A single bolt lay within the inner-cushioned box. Esconti withdrew the arrow-like missile and set it in the groove of the crossbow.

Now everything was set. Esconti could have left out a window and down the fire escape, but his services didn't come cheap, and he believed in giving his clients what they paid for. He replaced his electric screwdriver and black box in his suitcase and took a chair from the small kitchen and placed it facing the door, but not too close to any part of his trap. Esconti would ensure his success and enjoy a free show in the process. He was certain his trap would work, but in case it didn't he could always take his mark out with his bare hands.

Alfred Younce was a common stoolie for the cops. If he saw it, he reported it. In exchange, the cops never hassled him over the petty robberies and small-time drug sales he scored. Younce witnessed a murder a week ago. Some yuppie did his mistress to keep her from blackmailing him and he ditched the body in a dumpster. Younce had seen everything and was more than happy to tell the cops about it. The yuppie was arrested, but he made bail through Lanner and Lanner.

Lanner and Lanner were two brothers who ran a law firm that hired the likes of Esconti to deal with their clients' indiscretions. Through Bobby and Richard Lanner, the assassin made an enviable living. Of course, Esconti had been known to go freelance on occasion, either for a stiff fee or for personal reasons. Bobby Lanner, who had initially hired Esconti, truly liked the assassin. But even he had to shudder whenever his most-prized employee mentioned "attending to personal business." Whoever that phrase pertained to usually met with a truly gruesome end. Richard Lanner was terrified of Esconti and always let his younger brother deal with the killer.

A smile lit Esconti's face when he heard someone coming up the stairwell. Younce had a special surprise awaiting him. The tip of the crossbow bolt had been hollowed out. Esconti had placed within it a pill capsule containing a few drops of nitroglycerin. The assassin wasn't about to chance his mark surviving an arrow in the gut.

The metallic rustling of keys heightened Esconti's excitement. This was going to be good! He could hear the locks being unlocked. The doorknob started to turn…

Then everything seemed to happen at once. The high-tension spring snapped back, yanking the door wide open and pulling hard on the rope. The rope pulled the trigger to the crossbow. The bolt flew through the air and jabbed deep into Younce's gut. The impact jarred the unstable nitroglycerine. The rupture caused an internal explosion. Younce's guts sprayed out over the floor, wall, windows, and doorway. The man was dead before what was left of him hit the far wall of the hallway and slid to the floor.

Esconti grabbed his suitcase and ran out into the hall. "They got him! They got him!" The assassin yelled in feigned terror as he darted past people spilling out into the hallway, pretending to be just another onlooker.

Everything seemed fine until his eyes met those of Larry Alexander Scofield. Scofield was another "specialist" Lanner and Lanner used from time to time, but was more of a leg-breaker than a professional hit-man. He was great at intimidating greedy ex-wives to leave well enough alone and convince people of smaller stature to recant their testimonies on lesser cases, but the big man never rated very high on any intelligence scale and he lacked the nerve to kill for a living.

Scofield had recognized Esconti's voice and knew of the man's reputation. He thought it was mostly bullshit, but he didn't want to start an unnecessary war. So the big man kept his opinions to himself. Scofield gave the assassin a bemused smile as the man ran by.

Esconti continued to run the length of the hall and down the steps. Scofield must have just moved here, the assassin thought. Chances were good the goon would keep his mouth shut. But Esconti never played the odds. He would have to have a chat with Scofield sometime to make sure the muscleman had no intentions of informing on him.

It never hurt to make sure.

Esconti ran down the stairs to the ground floor and dashed outside. He fled around the outer corner of the building and into an alley where a white, rusting Chevy Citation awaited. Esconti opened the driver's side door and threw the suitcase in the front passenger seat before getting in himself. Despite the car's shabby appearance, it started on the first turn of the key. By the time the car exited the other side of the alley, the beard, coat, and latex gloves rested in the suitcase, and the silver hair had been neatly combed. Now the driver looked like a dignified gent in a light sports jacket, shorts, and sunglasses.

Esconti drove the Citation to a local auto repair shop. He pulled up to an overhead door and tapped a signal on the horn. Four, one, and two. A mechanic got in the car after Esconti got out with the suitcase and coat and drove the getaway car into an open repair bay. The assassin silently walked into a closed repair bay where sat a cherry-red Chrysler 300M. Esconti placed his coat and suitcase in the trunk as well as the wig he had worn. Then he pulled out a pair of new socks and jogging shoes. Esconti removed the other shoes and wrapped them in newspaper to keep them safe until their disposal later. He shut the trunk, slipped on the new footwear, and got in the driver's seat. Esconti grabbed a garage door opener from the glove box and pushed the button. The overhead door to the repair bay opened, and the 300M backed out. Another push of the button closed the door. The 300M rolled out into traffic and toward his employer's office.

Esconti walked into the lobby of Lanner and Lanner's law offices ten minutes later. He took a seat directly across from Larry Scofield. Esconti appeared to pay the leg-breaker no mind.

"Can I help you, sir?" The receptionist addressed Scofield.

The big, husky man shrugged. "I just came down to tell Bobby that his boy's getting sloppy."

"I beg your pardon?" the woman asked. She looked over the rims of her glasses at the crude, boisterous man. The middle-aged woman knew good and well what kind of things her employers dabbled in, but intensely disliked being spoken to as though she were directly involved in it. Her green eyes narrowed with irritation.

"Just tell Bobby Lanner his boy- Ah, there you are!" Scofield turned to the tall, stout man coming from down a hallway toward the lobby. "I was just telling your secretary about your boy."

"I heard you from my office," Bobby Lanner said. His face and forehead began to turn an angry red. "Why don't you just announce it over the fucking radio?"

"Chill out, man," Scofield said. "I just thought you might want to know, maybe talk to your boy and give him the word to be more careful."

"I think he's none of your business," Lanner replied. He ran a hand through his curly, graying black hair. "Look Larry, you're great at what you do. I mean that. But if you know what's good for you, you'll stay the hell away from our friend."

"That a threat?" the big man asked. He was more confused than anything else. It wasn't like his boss to intimidate people.

"Not from me." The heavy-set, mustached man shook his head. "But trust me, our friend is the last person you want to make an enemy out of. There's a lot of people out there who would agree with me on that, if they were alive to do so. You get what I mean?"

Scofield nodded and rolled his eyes in derision. "Yeah. I won't give him any problems. I ought to make the fucker pay me to keep quiet, but I'll coddle him like everyone else does." He turned to leave. "You need me, you got my number." He looked to the lone man sitting in the lobby as he walked outside. "Okay, your turn."

Esconti stood up and walked to Bobby Lanner.

"May I help you?" the lawyer asked impatiently.

"I won't need any help with that one," Esconti said. He crossed his arms in front of his chest.

Lanner's face whitened as he recognized the man's voice. "Oh shit. You know, he's all talk. I don't think he'll try to knock down on you."

Esconti chuckled as his boss led him back to an empty office.

112

"Put your mind at ease, Bob. If I have to deal with that one personally, I'll find a suitable replacement for him."

"Turnovers in personnel are bad for morale," Lanner said. "Our other associates might not appreciate losing a co-worker because of a personal squabble. It hurts their loyalty which hurts us."

"I said *if*." Esconti sounded noncommittal. "Anyway, I came by to tell you that the trash has been removed. Your client should have no more odor problems."

"Good. Wonderful." Lanner reached inside his suit coat and fished out a brown envelope stuffed nearly to overflowing. "Your mail."

Esconti accepted the envelope with a smile and slid it inside his jacket. "Heavy."

"The mailman is as generous as he is grateful."

"He should let me remove his family and friends' trash, as well." Esconti shared a laugh with his employer.

May 16th.

The hunger. Always the hunger. Hunger for the victim's fear, the victim's humiliation, the victim's blood.

Hunger for conquest.

The predator stalked this newest mark with an animalistic lust for the hunt. He was in his early, perhaps mid-thirties, average size, with light brown hair. The predator had been watching the area carefully. The law knew a hunter was in their midst, but this scenario was no set-up. The mark was alone, unaware, and prime.

The mark was irresistible.

The predator was upon him with a zealous frenzy. Again the predator knew the unrivaled ecstasy of domination, forced sodomy, and murder.

May 17th. 1:55 p.m.

"What the hell happened here?" Terry Fitzpatrick asked. Blood, accentuated by various bits of flesh, decorated the walls and floor of the dingy apartment. Fitzpatrick regarded the blood on his newly bought and newly shined brown leather shoes disdainfully.

Lieutenant Styvik led his superior through the crime scene. "Looks like a professional hit. The door was rigged. When mister Younce here turned the knob to go in, a high tension spring pulled the door open. A cord attached to the front door was rigged to pull the trigger of a crossbow. The arrow from the weapon lodged in Younce's mid-section. What we can't understand is what caused the victim's guts to explode. Coroner's gonna be pulling some major overtime on this."

"Younce...Younce..." Fitzpatrick mulled over the name, trying to recall where he knew it from. He started to run a hand through his hair, then pulled it away, almost aghast at the thought of ruining the styling job. "Oh yeah. He was the witness for that Overdorf case. Damn. Well, I guess that's one more rich asshole who's gonna walk. Unless the lab guys find something. Any trace of the killer?"

"None." Styvik shook his head. "Whoever did this knew exactly what they were doing and knew how not to get caught. We can't find a single print in the entire apartment other than the decedent's."

"If it's a professional hit, I wouldn't be surprised." Fitzpatrick looked around. "Time of death?"

"About one-thirty this afternoon," Styvik replied. "The bloody footprints end in the alley. The hitter probably drove off, but no one's seen anything."

The detective's cell phone rang. He hit the 'talk' button. "Yeah, Fitzpatrick."

"Detective Fitzpatrick." A feminine voice on the other end brought a smile to his face. "Would you please make sure my boyfriend doesn't forget our next dinner date? Tomorrow night at six. Oh, and please have him pick up some good white wine, not that drugstore variety, if you would please?"

The detective laughed. "I'll make sure he gets the message. Any other messages, ma'am?"

"Just that I'd be extremely grateful if you would let him borrow your handcuffs," April Cochran teased.

"I think we can arrange that," Fitzpatrick said. "By the way, I tried to call last night, but you were out. It was pretty late. Is everything okay?"

"Fine," she replied. "I got bored last night, so I went to the all-night gym."

Styvik tapped the detective on the shoulder. "Sorry to bother you, sir, but another body's been found. Looks like another serial hit."

"Goddammit," Fitzpatrick said. "April honey, I gotta go. Something's come up. I'll be there tomorrow night."

"Okay," she replied. "Be careful out there."

"I will."

May 18th.

Terry Fitzpatrick sat in front of a computer terminal alongside a police psychologist. "Our boy likes to target men of average size," the detective said. "He beats them with blunt objects, but never kills them right away. He leaves them alive but unable to fight back. Then he sodomizes them and slits their throats afterwards. We think it's with a large blade, like a sword or a butcher's knife. But our killer never leaves any semen or hair samples on the victims or anywhere in the vicinity of the crime. And since the crimes take place on or near paved areas, approximating the killer's height and weight by examining the footprints is impossible. All we know is that this guy's athletic and pretty strong."

The psychologist, a bespectacled, clean shaven man of about forty, pondered the information then began hitting keys. "This person is taking a lot of precautions not to get caught, which implies an older man's self-control and a high degree of intelligence, yet is still in his physical prime. And because of the nature of the crime, not only anal rape but also desiring the subject to experience the humiliation of such before the killing, I would venture to guess he's been sexually assaulted himself.

"So basically we're looking for a man of large build and in good shape, between the ages of thirty and forty-five who has been the victim of sexual battery. Let's see what we've got."

"Kevin Andrew MacGraw." The detective read from the screen. "Neil Edward Pyrmont, Lawrence Alexander Scofield, Theodore Gregory Gilson, and Vincent Xavier Jefferson."

"All of them are known felons of the right size and shape and between thirty and forty-five," the psychologist said. "All of them have been sexually assaulted, most of them as children."

"Forget Jefferson," Fitzpatrick said. "He's doing time for grand theft auto. Won't be out for another two years. MacGraw's up the river for life for assaulting and killing his step-daughter. Can't be Gilson, he got shot breaking into an old lady's house a few months ago. So unless the dead can walk, it can't be him. I'd say its Pyrmont, but he lives at least five hundred miles away. It doesn't figure he'd come all the way back here where he's known to start killing people."

"That leaves Scofield," the other man said.

"Long shot at best." The cop folded his arms across his chest. "We've crossed paths before, and I don't think the man's smart enough to pull it off. He matches the other criteria, though. He's thirty-four, six-two, two thirty-five, did time in Pendleton ten years ago for a strong-arm robbery, and was molested by his grandfather when he was nine. If the man had a brain, I'd say he's our guy."

"Gonna pick him up?" the analyst asked.

"Oh, you bet," Fitzpatrick said. "He lives where that Younce guy was killed. We're gonna ask Scofield about that, too. Thanks for your help."

"Anything to help the police," the psychologist said. Both men laughed.

Larry Alexander Scofield climbed the steps to his apartment. He pointedly ignored the stains on the walls and floor. The building's janitor had cleaned up the mess, but reminders of Esconti's handiwork would remain for years. Scofield looked at the young, scruffy-looking blond man using the payphone in the hall. The man gave him a casual glance and turned away. Scofield opened the door to his apartment. He was greeted by a plainclothes cop and three uniformed officers who stepped out of the apartment that had belonged to the late mister Younce.

"Larry Scofield," Fitzpatrick said.

"Yeah, that's me. So what?"

"I'm detective Terry Fitzpatrick." He held up a finely crafted scimitar. The weapon's hilt was six inches long, its pommel crafted in the image of a dragon's head. The sword's curved blade was nearly three feet long, its edge ground to razor quality sharpness. "Is this your property?"

"Yeah. What about it?"

One of the uniformed cops deftly spun the big man around and slapped a pair of cuffs on the small-time enforcer. Fitzpatrick's voice became monotone. "You're under arrest on three counts of first degree murder. You have the right to remain silent. Anything you say can and will be used against you in a court of law..."

Scofield's bravado was gone, replaced by a look of fear. "I didn't do it. I didn't do none of it!"

The policemen roughly escorted Scofield down the stairs and eventually outside and into a squad car that had pulled out from its hidden location to take him downtown. No one noticed the blond man on the phone studying the scene intently. Esconti hadn't planned on the police becoming involved. The assassin hung up the phone and considered his next move.

Scofield looked at the mirror in the interrogation room. He knew someone was watching; he wondered how big the room behind the mirror was and how many cops were now sitting behind it. Scofield pulled a cigarette from a pack in his shirt pocket and lit it. He blew his first cloud of smoke into the air when Fitzpatrick walked in.

"*Now* would you mind telling me what the fuck is going?" Scofield asked.

The tall cop sat down at the table, seated directly across from the detainee. "What's going on is that we have three dead men who would very much like to have their killer brought to justice. Phillip Deacon, Frederick Habner, and George Zent. Any of those names mean anything to you?"

Scofield shook his head. "Never heard of any of them."

"All three of them have been murdered the same way. First they're beaten into submission with some kind of blunt object, then while they're still alive and conscious, the offender rapes them. When he's done, the killer slices their throats. Does this sound familiar to you?" Fitzpatrick's eyes never left Scofield's.

"I don't know any of those guys, and I never killed nobody," the suspect answered. "And why are you guys coming to me?"

"You fit the profile," Fitzpatrick explained. "Tall, lots of muscles, own a sword, in your thirties, got a criminal record, and you were sexually assaulted."

116

Scofield leaped to his feet and shoved his chair backwards. He stabbed an accusing finger at the cop. "Hey fuck you! Fuck you for saying that! No way in hell I'd do that to someone just cause it was done to me! Never!"

"All right, all right." The detective motioned for Scofield to sit back down. The suspect picked up his chair, flopped down into it, leaned back, and crossed his arms.

"What else?" Scofield asked.

"Look, I didn't mean to hit a nerve," the cop said. "I understand that's a sensitive subject, but its my job to cover all the bases. That means questioning everyone who fits the profile. You just happened to be on the list. I'm sorry for causing you any grief." Scofield accepted the apology with a wordless nod. "The other thing I wanted to ask you about is something a little less personal. That guy that was killed in your building, you know anything about that?"

"I didn't do that, either." Scofield's expression was glum.

"That's not what I asked," Fitzpatrick said. His voice regained it's sharp edge. "Do you know anything about the killing, like who did it, why'd they do it, anything like that?"

The suspect ground out his cigarette and looked away. "No. Can I go home now?"

"We'll see." Fitzpatrick got up and left the room. He walked into the room next door. An African-American woman of average height and weight, looking about fifty stood between a pair of younger plainclothes men.

"What do you think?" she asked.

"Well Captain," Fitzpatrick said, "I don't think he had anything to do with the serial killings, but I'd bet my last nickel he knows something about that hit that was pulled."

"Think he did it?" she asked.

"No, a guy like Scofield would just ambush the guy in the shadows and crack his head open with a bat. But if he's not our man, he might lead us to him."

"Let him go and put a tracer on him," the captain said.

"Consider it done." Fitzpatrick walked out of the room.

Scofield trudged up the steps to his apartment. The young, blond-haired man was talking on the phone again. Scofield didn't notice him. The big man unlocked his front door and walked in. He started to close the door when the youth dropped the receiver to the phone and slid inside.

"Hey punk, get out!" Scofield reached forward to throw the intruder out into the hall. He found himself being spun around, the scimitar knocked from his hand, his nose pressed hard against the door, one of his arms twisted behind his back.

"What did you tell them?" Esconti asked.

"Nothing. I didn't tell them nothing!"

Esconti slowly released Scofield. The bigger man turned around. "How many faces you got, anyway?"

"As many as I need," the assassin said. His eyes scanned the burly man in the same manner a snake looks at a bird it's about to eat. "What did they want to know?"

"They wanted to know about those serial killings that's been going on," Scofield said. "They said I fit the profile."

"Did you do them?"

"No, I didn't do them!"

"What else?"

"They wanted to know about that hit you pulled. I said I didn't know nothing, but I don't think they believed me."

Esconti nodded. "But they'll be watching you, which will make you nervous. You might even be tempted to turn me in to encourage them to leave you alone."

"I'm not a squealer," Scofield said.

"Maybe not," Esconti said. His tone and expression revealed a great deal of doubt. "But the sooner the serial killer is stopped, the sooner they'll lay off of you."

"And you think you can do what the cops can't?" the big man asked. Now it was his turn to doubt the competency of his counterpart.

"Correction. I'll do what the cops *won't*." Esconti opened the door and started to walk out.

Scofield interpreted his associate's unexpected helpfulness as a potential emotional weakness and decided to send a final remark. "Add ten grand in small bills to me and I'll forget everything I saw."

Esconti paused, but didn't turn around. The assassin knew blackmail when he was being threatened with it. Yes, Esconti would keep Scofield safe and find the real killer. But afterwards, oh afterwards…

"Fine." The assassin continued about his way.

"I thought you'd see it my way." Scofield shut his door. The leg-breaker rubbed his sore arm. Esconti was just lucky, he thought. If Scofield had known it was him, he would have snapped the so-called "professional" in half and dropped the pieces off in front of Lanner and Lanner's office. Yeah, that's what he would have done…

April Cochran opened her front door and let Terry Fitzpatrick into her living room. The house was small, but sported a variety of decorative influences. Foot tall effigies of Victorian women adorned the Art Deco lamps that rested upon the marble topped end tables at either end of her sofa sleeper. The carpeting was old and somewhat frayed. This Cochran had hidden well with colorful rugs of Native-American design. The walls were an off white with the barest hints of sky blue. In all, the room seemed inviting, if a bit incongruous.

April wrapped him in a tight hug. "I thought I'd never see you again with all those hours you've been working." She led him to the sofa and motioned for him to sit.

Terry smiled. "Well, they've got me pretty busy. We've got some idiot running around loose. You know who I'm talking about."

April nodded. "Yeah. The guy raping and killing all those men. Found anything out about him?" She walked into her kitchen and opened a small liquor cabinet. The woman looked for some wine glasses.

"I really shouldn't talk about it."

"Oh come on. I think its so neat what you guys do. And you know how much I love police stories."

Terry sighed. "If it gets out I said anything..."

"It won't." She couldn't have sounded more assuring. "I promise not to tell anyone, not even my friends."

"Okay." He repeated the description of the suspect, removed his suit coat, brushed it off, and laid it upon a recliner before resuming his seat. "We're looking at this one guy because he fits the profile in most aspects."

"Do you think he's the one?" April asked.

Terry shook his head. "Whoever's doing this is smart enough to take tons of precautions and cover his tracks. The only suspect we've been able to come up with has barely a seventh grade education. If it had been him, we'd have caught him after his first slaying."

"Are you sure he's not playing possum with his brains?"

"Not unless he's been playing possum all his life."

April give him a look of mock irritation. "You forgot the wine."

"Shit." Terry almost slapped his forehead. He stopped, realizing the damage that would do to his hair style. "I'm sorry, honey."

She giggled. "That's okay. I'm in the mood for scotch, anyhow. Want some?"

"On the rocks," the man said. "Just like my career if I don't catch our serial killer."

"Oh, it's not as bad as all that." April returned with an iced glass of scotch for him, and a straight one for herself. She sat down close beside him upon the navy sofa sleeper.

"Appearances are everything. I can't afford to look bad. Besides, you haven't met my captain." He sighed. "That woman has a fetish for my ass. She can't pass up a chance to chew it out."

"Now there's a new approach," she said. "Is that what I have to do to keep you around more? You like being nibbled?"

"Keep that up and we'll never get around to dinner," Terry said. He drained his glass with a single swallow.

"Maybe I lied about dinner." April took in all of her drink with a long gulp.

"Maybe I'm not hungry. For food, anyway."

April got up with Terry and led him toward her bedroom. April Cochran was the kind of woman Terry Fitzpatrick had always dreamed about. She was twenty-seven, a six-foot tall natural blond with short hair who worked as a fitness instructor. She possessed a hard, lean body with blue eyes and small, cone-shaped breasts. Terry knew as the bedroom door closed behind them that he was in for a long night of rough, passionate sex. A smile lit his face.

Esconti sat in the driver's seat of a plain, white, almost totally windowless van, aiming a long-range microphone at April Cochran's home and wearing headphones. He knew the conversation was over when he started hearing moans, grunts, and cries to God. Esconti removed his headphones and thought about what he'd heard. The cop, Fitzpatrick, didn't know too much. He doubted Scofield's guilt, but would probably continue to lean on him until the man broke and started talking about the hit on Younce. If he couldn't solve one crime, the policeman might save face by solving another. However, it might be a while before that happened, especially since Scofield had been assured of his ten thousand dollar payday.

Esconti continued to stare at the house. Fitzpatrick might just get lucky. The man was smart but not exactly a genius, and who could tell when the cop might get a break in the case? Esconti would bug the woman's house. The detective revealed his willingness to divulge sensitive information, but even more important, the assassin wanted to get to know the woman better for future reference. If Esconti needed to use her either as a pawn or as a bargaining chip, he intended to be ready to go either of those routes should it become necessary.

Esconti continued to watch the house, listening in periodically. Eventually the bump and grind was over. There was some muffled conversation, but nothing important. A while later, Fitzpatrick opened the front door, gave a barely-clad April a long tongue-kiss, then turned around and walked to his own car. The cop got in and drove away. Esconti would eventually get inside the detective's home, but the woman, April Cochran, was his Achilles heel. Esconti would take advantage of that first.

Esconti watched the house throughout the rest of the night. No phone calls, only a little TV before going to bed. Dawn came about five hours later. Esconti heard the woman get up an hour after that, shower, have a light breakfast, and get dressed. She did a half hour of calisthenics before getting in her car and driving off to work.

The assassin got out of the van, now dressed as a meter reader holding a metal clipboard, and walked around to the rear of Cochran's house. Less than a minute later, Esconti was padding lightly throughout the woman's home. Nothing out of the ordinary in the kitchen or the dining room. The living room was as it should be. A spare bedroom had been turned into an office. Nothing special in there. The bathroom, too, seemed normal at first glance. Esconti paused before he left. There were no feminine hygiene products anywhere to be found, with the exception of some douches. The assassin assumed the woman had had some medical problems in the past, though it seemed strange considering how good of shape she was in. He filed it in his memory and kept on looking.

The master bedroom seemed ordinary enough. Esconti searched the dresser and discovered only some shirts, panties, and lingerie. He searched the closet. Pants, some business suits, some dresses, and blouses were hung neatly. The bottom of the closet revealed only numerous shoes, a couple of old purses, some barbells, an old video game system with cartridges, and some toys dating back to Cochran's childhood. The shelf of the closet was a little too high for him to see. The assassin went back into the dining room, took a chair, and returned to the bedroom. Esconti looked around the shelf. Some old baseball caps, a couple board games, and a black satchel. Of everything here, only the leather bag didn't have dust on it. Esconti carefully removed the bag, taking note of exactly how it had been positioned before opening it. The assassin looked inside, chuckled, then closed and replaced the bag exactly as it had been. Esconti put the chair back in the dining room, smoothed the carpeting in the master bedroom, and walked out the back door without bothering to bug the house. He locked the door and went back to the van, pretending to check over the clipboard.

Esconti drove away from Cochran's house. Now his mind was more full of questions than ever before. Still he didn't worry. He would just have to do some homework.

May 26th.

There would be no stopping now. The predator would never-could never- be satisfied. A thousand conquests, a thousand kills, and the beast within would still cry for more. And more. And more...

A gleam appeared in the eyes of the predator who now stalked a park close to home. Here was another delicious victim, almost close enough to touch. The predator could smell his sweat. Soon it would be blended with the sweet aroma of fear.

The hunger and the lust urged the predator into action. This one, while so similar to all the others, carried his own distinctive flavor. The victim's feeble struggling and fearful grunts signaled to the predator his need to be dominated. The predator hungrily pushed onward, inward... until a tranquilizer dart jabbed into the victim's side, knocking him out.

"My name is Deiter Esconti," the assassin said. Esconti now sported hair and features similar to that of the victim's. He tossed the dart gun aside. "Its so good to make your acquaintance at last, miss April

Cochran."

The predator extricated herself and stood up. She removed the prosthetic penis she had been wearing. "You know you're going to be next," she said. Her voice was steady, not a muscle twitched to indicate worry.

"Was that what your father said when he raped and sodomized you?" Esconti asked. A faint smile played about his lips. "My original plan was to bug your house so I could hear anything else your cop boyfriend might want to talk about. But then I found the strap-on you keep in the black leather bag in your closet. A little background check told me everything else I needed to know.

"The repeated assaults left you so damaged that by the age of eleven you required a hysterectomy. When you were twelve you were placed in the first of four private schools for girls. You were thrown out of two of them for attacking your classmates, the third for having sexual relations with a fellow student. You graduated from the fourth and went on to college. You turned your energies to athletics, but the rage remained. It grew until you couldn't hold it in anymore. So you started raping and killing men who resembled your father as he looked at the time you were attacked."

"So are you a private investigator?" she asked. Her eyes never left the dangerous man before her.

"Of sorts," Esconti replied. "You see, the police are leaning heavily upon an associate of mine. They think he's committing your crimes. And he has information about some of my activities that the police also want."

"So catching me helps your friend, which helps you," she reasoned. "Are you going to capture me and turn me over to the police?"

"No," Esconti said. "I'll settle for killing you."

Cochran reached into a nearby bush and pulled a machete from its scabbard. "Tall boast."

The assassin drew a machete of his own from a sheath belted to his hip. "The best kind."

Without another word, both predators circled each other. Only fools blindly jump in without appraising an enemy. Neither would make that mistake. She was confident. He was determined.

Cochran leaped forward and slashed out, aiming for the assassin's neck. Esconti blocked the swing. She put more power behind her blade, and slowly forced both blades uncomfortably close to his face. The assassin saw her tense up for a follow-up strike and fell back as the woman thrust out a leg at waist-level. The hit should have shattered the man's hip, but his reflexes limited the strike to a glancing blow.

Esconti rolled away and sprang to his feet. Cochran waded in fearlessly, her blade coming in fast and high. The assassin threw his head back in time to keep from being decapitated. Her blade nicked the edge of the man's nose.

The sight of his blood drove her onward. Cochran spun to deliver a roundhouse kick to break the man's neck. Esconti dropped his weapon, rolled with the kick, and grabbed her foot. The assassin twisted hard and fast, snapping the foot out to one side. Cochran's ankle shattered with a loud, grating crunch. She stifled a scream and hobbled backwards. Esconti retrieved his weapon.

They circled each other again, both having new respect for the other. Cochran's gait was unsteady, her crippled foot dragging behind her. Esconti moved in with his blade spinning rapidly. She knew she had to prove superior with her machete. It was her only hope.

Their blades met and sang out a metallic tune as each swing was blocked, death avoided at instances by less than an inch. Cochran blocked a low swing aimed to slice her abdomen open. She landed a hard punch with her left fist to Esconti's right eye. The assassin ignored the pain and returned the punch with one of his own, his fist hitting her hard in the neck, barely missing her windpipe.

One of Esconti's eyes was puffed shut and the side of his head ached badly, Cochran's ankle had been shattered and she was coughing up blood. Both of them knew the time had come. They were both seriously hurt and a winning blow had to be told soon. The alternative was a stalemate, and neither of them had any desire for a second fight.

Cochran cut a slash across Esconti's left forearm. The assassin thrust his blade forward, digging into her chest. The serial killer jumped back before her foe could drive it home. Cochran accidentally put her weight on her wounded foot and fell to the ground in a twisted heap. Esconti brutally kicked the blade out of her hand, breaking her wrist in the process. Cochran scrambled to her feet. She had to leave! She had to escape this terrible man and his promises of death!

With his enemy crippled, weaponless, and unable to fight back, Esconti leaped forward one last time and ended the battle once and for all. The assassin paused to catch his breath. He regarded the woman and her victim. One was dead, the other safely unconscious.

"Yes, my friend." Esconti spoke assuringly to the slumbering man. "I'll bring the police to you. I'd stay longer to hear you thank me, but I have to attend a picnic."

Fitzpatrick sat at his desk, staring blankly at the computer screen before him. No one else matched the profile except Scofield. The detective took a sip of his black coffee from a ceramic mug bearing the images of the Three Stooges and continued to wrack his brain for possibilities. He was completely oblivious to the ringing coming from behind him.

"Terry." Styvik called out from a desk at the other end of the room. "Answer the phone. It's for you."

Fitzpatrick picked up the receiver and hit a button. "Yeah, Fitzpatrick." The man's voice sounded disinterested.

"I have your killer." The voice on the other end of the line sounded casual, almost bored.

"What?" Fitzpatrick now gave the caller his complete attention.

"I did your job for you," the voice said. "I've captured your serial killer and gathered a file detailing the motives, background, and so on."

"Who is it? Where is he?" the detective asked.

"Come to 1717 East Foster road and see for yourself."

"1717...hey! That's-"

"That's where your killer is. So go get what you're looking for and give that lovely girlfriend of yours a big kiss for me." The voice hung up.

"What- Hey!" Fitzpatrick slammed his phone down. He turned to lieutenant Styvik. "Get some uniforms over to April's place! Tell them not to go in first. I'll do that!"

Within five minutes, the home of April Cochran was completely surrounded. Terrence Fitzpatrick dashed from his car, pulled his .44 from his shoulder holster, and approached the front door. All the curtains had been drawn; it was impossible to see in. The head cop knocked on the door, calling for his girlfriend twice. He readied his gun and kicked the door in.

Fitzpatrick barged in just in time to see the nylon cords stretching from the door to the limbs of the headless woman's body loosen. The body was strung up into an upright position, the hands clasped around her machete and tied together with more cords. She was wearing her strap-on genitalia. Laying atop a table in front of the dead woman, just above waist level, was an unconscious man resembling Cochran's other victims. He had been shot with three additional darts. The woman's head rested atop a shelf, watching silently as some of the cords loosened, causing the arms to lower quickly and drive the blade into the victim's chest.

April Cochran had claimed her last victim.

Fitzpatrick stood numbly as other policemen spilled into the house. Someone had found a folder with some kind of information in it somewhere and was trying to tell him something. Fitzpatrick didn't care.

Appearances are everything.

Fitzpatrick had slept with a serial killer who was also a sex fiend. He had given sensitive information to this monster. They had gotten together right before the killings started. She had probably kept him around to stay informed as to how close they were getting to her. And everyone knew about them. He had loved her, now she had been cut in two by another killer, but she was the murderer he was looking for.

Grief, anger, and shame whirled uncontrollably within the detective. He was so sure she was the one for him! Now it was over. It was all over.

Appearances are everything.

Terrence Fitzpatrick walked into the woman's bathroom and shut the door. A picture in a small yellow plastic frame of a smiling April receiving her college degree sat upon a shelf. She looked so very incapable of such heinous crimes. He could almost bring himself to believe...

But he couldn't. The detective turned away from the picture. She was guilty, and he still loved her. Loved her and hated her at the same time. He, Terrence Fitzpatrick, was now, and forever would be, the disgrace of the police force, even if they didn't fire him. He had been literally within arm's reach of his prey and didn't even know it. Worse, the crime had been solved by a second killer for whom Fitzpatrick didn't even know where to begin looking. In both cases, the detective faced undeniable, ignominious defeat.

Appearances are everything.

Terry Fitzpatrick put the barrel of his gun in his mouth and pulled the trigger.

May 28th.

Larry Alexander Scofield sat in his old, haggard-looking recliner. The only light in the apartment came from the TV set. He wasn't wealthy by any stretch of the imagination, but the man had two luxuries he tried to maintain. The first was his collection of swords, most of which he had purchased from various shopping channels. The other was his cable television. He loved ESPN, but he also enjoyed Comedy Central and VH1. With a cold beer in one hand and the remote in the other, Larry Scofield didn't think life got any better than this.

Scofield didn't see the hand holding the handkerchief until it was clamped firmly over his nose and mouth. If he had already been standing he could have broke free, but now he was prone. And then he was asleep.

Scofield had no idea how long he had been out. He awoke with a headache from the anesthetic. Scofield heard a pair of ticking sounds, one coming in regular intervals like a clock, the other totally random and sounding a little like pins scratching plastic. He tried to get up, but his wrists and ankles were in metal restraints chained to the bed he now lay upon. A putrid smell assailed his nose. He tried to turn his face away from it, but it was all around him. It was then he noticed something sticky was covering his naked body from head to toe. Scofield saw some kind of amber colored glop coating him.

"I see you're awake in time for lunch," Esconti said. He leaned against a cushioned wall, chewing absently on a chicken drumstick.

"Let me go, you fucker!" Scofield struggled uselessly against the restraints.

"No one can hear you." The assassin was calm. "I did some hasty renovations to one of the storage areas in the basement of the building next to yours. Right now the police are in your apartment wondering what's happened to you. You can shout if you please, but no one will hear you unless they're standing right outside the door. Of course I doubt anyone will come this way for some time. I'm putting a padlock on the door leading down here as soon as I leave. It could be days before the manager gets around to prying off the lock and investigating the basement."

"What's this shit all over me?" Scofield tried to sound intimidating, but his words ended up sounding terrified.

Esconti smiled. "It's a concoction I made especially for you. Honey, ground-up rotten oranges and onions, and fish oil. Actually, it's not for you. It's for them."

Scofield followed Esconti's gaze to the far right corner of the room. Inside a pet carrier, the prisoner saw two, perhaps three, huge rats. Their claws raked against the plastic carrier, making the random ticking.

"NO! Oh God, please! Don't do it! Let me go!" The big man began to cry. "Why are you doing this?"

Esconti's gaze hardened. "Because I won't put up with being blackmailed."

"Never again! I swear!" Scofield's pride was gone, exchanged for terror. Pleading was all he had left. "I promise to God I'll never do it again!"

"I know you won't," the assassin said. "You see, you made yourself my enemy. And I never allow my enemies to live. If I did, their fear would over time be replaced by a desire for revenge. No, I'll never let an enemy live long enough to strike back at me when I least expect it.

"Well, I've kept you long enough. I have things to do and so do you." Esconti walked to the door, pointedly ignoring the rat cage.

"You mean you're not going to feed me to them?" Scofield asked. A sliver of hope pricked his frantic mind.

"I am," the assassin confirmed. "There's a timer by the cage's latch. I'm not sure if the beasts have any kind of diseases, so I decided not to take the chance. They'll be out soon. The timer's set to go off in about a minute or so." Esconti took a final bite of his drumstick, then flung it toward his prisoner. It landed on the man's chest and stuck there.

Both men heard the 'ding' of an egg timer attached to the cage's latch. A whiskered snout, and then a second, poked against the carrier's gate. It gently swung open.

While Esconti's gaze was expectant and amused, Scofield's was nothing short of terrified. A third rat, the smallest of the three and about the size of a raccoon, joined the first two. The largest rat, as large as a fat groundhog, skittered up onto the bed first. Then up came the other two.

"Screaming makes them jittery," Esconti said. "By the way, I haven't fed them for several days. I believe they are quite ravenous by now."

The smallest of the three rats began sniffing the prisoner's chest, its snout close to the man's nipple. The rat in the middle crawled between Scofield's bare legs and began nuzzling close to the man's crotch. He couldn't see the third one! Where was it?

Esconti watched with amusement as Scofield fought desperately to keep from screaming.

Scofield felt a heavy, clawed paw land upon his chin. A second came to rest upon his forehead. Then he saw the snout, sniffing just below an eyebrow. Scofield could smell the stink of the rat's reeking breath, could feel its coarse, oily hair brush against him. Something warm and wet began to lick his right eyelid.

Esconti started to laugh as he left the room. Let the fool face his death alone, he decided. The assassin locked the door from the outside and waited.

Then he heard, barely, a muffled shriek.

Esconti laughed harder. The screams continued. The assassin knew they would continue for some time. Hours, perhaps.

Deiter Isaac Esconti listened to Scofield's agonized wails a moment longer, then sauntered away. He began whistling "Three Blind Mice" as he walked up the stairs. At the top, the assassin shut the door and clicked a padlock shut, securing the door from casual passersby.

And then Esconti left.

Victims of The System

Cedar Ridge, Missouri.

October 12, 1995.

People had said they made a cute couple, and perhaps they did. Danny and Carla were both fifteen and sophomores in Cedar Ridge high school. They had known each other four years and always seemed to be hanging out together.

When Homecoming came around, there had never been any question of whether they would be going to the dance together. They both had simply assumed so. The only question was which of the four parents would be driving the couple to the school and back.

Danny was a straight 'A' student with aspirations of going on to college after high school. He and Carla had talked for hours at a time about their futures. Mostly it was Danny who talked. Carla didn't have any big plans except maybe to graduate high school. Danny's plans included medical school after taking his basic courses. Carla had listened to him indulgently, silently not believing that anyone from a little redneck town such as theirs stood a chance at becoming any kind of success story. Aside from this, the two were like bookends; where you saw one, you saw the other.

Danny and Carla sat in the back of his father's van. The young man stood five-six, wore short, dark hair, and had dark green eyes more than a few girls said were 'dreamy.' She was five-two, sported shoulder-length naturally blond hair, and eyes as blue as the morning sky. He looked handsome in his suit, she looked beautiful in her dress. Both of them wished they could get out of the stuffy duds and put on normal clothes.

"Two more years." Danny spoke with a tone of voice Carla knew only too well.

"Two more years til what?" She hoped he would give the subject a rest, but indulged him anyway. Carla couldn't understand why he didn't have normal obsessions like trucks or guns or titties.

"Two years from now we'll be in college." Danny's eyes seemed to stare off into space. "After that, med school."

"You mean med school for you." Carla felt like she always had to correct him at this point.

"You could do it, too," Danny said.

"Nobody from a town like this ever gets to be a doctor or any other kind of big thing like that. Like a lawyer or something," she replied. Carla sounded firm in her opinion.

"There's always a first." Danny's father, Ray, spoke up.

"Well, *I'm* going to do it." Danny was adamant. "You could, too, if you wanted. It doesn't have anything to do with where you come from. You just have to want it with all your heart and let nothing get in the way."

"You think Rosalee and George'll be at the dance?" Carla decided to change the subject.

"I don't know." The young man let it slide. He'd show her. Danny would show her that anyone who wanted an education and a way out of Cedar Springs could get it if they kept at it and worked hard enough. Then, hopefully, Carla would think seriously about college. "George said Rosalee wanted to go pretty bad, so they'll probably be there."

"Good." Carla looked out the window. It was getting dark already. The air was still mild for that time of year, but the van was built so that only the driver and whoever rode shotgun could lower their windows, so Carla tried to forget the stuffiness of the vehicle's interior and contented herself with staring out the window. Every time she tried, she couldn't help but feel as though she were still a little girl being carted around by grown-ups.

Carla forgot all about Danny, his father, and school dances for the moment. Her resentment for The System which society revolved around dominated her mind. Never mind that she was almost grown and could take care of herself. According to The System, eighteen was the magical age. Before that special birthday, nothing else mattered. Carla felt she might as well still be wearing diapers and nibbling a pacifier for all the respect the world had shown her up to this point.

And even after turning eighteen, The System didn't let up. After high school, if she bothered to finish, it would be time to look for a job wherever work could be found. The System, as it existed in Cedar Ridge, virtually guaranteed that if you lived there, you would eventually die there. People like Danny, Carla believed, were dreamers. Sure, he'd finish high school. He might even make it into a junior college somewhere. But he'd see. The people who ran The System would show him that no one from Cedar Ridge could ever make it out there in their world. Then, Carla was sure, Danny would see the light and grow up and try to find a real job.

Carla saw the high school in the distance. As it got closer, she began to feel even more frustrated. High school. Just another building to keep the kiddies in until The System said they were all grown up. Then came the big shove out the door and into Loser Land. Carla shook her head. What sense did any of it make? Why do so many people like Danny fall for the lies they hand out there? With or without a diploma, there was no chance of getting a decent job anywhere. Carla knew the truth, and so did some of her friends. Why was everyone else so blind? Next year, when she turned sixteen, she planned to quit. After all, high school was part of The System, and The System was always against her, so why shouldn't she just tell The System to go to hell and make her own way?

"Here we are." Ray pulled up close to the double doors leading into the main building of the high school. The two teenagers got out. Danny bid his father good-bye, then walked into the building with Carla. The couple walked through the lobby arm-in-arm, past a crowd of attendees, and into the gymnasium. Thanks to the wonders of streamers, posters, and papier-mache, the "Home of the Elks" had been turned into a Midwestern, underage version of Club Med. With the lights turned down and the music blaring, no one noticed the difference.

Right off, Carla spotted George and Rosalee. She tugged on Danny's arm, and the two of them walked over to the other couple. The four friends chatted through a set of fast-paced songs. George and Rosalee were a year ahead of their friends, and were already talking about getting married after George joined the Navy. Danny kept up keenly with the conversation, but Carla wanted to shout at all three of them. They were slaves to The System and too blind to realize it.

Carla excused herself, claiming a need to use the bathroom. Once she was out of the gym, she went straight outside. The company had become as unbearable as the stuffy atmosphere, and Carla needed a drastic change in scenery. She stood outside in the parking lot with some of the older girls. Carla reached inside her purse and pulled out a pack of cigarettes and a lighter. She withdrew a single generic menthol and replaced the pack. After lighting up her puff, she stuffed the lighter back where she got it.

One lungful of tar and nicotine followed another until Carla finished the smoke. Now she felt in better company. Most of the girls here were seniors, all of them the kind of girls that act far older than their eighteen years and possess over-inflated opinions of themselves. In Carla's eyes, their tolerating her company meant they saw her as a kindred spirit. To them, she was an evening's entertainment, someone new to corrupt.

The sound of a pickup truck, sans muffler and in desperate need of a tune-up, came down the road toward the school. Once, the truck might have been the pride of the showroom floor. Now, with its dented and rusted out body, bald tires, and badly cracked windshield, it resembled the aftermath of a demolition derby. The fake raccoon's tail adorning the tip of the radio antenna seemed to wag of its own accord as the truck raced into the parking lot and skidded to a halt barely three feet from the cluster of young women.

"Oh, God." One of the snootier girls in the pack rolled her eyes. "Here comes Shane the Shithead."

"Wonder if he's ever had a girl who wasn't jail-bait?" Another senior in the group couldn't resist making the comment.

The truck's engine shut down, and a giant stepped from the cab of the shabbily-kept vehicle. Shane stood over six and a half feet tall and sported long, unkempt brown hair that dragged past his shoulders with stubbly whiskers and a thick mustache. His pale green eyes settled immediately upon Carla.

"Now who's this?" The big, twenty-eight year old man walked up to the young girl.

Carla found herself strangely impressed with Shane's large build and confident stride. He seemed powerful enough to have molded the world with nothing but his thick, hard hands. "Carla." Her voice was quiet. Something in his eyes seemed to suggest that he expected obedience. Something in her mind was happy to hand it over in exchange for being treated the same way the older girls got treated by the men they attracted.

"Bet you never had yourself a *real* man before." Shane had known dozens of girls like Carla. To him, it was like fishing. You caught one, tried it out, then threw it back in when you were done with it. You only hung on to one if she did everything you wanted with no sass or backtalk. Carla, he noted, was prettier than the others. He might just hang on to this one.

"Well...no." Carla could feel the heat emanating from her cheeks as she started blushing. A man, a *grown* man, was talking to her! Talking to her the way a man talks to a woman.

"'Bout time you had one." Shane spoke confidently and took a step closer. "How d'ya like my truck?"

Carla couldn't tell what color it had originally been. Now it sported a wonderful shade of rust. She started to speak when an arm draped protectively across her shoulders.

"We don't." Danny started to lead Carla back when Shane pulled them apart and grabbed the boy by the front of his shirt.

"I wasn't talkin' to you!" Shane shoved Danny backwards, putting the young man off balance and sending him down hard on his back.

Carla had to admit, Danny was no coward. The youth was back on his feet and ready to give it his best shot. Danny was put back down a second time. Sadly, he didn't know when to quit. Danny got up again, trying to discount the pain in his face and ribs. He was no quitter. Neither was Shane. Danny was on his back again. This time he wouldn't be getting up by himself.

Carla stared at Shane's handiwork. The man had barely a scratch for his troubles, with the exception of his knuckles. A voice deep within her said she should be by her long-time friend's side, trying to help him up. That voice was overwhelmed by her awe of what had just happened. The thought of a grown man, one as big and tough as Shane, taking such an aggressive interest in her sent a shiver up Carla's spine.

131

"A real man don't take no shit from no one." Shane spat on Danny. "Fuckin' pussy." He turned to Carla. "You're coming with me." Carla didn't argue when he opened the passenger door of his truck, picked her up, and promptly set her on the seat. Shane walked around and got in the driver's side door. Carla shut her door as the truck again roared to life. The tires squealed mercilessly loud as the rusty pickup tore out of the parking lot.

A few of the girls cheered Carla on as she accepted Shane's invitation. Most of them shook their heads. She would just have to learn the hard way, they muttered among themselves. The girls looked down at Danny. One of them would eventually have to tell a teacher chaperoning the dance that he was laying out there, broken and bloody.

Carla felt a surge of excitement. No more riding in the back of mommy and daddy's grocery-getter, feeling a short step away from needing a car seat. A grown man had come along, literally swept her from her feet, and was now taking her off into the night! The thrill of mystery and adventure made her giddy.

Carla looked at herself in the outside mirror. Her golden hair blew in the breeze. Now, she knew, she had stepped past the line. She had gotten around The System. Now she'd make her own way. Shane would see to it. They'd make their own way together. How many fifteen year old girls can say they're this lucky, she wondered. Too bad about Danny. I hope he isn't hurt too badly. But this is so cool!

Carla's thoughts drifted off to the wondrous future in store for her and this man who was obviously smitten by her.

September 23, 2005. 7:04 a.m.

Shaking hands closed the medicine cabinet. Carla stared into the mirror, taking stock of the woman looking back at her. Her blond hair was already turning gray, her nose bent to one side as a result of too many beatings. Some of her teeth were chipped, others were missing entirely. But what she lingered on the longest was the black eye and swollen cheekbone, compliments of last night's argument. Carla remembered the night she rode off into that wonderfully unknown future with Shane. It was hard to believe it had been only ten years since that night. Although Carla was twenty-five, she looked past forty. Lines of worry creased her once-girlish face, and she knew the gray smudges underneath her eyes would probably always remain there.

Carla thought, for perhaps the millionth time, how things might have been different. "Danny would never have hit me." She muttered to her reflection, a habit she had been accustomed to since childhood. What a goddamned fool she had been for leaving him to lay on that asphalt! "He needed me, and I let him lay there." Carla forced the thoughts away. The more she dwelled upon them, the more clearly she saw her own situation, and things were bleak enough. Her war against The System hadn't been very successful.

Carla didn't even bother with makeup. Shane wouldn't let her work as he didn't trust her around any other men. With no one left to try to fool, for everyone in her family knew what her home life was like, Carla didn't see the point in trying to cover up the bruise. She turned off the light and left the bathroom.

November 26, 1995.

Carla stood beside the leather recliner in the living room, smiling meekly as she handed Shane a beer from the fridge. "Honey." Her voice was timid.

"Goddammit, shut up!" He flashed her a malevolent glare. "The game's on!"

Carla bit her lip and waited patiently. After an eternity of minutes, a beer commercial came on. She remained quiet. He would address her when he was ready to talk.

"What do you want?" He popped the can open and took a long guzzle of the foaming amber liquid.

"I'm pregnant." Her eyes searched for something, anything, that resembled joy. After all, Carla thought, this baby is part of him and part of me. How could he not be happy?

"It ain't mine." Shane's voice was flat. He kept his eyes fixed on the TV and on the nearly naked women advertising the glories of some new kind of malt beverage.

"It's yours because there ain't been anyone else." Carla's voice was firm, but contained a healthy amount of respect.

"I said it ain't mine, and I don't wanna hear no more about it!" His tone carried the edge of a threat.

"I'm fifteen." She sat on the couch and wrung her hands together nervously in her lap. "Daddy said it was up to you, but if you didn't do right and marry me, he'd have you locked up for statutory rape. And even your cousins in the sheriff's department can't help you out of it like they did when you beat up Danny."

"Don't you never bring up that pussy motherfucker's name again, you hear me?" Shane sighed angrily. "Shit! I guess I better marry your sorry ass. Either that or make license plates for a few years. Fuckin' whore."

Carla's face sagged. "I thought you loved me! This baby's yours, no matter what you say!" She relaxed and put a hand on his meaty arm. She could feel him tense up, but continued anyway. "We can make this work, baby. We can have a nice life, all of us. We got the trailer, your job, and the truck still runs okay. We're all set. 'Sides, you might like being a daddy."

Shane kept quiet. Carla was about to speak when the game came back on. She stood up. Maybe once the baby's here he'll change his mind, she thought...she prayed.

September 23, 2005. 7:18 a.m.
Carla stepped out of the bathroom and walked into the front room just in time to see her oldest, nine year old Shane junior, thrust his fist into the stomach of their youngest, three year old Tonya. The middle child, seven year old Tammy, tried to intervene on her sister's behalf and ended up getting kicked in the face. Both girls sobbed and backed away from their older brother.

"We watch what *I* want on TV!" Shane junior looked down triumphantly at his sisters. His expression became one of pain when he felt Carla pull his ear and forced him to look at her.

"You learn to share with your sisters." The mother was in no mood for trouble today. "Or I'll set your little ass on fire, boy!"

The boy wailed in pain. Carla's eyes widened in poorly-concealed fear as her bedroom door came open and a haggard-looking Shane staggered out, wearing only worn and holey underwear. "Let him alone." His voice was deathly calm.

"He was beating the girls up...again!" Carla tried to make him understand. "He can't be doing that!"

Carla found her own ear being pulled as Shane dragged her across the room. "Ain't no woman gonna get the best of no man! Not in this house." He gave her a sudden jerk, causing tears of pain to well up in her tired eyes. "Now, you ain't never gonna whoop that boy or lay hands on him again. Not no more. Got that?" She didn't answer quickly enough to avoid another violent jerk. "Got that?"

"Yeah, yeah, I got it." Her words came out as a squeak. Carla bowed her head when Shane let go. She kept her head down even after he went back to bed, trying to hide the burning tears in her eyes from Shane junior's gloating face.

"Dad really told you, huh?" The boy looked smug as he shoved the nearest sister out of his way so he could watch his cartoons on TV.

December 1, 1995.
Carla smiled as Shane pulled up in his truck. It looked and sounded as bad as before, only now the truck was jacked up a foot higher than it had been yesterday. Shane got out and walked up the three steps to the porch. Carla couldn't remember ever seeing him so happy.

"Got it all fixed up now?" She smiled at him.

"Yup." Shane grabbed a beer from the fridge and popped it open. He took a big swallow from it before heading back outside.

"Gonna take me for a ride?" She hoped he'd take the hint.

"Naw." He thought she should know better. "Gotta show Leo and Buddy. They'll shit when they see this!"

"Can't I go, too?"

"Its gonna be just us guys. Having an old lady around'll ruin everything. See you later. Don't wait up."

Carla wanted to cry. She tried hard not to, even managing to look happy when she waved good-bye to Shane as he drove off. He didn't even look back at her. Carla turned around and headed back into the trailer. She'd make him see, she believed. She just had to be patient. Shane will come around, Carla told herself. She just had to try harder.

Everyone said she was a fool for sticking with that bum, but they just didn't know him like she did. Being a mechanic is hard work, Carla had said in defense of her new boyfriend. She had said that many times. When a man comes home from a job like that, he needs to just be himself. And sometimes he says things he doesn't really mean, but you have to stick with him...make sure dinner's on time...make sure there's plenty of beer...make sure you do all the right things, things he needs so he'll know you really care...make sure there's clean clothes for the next day...

September 23, 2005. 8:11 a.m.

A final push secured the fifth bag of clothes in the back of the dented and rusty Chevette. Carla took a breath, then gathered up Tonya and put her haphazardly into the ancient car seat in the front of the car. Tammy and Shane junior were squeezed in the back seat. Carla had to tell the boy twice to get his leg in the car before she accidentally slammed the door on it. Finally she got the clothes and the kids situated. Carla got in the driver's seat and started the ignition. It took a couple tries, but the old car eventually woke up and reluctantly went about carrying its passengers to the local Laundromat.

In Cedar Ridge, like so many other redneck towns, the local social life was split into two groups. The men who weren't working were at the bars. The women who weren't working the men in bars were either at the local supermarket or the Laundromat.

Carla found a parking spot and pulled in. She got out, as did the two older children. While Tammy helped carry in the laundry, Shane junior began running around the parking lot and picking up rocks to throw at passersby.

After three trips to the car, Carla finally got the kids inside the building and the five trash bags of laundry placed near the washers she intended to use. While she started to sort the clothes, her children played with the other kids who had come here with their mothers. One child, being no more than two, ran around shrieking happily despite being unwashed and naked except for the soiled diaper clinging to its backside. The toddler chased after two boys, both about four and both afflicted with chicken pox. Another toddler entertained itself by collecting ground out cigarette butts. This went on until the tot came across one that was still partially lit. The child's screams went unanswered.

The mothers and grandmothers talked and laughed while they did their laundry, some of it being no more than rags, and did their best to ignore their raving offspring. Occasionally a housewife would have to put her chores and chat aside long enough to backhand a particularly belligerent child, but these interruptions were always only momentary. Then they were back to carrying on a full conversation, and every now and then having a belly laugh, without ever dropping the cigarette from the corners of their mouths. For most of them, this was all the social life they had. For some of them, this was all the social life they were allowed.

Carla wasn't the only woman in the Laundromat to come in bruised up. She found a modicum of solace by talking with a couple other women who, like her, had chosen their mates poorly. Like they say, misery loves company, and Carla was no exception. She didn't feel quite so alone when she consorted with other battered wives.

December 5, 1995.

Carla monitored the sizzling steak anxiously. It had to be cooked just so. Shane wouldn't eat it otherwise, and he was doubly grouchy when his dinner wasn't fixed right and fixed right on time. Carla stirred the mashed potatoes to keep them from burning.

The teenager felt, at long last, like a real woman. While her friends trudged and slaved their way through the tenth grade, she was fixing dinner for her man, a *real* man. Let them wait outside and freeze their asses off waiting for school buses, she was in a warm home cooking a meal for her and her man. Carla opened the fridge and put a hand on one of the beer cans stored within. Yep, it would be ice cold by the time Shane got home. Carla laughed. It felt so good to beat The System.

Carla tended the steak with the same skill as a surgeon would use when operating on a patient. The potatoes were exactly the right consistency and not burnt. The peas were heated to just the right temperature. Everything was set. Carla felt impressed with herself.

"System, kiss my ass." Carla nodded primly, thinking the statement appropriate.

September 23, 2005. 2:37 p.m.

Carla held the phone between her ear and left shoulder while scraping gunk off a plate she had pulled from the grayish-brown dish water. "Yeah, Momma. Uh-huh. Hold on." She turned to Tammy and Tonya. "Girls, settle down! I'm not gonna tell you again! Quit running around when I'm on the phone!" Carla set the clean(ish) plate with its mates and turned to stir the potatoes.

"Yeah, I know. I shoulda stayed with Danny." Carla's mother worked the subject into the conversation almost every time she called. "Every time Shane gets rough with me, that's what I think. And, God help me, but I think it every time I look at that oldest one, too. He's as much a monster as his father. You know he won't even let me scold him? Yeah, it's that fucking bad around here!" Her voice began to reflect her fear and frustration. "And where the fuck am I gonna go? They all know him around here. Shit, he's got family in the sheriff's department, they won't do a goddamn thing to protect me from him! If I left, he'd beat my ass like he did Danny's. And the fucking cops would sweep it under the goddamn rug, just like they did back then!" She sighed. There was no use getting upset over things she was absolutely powerless to change. "Look, my ass is stuck here. If I came home with the girls, it'd just cause trouble for you and Poppy. And I'd wind up right back where I'm at now, with a few extra bruises to boot." She looked at the clock. "Oh shit. Look Momma, it's almost time for Shane to get home and I still got dishes to do. I'll call tomorrow, okay? Yeah, love you too. Bye."

December 8, 1995.

Carla looked at the bottle's contents with a wary eye. It looked a little like tea, but she knew it was a lot more powerful than anything Lipton ever put out. She'd seen Shane pour the rotgut stuff down his gullet on special occasions. Carla figured this was one of them, but what it was exactly, she had no clue. Shane poured a double-size shot glass full of the whiskey and handed it too her.

"Go on." He nudged her arm encouragingly.

"But what about the baby?" She started feeling nervous. "I mean, that ain't good for it."

"I don't care." Shane shrugged. "Now go on. I told you to drink it."

Carla slowly brought the glass to her lips. He'd make her drink it, she was sure, even if she didn't want to. Sipping it slowly would only prolong the miserable experience, so Carla downed it in one burning gulp. She coughed violently as it made its way to her stomach. She felt a warm sensation generating from the pit of her stomach as her body began to absorb the alcohol. Again the glass was filled and handed to her, and again she drank. Soon Carla felt the buzz from the whiskey.

"Must be something special going on." Carla watched Shane gulp the stuff straight from the bottle. "What is it?"

"You're ready." He didn't elaborate.

"Ready for what?"

"For what we talked about."

Carla looked at him curiously for a moment, the liquor slowing her thoughts. Then her eyes widened as much with disgust as fear.

"Shane, I can't." She began to plead. "That'll hurt too much. Can't we do something else?"

"I said you're ready." Shane's voice came out a growl. His eyes seemed to hint at an explosive outburst floating barely underneath his relatively calm outward appearance.

Carla was sure he'd never hit her, but she didn't want to press her luck any farther than she had to. Still, what he wanted would hurt just as bad, maybe worse. Caught between fear, loyalty, and her own stubborn pride, Carla hung her head. Her golden hair covered most of her face. Even that couldn't hide the quiver of her lip as she decided to risk it all. "Please, Shane." She was determined not to cry. "I don't want to."

His hand wasn't overly rough, but neither was it gentle when he raised her face to meet his. His stern green eyes locked mercilessly upon her sad blues. "Who's man of the house?"

"You are." She turned her eyes to the floor, her voice a whisper.

He lifted her face again, this time with a little more force. "Who?"

"You are." Carla said it a little louder as she looked right at him.

"Uh-huh. And the man of the house makes the rules, right?"

"Yeah."

"Then the rule for you is do what I tell you," Shane said. "And I say you're ready. Now, are you ready?"

It's all part of being a good woman, Carla told herself. Maybe if she did this he'd see how much she loved him. He might even come to love her, too. Carla nodded and offered no resistance when Shane got up and led her to the bedroom. Her last thought, before the door closed, was how much of the pain the whiskey would numb.

September 23, 2005. 5:03 p.m.

Carla watched wordlessly as Shane put on his best baseball cap and got ready to leave. It was Saturday night, and there was no way Shane was going to miss out on spending the evening with his buddies at the tavern. He might even meet up with some pretty young thing and score another victory for his manhood. Carla wished he would find someone else and tell her to go. Or better yet, she thought, maybe he'll get himself killed before he comes home.

"I'm leaving," Shane said. He headed for the door.

Nope, Carla thought. Her luck never ran that good.

Shane stopped and turned to face her. "You have them kids in bed before I get home. But don't you go to bed. There's something you gotta do when I get home, and I don't wanna be bothered with them fuckin' kids. And I don't wanna hafta wake your ass up, neither."

"All right." Carla revealed no emotion at all. Although the task didn't hurt as much now as it did in the beginning, she still hated it. If

God had intended for that to go on between men and women, she figured, assholes would have been made wider by nature, not by force.

"And better not be no problems when I get home," Shane said. "I wanna have a beer and get some of that ugly ass of yours 'fore I go to bed."

"You didn't used to think it was so ugly." A meek defense was all she dared come back with.

"Not my fault you're gettin' to be an eyesore." He shrugged. "Now you remember, woman. No kids, and you be waiting."

"Everything'll be fine," Carla said.

"Better be." Shane slammed the front door behind him.

December 12, 1995.

Every little noise made Carla flinch. There had been three break-ins in the trailer court within the last two weeks. The burglars hadn't been caught yet, and no one had any idea who was doing it. An old woman was beat up during the last robbery, and Carla was afraid of, perhaps, being next. Shane didn't have anything of value, but lack of precious goods didn't seem to stop these thieves on the loose, who burgled trailers at random.

Carla's parents had argued vehemently against her moving in with Shane. They had said she wasn't ready for that. Of course, they also hated Shane with a passion. Carla's parents said that any man who beats a fifteen year old boy almost to death for trying to defend his girlfriend, and then seduces the girlfriend, isn't a man at all, but a goddamned coward and a bully. Danny's parents had expressed similar views.

Naturally, Carla took these things to mean that her parents were just trying to control her and that, out of jealousy and revenge, they were attacking the man who had swept her off her feet and, therefore, threatened to break their death-grip on her. So, of course, Carla felt she had no choice but to move out and shack-up with Shane in the middle of the night.

That had been three weeks ago. Carla missed only the security of her parents' home, which was located in a better neighborhood. She wished Shane would hurry up and get home. She'd feel a lot safer with him nearby. After all, who would be stupid enough to try anything with a giant like Shane around?

The sound of glass shattering shocked Carla out of her reverie. Her body trembled as she slowly got up and walked into the kitchen. She grabbed a heavy iron skillet and padded silently toward the source of the noise, which was the bedroom that faced the road.

Carla gingerly opened the door. A crack at first, then wider. Her brow wrinkled with confusion when she saw that the bedroom window wasn't broken. Carla looked outside to see two neighbor men standing by a car and drinking. One of them had dropped a beer bottle.

Cursing herself for a fool, Carla put the skillet back and returned to the living room. She sat down on the worn-out couch and went back to watching TV. Carla felt a little easier. At least if there's people outside, a robber won't come around, she figured.

Carla heard Shane's truck pull into the gravel driveway. For an instant she was even more afraid than she had been when she thought burglars had broken in. They had argued earlier. Shane had slapped her, but it had been Carla's fault. She should have known not to sass him when his friends were around. But now she was safe. Shane was home, and no one'd be dumb enough to mess with Shane.

September 23, 2005. 10:31 p.m.
Carla's blood ran cold with fear when she heard the sound of the engine coming closer. It was only ten-thirty! Shane usually stayed out until at least one. He must have struck out at the tavern, Carla figured. The girls had been put to bed at nine, but Shane junior was in one of his moods and insisted on staying up.

"Come on, Shane!" Carla tried to hide the urgency and fear from her voice. "You need to go to bed now!"

"I ain't going to bed." The boy stood defiant against her command.

The truck pulled to a stop in the driveway. Carla could hear the radio screaming some country tune.

"Shane, *please*." The woman clasped her hands together fearfully. "Go to bed, or at least go to your room. It'll go really bad for me if you don't! Please?"

"Fuck you." The boy sat back down in from of the TV.

The engine and the radio went dead silent.

"For God's sake, Shane, *please*!" The mother pulled her son to his feet. "I don't want to be mean with you, but I need you to go to bed. Now!!"

"Lemme go!" The boy knew his father must be close by for her to get so riled, and started shouting as though she were trying to kill him. "Leemee 'lone!"

The pair heard angry grumbling and footsteps on the porch. Carla tugged more insistently on her son's arm. The boy pulled back with equal intensity.

The front door exploded.

Carla had barely gotten the first word of an explanation out of her mouth when the first impact caused the room to spin. So fast and furious were the blows that there was no time to register the pain from one before the next came. And the next. And the next. And the next.

From someplace far away, Carla thought she could hear the girls screaming and crying. The world swam around and around through a sea of inky blackness. For a moment she thought she could hear a young voice shout, "Get her, dad! Get her!" Then it, too, was gone, swallowed by the all-pervasive darkness. Only when a spike of pain ran through her body did Carla gain a sliver of awareness.

Carla had the vague sensation of…what? Was she floating? Was she being carried? It didn't matter, the woman fell back into oblivion before she could discover the cause of this strange sensation.

January 12, 1996.

Carla stared at Danny impatiently, as though he were a mosquito that had flown too close to her ear. It was no coincidence that he had run in to her here at the grocery store. But, she reminded herself, he had taken a world-class beating on her behalf. For that, Carla would hear what he had to say.

"Look, I just want to know what the hell happened." Danny wasn't sure how to approach the subject, but hearing the sound of his own voice bolstered his self-confidence. "I mean, what is it about that asshole that you can't resist? Is it his truck? Is it because he's as big as a mountain? I don't understand what you saw in him that made you want to dump me. I mean, we went everywhere and did everything together. I just don't see how he could turn your head around the way he did. Your parents are freaked out over it. They don't understand, either.

"Carla, there's a lot of people who love you that you've hurt. Me, your parents, my parents, our friends…you've just turned away from everyone. And this guy doesn't care about you, you're just another pretty face to him."

"First of all, Shane's a *real* man." Carla took silent pleasure in Danny's defeated look. "He took care of you pretty good. I mean, he's big, he's strong, and he treats me like a real woman. I'm tired of being mommy and daddy's little girl!"

"But I thought we had our future all planned out," Danny said. "After graduation, we'd go to college and-"

"Aw, come on!" Carla scoffed at him. "You know good and well no one from around here's ever gonna go on to no college. You, a doctor? You're no better than anyone else around here! You'd be lucky to get a factory job. You'll probably end up like most people around here, making French fries for the factory folks. And that's the truth!"

Danny gently took her hand in his. "Stay with me, Carla. Don't leave. Things will get better, you'll see."

"You're the one who needs to see!" She didn't care if people stared at her. It was time to tell it like it was. "You, my parents, the whole goddamn world, everyone is so blind! I can't fucking believe it! You believe in The System. The System says you need to finish school and try to make it out of Cedar Ridge, so that's what you'll try to do. But you don't get it. You'll never make it, and that's how The System is set up. They lie and say you can do the impossible. Then when you fall flat on your ass, they'll laugh and say they told you so.

"Well I'm past all that now. I'm past The System. I'm my own person. And not you, my folks, your folks, nobody's gonna change that!"

"We can make The System work for us." Danny knew what she was getting at, but he had to try to save her from herself. "The System won't kill you like Shane will. I don't want that to happen, Carla."

Carla wouldn't acknowledge his nonsense. She turned around and walked away from Danny. The young man looked after her with sad eyes. Why couldn't she see the danger right in front of her?

Danny turned and walked away. He had done his best. There was nothing else to do now but let events take their own course.

September 23, 2005. 11:19 p.m.

Midnights in E.R. were never pretty. Danny had seen more shootings, stabbings, drug overdoses, and car crash victims in the last two months to last him a lifetime. But, such is the lot of an intern. You didn't choose your hours or your surroundings, the people with degrees did. A few more years, the twenty-five year old medical student told himself, and he would be among that lot.

"Incoming." A middle-aged nurse wheeled a slight, bloody body on a gurney. "House party, but the husband says she fell down."

"Right." Danny spoke sarcastically, recognizing the hospital lingo for a victim of domestic violence. "How bad?"

"Bad." The nurse's voice was grim.

The two of them wheeled the gurney into an examination room. The nurse hooked the victim up to a monitor and turned to leave. "Keep her conscious if you can. I've got to get Doctor Leeds." She rushed out of the room.

Danny looked down at the woman on the gurney. She bled from the eyes, nose, and mouth, and had a purple gash in the side of her head. He looked at her curiously until it dawned on him who she was. "Carla? My God!"

Her eyes weakly fluttered open at the mention of her name. She recognized the voice immediately. "Danny?"

"It's me, Carla." He smiled sadly.

Carla began to cry softly. "What'll he do to my girls? He never liked them, neither did the boy."

"Don't worry." He tried to sound reassuring. "His days of pushing people around are over. The police won't ignore it this time."

That would have to be enough for her.

The intern's eyes grew fearful when he saw her vital signs fluctuating erratically. Danny took her hand gently in his. "Stay with me, Carla. Don't give up. Things will get better, you'll see."

"I can't." Carla's voice was slurred by the damage to her lower jaw. "My girls...I was wrong...thought I could change him...sorry...should've waited..."

"Don't go, please!" Danny whispered fiercely.

Carla said nothing. Her eyes closed, her hand fell limp.

Shane sat in the emergency ward waiting room. The burly man was uncharacteristically quiet. Sitting across the room from him, Greg, Carla's father, sat silently, his lips pursed tightly together, his eyes revealing only a seething hatred for the lump of human waste seven feet away. Carla's mother was at the trailer, watching the children.

Both men were surprised to see Danny walk into the waiting room. The intern didn't bother hiding his tears. He could see through them well enough. Shane's face turned chalk white with fear as Danny spoke to him. "I hope you're happy, you big hunk of shit."

"My girl..." Greg's voice trembled.

"I'm sorry." Danny turned to the short, blue-eyed, middle-aged man. "The damage was too extensive. The doctor will be in shortly to give you the official notice. I thought you'd rather hear it first from a friend."

"She fell down." Even Shane thought the words sounded pathetic. He let his voice trail off.

"I swear before God, I'll kill you!" Greg wanted to throw something at the monster he'd called son-in-law for almost ten years. He wanted to shoot him, leap on him and smash him as Shane had smashed Carla. But he couldn't. All the man could do at the moment was think about his little blue-eyed girl and her short life and sob bitterly.

"She always thought that staying with you was her way of beating The System." Danny's words were laced with venom. "Now we're going see if you can beat The System any better than she did."

Shane saw two uniformed police officers walk into the room. Fear such as he had never known pierced his heart. No more nights at the bar. No more driving his truck. No more chasing high school girls around. That was all over. When he felt the cold steel wrap firmly around his wrists, Shane began to cry.

The System had won again.

143

Wesley

Gotta hurry, gotta get to work! Have to be on the assembly line by three, and it's a quarter till. I'll never make it in time! Boss'll chew me out good for this! Shirt's on, pants, socks, work shoes. Going through the kitchen, got my lunch box.

I oughta say good-bye to Wesley. I always do, but I'm really late today. I'll make it up to him tomorrow. He knows I love him. Wes'll be two tomorrow. Terrific son, and Carol's a great wife. They know I work hard so they can have a good life. I'll make it up to them this weekend.

Garage door's already open. Good. The truck starts up on the first try like always. Backing up fast...

Whoa! What the hell was that? I hit something! Better get out and see what it was. Oh no! Carol! I'm sorry! So sorry...

The blond-haired man awoke. Nine-thirty. "Wes'll be up." George Caine sat up in bed. His blue eyes adjusted to the sunlit room as he stood up and pulled on a pair of pants. Caine was slender, lean, and youngish. He walked from his bedroom down the hall to the living room.

"Hi Daddy!" The little boy's voice was squeaky. He played contently with his toy cars on the floor.

"Morning, Wes," Caine said. "How's my little man today?"

"I'm okay." The sandy-blond haired boy looked up at his father. "You had bad dreams last night, didn't you? I tried to wake you, but I couldn't so I stayed up."

Caine silently stared and smiled at his son. Wesley had just turned six and, except for having brown eyes instead of blue, was the spitting image of his father; a bit tall and lean for his age. The boy wore blue shorts and socks, a T-shirt with a picture of some cartoon character on it, and a baseball cap turned backward. Wesley's smile, looking so much like the smile that his mother had used to charm Caine, made the grown man grin turn bittersweet.

"Are we going to see Mommy today?" Wesley looked at him expectantly.

"No." Caine's voice was short and tight. He decided it best to change the subject. "I thought we'd just spend the day together."

"Okay! Let's go, Daddy!" The boy stood up and put on his shoes.

Caine threw on a shirt, put his own socks and shoes on, and led the boy outside after grabbing his wallet and keys. He opened the door to the van and the child climbed in. Caine smiled as Wesley put his seat belt on, proud as could be that his son was quickly learning how to ride safely inside a vehicle. The man shut his son's door and got in the driver's side. He put his key in the ignition and started up the van.

144

"Well Wes," the father asked, "where do you want to go?"

"Let's go to the park," the boy said.

Caine nodded and pulled out of the driveway. Before long the two were in the parking lot of a local playground. Caine got out and opened Wesley's door. The boy eagerly undid his seat belt and jumped out. The father closed the van door and jogged after his son, who was by then swinging from the monkey bars. Caine stood by, taking in a lungful of warm, fresh July air. It was supposed to rain later, but now it was clear and eighty-one degrees. He started to think about how nice it would be for the two of them to share this day with Carol. Caine instantly pushed the unwelcome thoughts aside. He wouldn't let those depressing images interfere with his day out with Wesley. The boy was getting older and would soon demand to know the truth, the man knew. He hoped that day was far off, but he knew it wasn't.

"Hey, Daddy." Wesley called to his father. Caine looked over to his son, who was hanging upside-down by his knees from one of the bars. "Lookit me! See what I can do?"

"You're doing great, son," the father said. "Be careful now. Don't fall."

"I won't." The boy's voice was confident. He righted himself and jumped down. "Swing time!"

Caine laughed and followed his son to the swings. By the time Wesley tired of the playground, the sky was starting to cloud up. Father and son got into the van and drove to a nearby frozen yogurt shop. After pulling into a parking spot, the two got out and went inside. Caine ordered two chocolate ice cream cones and walked outside with Wesley. They sat down at a picnic table where Caine handed the boy his cone. Wesley reached out for the treat...but promptly dropped it. The boy looked heartbroken as he watched the stuff begin to melt on the warm asphalt.

"I'm sorry, Daddy." The boy sounded pitiful.

"We'll share mine," Caine said. He offered Wesley the first bite. The boy accepted and before long the ice cream cone was gone.

Wesley wiped his mouth with the back of his hand. "That was good. Is it gonna rain soon?"

"I think so." Caine looked up at the slate-gray clouds. "Tell you what, pardner. Let's head back to the ranch and rustle up some cartoons on TV."

"Awright!" Wesley made a fist and pulled his arm back. "Cha-ching!"

The father laughed at his son's antics and took him home. Rain spattered the windows and siding, but Caine paid it no heed and flipped on the box and sat on the floor with his son. The man suggested turning on the TV to keep his son amused, but found himself actually enjoying the animated shows. For a few moments he wondered how such shows would have fared when he was a boy. Kids back then would have loved them, he decided.

While the boy sat transfixed by the TV, Caine soon found his eyelids getting heavy. Five minutes later, he was napping soundly. When Caine up, Wesley was still watching TV, but was also eating the last of a peanut butter and jelly sandwich the boy had made for himself. The son, seeing his father awaken, smiled and approached him.

"Let's play cars." The boy pulled a tiny version of his father's van from his pocket. Caine was ready for this, and pulled out of one of his own pockets a toy car he'd bought earlier that week. Father and son played cars together. Sometimes they had flip-overs, sometimes they were on high-speed chases, and other times they simply tapped their cars along with a single fingertip.

Caine looked up at the clock. "Okay buddy," he said. "Its eight o'clock. Time for bed."

"Aw, do I really have to go to bed?"

"'Fraid so, pardner."

Wesley obediently got up and trotted off to his bedroom. The boy stripped down and climbed into the old crib that served as his bed. "When am I getting a big boy's bed?" he asked.

"Pretty soon," Caine said. "Tell you what. Tomorrow you can go with me to pick one out."

Wesley nodded and pulled the blanket up to his chin. Caine smiled at him and started to turn off the light. "Daddy?" the boy asked.

"Yes son?"

"Where's Mommy?"

The father sighed. The moment of truth had come. "She went away." Caine's voice was quiet and tinged with sorrow. "See, sometimes moms and dads don't always get along. They have to live apart from each other."

"Does it mean that Mommy doesn't love me anymore?"

"No." The father's voice softened. "It just means that she moved away to another town and we can't see her right now. But one of these days I'll take you to meet her."

Wesley nodded, apparently satisfied with that answer. "I know you didn't mean to run me over with the truck."

"I did no such thing!"

"But I died," the boy said.

"No you didn't, because I wouldn't let you go!"

"Is that why Mommy went away?" Wesley asked.

"Go to sleep, son." He ignored the question and adjusted the blanket in the empty crib, ignoring also the several years' worth of accumulated dust that layered upon the long-unused piece of furniture. Caine turned and shut off the light.

"Goodnight, Daddy. I love you."

"Goodnight, Wesley. I love you, too."

Caine left the bedroom door slightly ajar and the hall light on before going to bed himself.

Gotta hurry, gotta get to work! Have to be on the assembly line by three, and it's a quarter till. I'll never make it in time! Boss'll chew me out good for this. Shirt's on, pants, socks, work shoes. Going through the kitchen, got my lunchbox.

I really ought to say good-bye to Wesley. I always do, but I'm really late today. I'll make it up to him tomorrow. He knows I love him. Wes'll be two tomorrow. Terrific son, and Carol's a great wife. They know I work hard so they can have a good life. I'll make it up to them this weekend.

Garage door's already open. Good. The truck starts up on the first try, like always. Backing up fast...

King of the johnnies

Hey there! How's it going? Me? Not too bad. I guess before we go any further, I should introduce myself. The name's johnnie. Not Johnny, mind you, but "johnnie." There's an important distinction to be made. Johnny is a name for male humans, but johnnie is a name given to us portable toilets. Port-a-Potty, Outhouse, Shithouse, Shitbox, we go by many names. But I prefer johnnie. It sounds respectable. Of course, how much can you respect someone whose purpose in life is to be full of shit?

However, you have to give me credit, I'm pretty well made. I've got a nice, sturdy seat. You should know, you're s(h)itting on it. Got a separate urinal device, handy paper holder, plenty of ventilation so you humans don't gag on each other's stench, I'm even handicapped accessible. All this, and with an attractive blue hard plastic exterior, too. Yep, I'm the King of Crappers, the Sultan of Shitters, the Pharoah of Feces, the Emperor of Excrement, the Overlord of Offal, the Premier of Poo-Poo. A real super deluxe model. Whoever rents me out pays top dollar for my unique services.

No, you are *not* tripped out on acid. We johnnies normally don't say much, but even we get lonesome from time to time. And you humans are notorious for doing your business and leaving. You never stick around to say, "Hello,", "Thanks for putting up with my shit,", "Want me to leave the seat up?", or anything else. So since you won't talk to me, I'll have to talk to you. No, don't try force the door open, and stop yelling for help. This conversation is just beginning. That's it, just relax. No one's going to hurt you.

First of all, you humans think you've got some kind of monopoly on having bad days. Did any of you ever stop to consider what it's like for us johnnies when *we* have bad days? No, I didn't think so. Too caught up in your need to take a piss to give us a second thought. You have any idea what it's like to be tipped over? Not much bloody fun, I can tell you! Being knocked over, hearing that crash and splash, feeling your insides gush out all over the place. At least you humans can get right back up! We johnnies have to just lay there until some poor bastard comes along and tips us back up. And if the wise-ass who knocked us down made us land on our doors, you ought to see the reactions of our owners when the fools lift us back up! The door flies open, and the guy gets splashed. Ha ha, very funny, asshole!

I'm lucky, though. I've never had to go through that bullshit. Not yet, anyway. But you ought to hear it from one of the older shitters, like old Uri over there. His full name is Urine Luck. He got that name because he's seen all kinds of shit, literally and figuratively, and he's still around to talk about it. But we call him Uri for short. Makes it easier. Hey, Uri!

Yeah?

You in a mood to talk?

Sure. Got a human in there?

Yep.

Okay. Guess johnnie's already told you my name and how I got it. Don't kick his door trying to get out! What the hell's the matter with you? Ain't many of your kind we talk to. You oughta feel privileged! That's better, just calm your ass down. Just 'cause we put up with your shit doesn't mean we have to take your abuse.

Like I was saying, I been all over. I used to be all new and pretty like johnnie there. But, like you can see if you look out the vents, I'm dark green. Not sky blue like johnny. Our makers, they didn't take the pride in us back then that they do now, that's for sure! Now, you'd think they was trying to create works of art or something. But not my generation. I'm all dented and scratched up, my door flies open if the lock ain't locked. But at my age, I guess I ought to feel lucky to still be around.

I remember one of my first jobs, I was at some city park. The sewer system was backed up, and me and my buddies were sent over to handle the situation. You know what a pain in the ass it is having to put up with a bunch of screaming kids all day? They're too short to hit the hole, so most of them piss on the floor. This one little bastard, him and some of his friends pissed on my door and walls. Then they laughed about it. One of them grabbed the end of the toilet paper and took off running out my door! It looked like I had streamers coming out of me! If you only knew how bad I wanted to tip myself over on the little shit! But no, I had to put up with it for three whole days. You don't know how glad me and my pals were to go back home after that experience. It felt good to be emptied out and hosed down.

You listening, human? This is a voice of experience talking! No shit.

Not yet, but it's still early yet. Give it time.

Go on, Uri. Tell this person about that kegger you hosted! I just about tipped over when I heard about it. Go on, Uri! Tell us!

Alright, alright, keep your seat down! I was just coming to that part, anyway. See, this rich kid, he'd just graduated from college or something, and his folks left town while he had this wild-ass party. Well take it from me, when forty college kids get together, there ain't no way a couple little house pissers' gonna get the job done, so they sent for me. I guess they didn't want to commit chemical warfare on the grass, so they put me on the patio. I mean, it feels nice to sit on that soft grass, but it's not always perfectly level. You never know when somebody's gonna put too much weight on the wrong side and send us both falling over. I don't like it and I know for damn sure they aren't too wild about it, either. Puts a whole new meaning to the phrase "getting shit-faced."

Anyway, the night started off okay. I mean, at first it was just business as usual, no biggie. There was this one college chick, though. I mean, she was hot! I was just too happy to serve her. That's one good thing about being a portable toilet. We get all the ass we can handle. It's just a fact of life.

But about an hour or so after it got dark, things started to get crazy. This one asshole wouldn't leave. I'll bet he spent every bit of half an hour smoking dope inside me. I didn't mind that so much, but his friends didn't like it at all. They kept hitting me with beer bottles trying to get him out. Yeah, like I can just spit the son of a bitch out! Finally the idiot managed to find the door and he left. It was one after another for about fifteen minutes after that. Then it got quiet for a while.

A while later, this couple came in. I thought, what the hell? I can only take one at a time! Then they started getting it on. They made me rock so bad, I thought all three of us were going down. Turned out, they were the only ones to go down. I guess they ran out of bedrooms to use. At least they were nice enough to leave something for me to remember them by before they left. Not like I would forget that.

Then the puking started. I'm used to the mess, but I can't take that noise. Trust me, if I could vomit, hearing that come from one human after another would get me heaving.

Go on! Tell us about that other thing!

Alright! Calm the hell down, why don't you? No patience, these youngsters! Anyway, I thought the party was over for the night. And brother, was I glad! But just as I was about to settle in for the night, these asshole kids from next door climbed over the fence and dumped me in the damn swimming pool! Actually, it was kind of nice to take a bath for a change. I mean, usually I get hosed down every time I get cleaned up, but I was the only one who thought the bath was cool. When the party's host got up the next morning, he was pretty pissed...er, angry, when he saw me floating in there. And all that pretty blue water had turned a funky brownish color. Well, it wasn't my fault. It's not like I tottered over to the diving board and jumped in by myself. It took them quite a while to haul me out of there. I wonder how they ever got that pool cleaned up?

Oh, that was great! What about you, human? Wasn't that cool? Hey, Uri! What about that time you were over at the plaza? Remember that one?

How the hell could I forget? That's how I got all dented up.

Tell us, then.

I guess you and your human won't shut up about it until I do. Fine. It was a while back. They were just starting to build that plaza across town. You know, the one on top of the hill. No big deal. Me and one of my buddies were put out of the way, over by a guardrail at the edge of the parking lot by the edge of the hill. I mean, no one wanted to take a chance on having a girder snap its cable and crush us into action-figure sized pieces of plastic. It was a typical job, we were supposed to sit there and take shit from people for a couple weeks, then head back to the shop.

Then these two pricks came along one night and start messing around. Can you believe those assholes knocked me over that guardrail? You know what that feels like, falling end over end down a hill? Talk about spilling your guts! I slid against some rocks, and my door was torn off. Then my seat flew off into space. I'd have landed on the pavement of the parking lot at the bottom of the hill if I'd been two feet over to either side. Then I'd have been smashed up for good. Lucky I landed on the hood of this BMW instead. Saved my ass, that's for sure! It didn't do the owner of the car any good, but that's his problem.

My buddy, he wasn't so lucky. Those shitheads set him on fire before they tossed him down. He was a goner just from that alone, but he ended up hitting the bare pavement; a double whammy for sure! I can still see him in my nightmares, pieces of burning plastic flying all over the place. Screaming for help, all banged up. Burned up before the fire department got there. Terrible. Just terrible! And shitters like johnnie over there, they think it's story-time when I start talking about it. Just you wait until you're an old shitbox like me and you've seen more of that violent world out there! Then you'll know old Uri wasn't always full of shit!

Sorry, Uri. I didn't know it was as bad as that.

Well now you do, by God!

Well I won't make you talk about anymore if you don't want to.

No thanks for small favors!

Okay, I said I'm sorry. No need to get hostile.

S'alright. Bad memories, you know. At least my owners were nice enough to give me a new seat and put my door back on. Kind of hard to do yourself when you're on your head and oozing gunk out of your chimney and vents.

Understood. Well, human, what do you think of that? Is that a true hero or what? He went through all that and he's still able to deal with people's shit every day. He's a real trooper, you know. Maybe someday I'll have stories of my own to tell like his. What? Oh yeah, you can go now. And please remember, if you're going to trash something, stick with things like shopping carts, they don't break as easy as we do. Especially in the winter. I heard of this one johnnie that got slid down an icy hill at a construction site one January. It hit the side of a bulldozer and smashed into a million pieces! Tough break!

Anyway, the door's unlocked. Come back again sometime! Bring a gun and we'll shoot the shit!

Watch your mouth.

Right. Sorry. Well, bye human!

Journey Toward the Light

The Present.

The sound of metal hitting metal was completely obliterated by the deafening explosion that echoed throughout the garage. Before the first waves of sound could blast his eardrums, Lance Dunphy felt the hole being blown into his chest. A nanosecond later, Dunphy's back slammed hard against the rear wall of the garage. Pain would not set in immediately. Dunphy could only be impressed by the force of the chain of events that had been set into motion. By this time, the blast had registered in the 37 year-old man's ears. Only a hint of pain there, followed by the constant ringing of sound waves that carried Dunphy's mind across the ethers of time. Rising to blend in with the resonance of the blast came the voice of someone calling from the distance, leading his descent into darkness...

Lance P. Dunphy, age 7.

"Get away from that window this instant!" Ophelia, Lance's mother, stormed into the living room of their house. Her bird-like voice struck fear into the little boy's heart. "There's nothing out there for you to see! Come away right now!"

"The boys next door are having a party." The boy's words were a lament. "I think it's Josh's birthday."

"Oh yes." Ophelia's voice virtually dripped with contempt. The slender woman put her fists on her hips. Her pale face and dark hair were severely set, looking almost inhuman to the casual observer. Lance had seen this look on a daily basis. "They're celebrating another year that little punk's been on this earth. How old is he now? Eight? Nine?"

"His dad's got him and his brother Teddy in football." Lance's voice was wistful. "They got to play their first game last week." The boy decided to take a big gamble and looked up at his mother. "When can I start playing football?"

"Never!" Her voice was adamant. "I'm not going to see any kid of mine get busted up or killed playing those goddamn roughneck sports! You just better put those thoughts right out of your head this instant, young man. In fact," she pulled the curtain closed, "I don't even want you looking out there. All those little pricks are doing is putting bad ideas in your head. And they're just playing outside. Can you imagine what kind of harm they could do if they ever got hold of you? Mark my words boy, you'll end up dead in an alley somewhere or locked up for being a drug addict if you hang around that crowd.

"Now go on into your room and play with your new toys. I bought them special for you."

"Always toys." In truth, Lance loved his new treasures. But there was something missing...something that always seemed to be missing. "Why can't I have friends over to play with my stuff with me?"

"Because all the other kids will do is either break your toys or take them away from you." Ophelia sighed and draped an arm around Lance's shoulders. "You know I buy you things because I love you. It's how all good parents show their feelings toward their kids."

"Then will you play with me?" The boy looked up at her with hopeful eyes.

"Oh honey I can't." She led him gently away from the window. "Mommy's got an important movie to watch on TV in a couple hours and I don't want to get so wrapped up in something that I end up missing it. Now I'm going to take a nap. If I'm not up by five, make sure you wake me."

"Yes mommy." Lance cast his gaze to the floor.

"I know things are hard for you sometimes." Her voice sounded almost sympathetic. "But this is the way it has to be if you want to stay out of trouble and make me proud. Now go play in your room."

"Yes mommy." The boy moped out of the living room and toward his bedroom.

"Now don't let me catch you looking outside again." Ophelia's voice became as stern as before. "I've still got your father's belt and you know I'll use it."

"I know." His defeat was reflected in his voice. Things had gone from bad to worse since his father had left. He used to be able to play with the other kids when his Daddy was around. But those days were gone. Daddy wasn't allowed to come around anymore and Mommy didn't like for anyone else to come around. No one.

"Good boy." The mother sounded pleased.

Lance walked into his bedroom. He would have closed the door, but Mommy said doors were forbidden. Mommy said if he had a door, then he would be alone in his room. And if he were alone in his room, Mommy said that God only knows what he would be up to. Lance decided to be a good boy. He sat at his desk and started playing. He had to keep quiet. Mommy had taken the door off her bedroom so she could make sure Lance wasn't doing anything wrong.

The boy grew tired of playing quietly, tired of playing, and just tired in general. He started to lay down on his bed when he remembered his promise to wake his Mommy just before five. Lance decided to stare at the clock on his wall until it was time and plopped down on the bed. Falling down, down...never stopping...always falling...

The Present.

Lance's legs gave out beneath him and he felt himself begin to slide down the wall toward the floor. He knew that whether or not he

153

fought to remain standing wouldn't matter; he would fall now as he had fallen his whole life. The parallel between this situation and his youth was inescapable. A ghoulish smile parted his lips as the darkness reclaimed him. Now Lance wasn't sure if it were he who was falling, or if the floor had become less than solid. Something liquid, maybe? Like water, perhaps...

Lance P. Dunphy, age 15.

The water slapped briskly against the docks. Lance's cousin, Brad, wanted to take his father's rowboat out for a short trip on the lake without telling anyone. Lance eagerly went along with the plan. Ever since the state had stepped in and placed Lance with his uncle, aunt, and cousin after forcing Ophelia to enter a psychiatric hospital, the two boys had become inseparable. The skies were cloudy and the weatherman had predicted rain, but the two cousins paid it little heed. They were near the middle of the lake when the wind began to pick up. Only then did the boys start to have misgivings.

"How fast do you think that wind is?" Lance asked. He eyed the waves that now rocked their little boat.

"About thirty knots or so," Brad replied. He was the better sailor of the two. "Rain's coming down pretty hard and the waves are getting rough. Let's head back."

Lance helped turn the boat around and the boys began to row back to shore. They made good progress, the docks were getting close. Then a strong gale caused the boat to rock violently.

"Hurry up!" Brad called. "It's getting worse!"

The boys picked up the pace and rowed frantically toward the dock when a high wave lifted the small craft and flipped it over. Lance broke the water's surface first. Seconds passed by mercilessly slow. Brad bobbed up twenty yards away. Lance could see his kin struggling mightily to make it to shore. Although Brad was the better sailor, Lance was the better swimmer. It didn't look like Brad was going to make it. Lance threw aside all concern for himself and plunged ahead, away from the dock, to help his cousin.

"I can't swim that well!" Brad cried. "Go home and get help!"

"I'm not leaving you!" Lance shouted.

"Go on! I'll be fine!"

Lance wouldn't hear of it. The rain was coming down in sheets, making it almost impossible to see Brad. Lance chopped through the water, unsure if he was getting close...or even heading in the right direction. The young swimmer pushed himself even harder.

Lance topped a wave. The rain lessened a bit. He could see Brad barely four or five feet ahead of him. The boy was exhausted, his strength spent. Lance threw himself to the edge of his endurance, knowing his cousin was in serious trouble.

Then Brad slipped under the waves. Horror and disbelief struck Lance. He dived under once, then again, for his lost kin. Nothing. Lance wanted to try a third time, but he knew if he went down again he wouldn't have the strength to make it back up. Reluctantly, the swimmer returned to the dock.

Lance climbed to safety atop the wooden planks. He looked back to the lake that had taken his cousin from him. Sobs wracked his entire body as the severity of his failure dawned more fully upon him with each passing moment. Lance was the best swimmer in his class, yet he had failed to save the life of someone dear to him. The boy's despair grew only deeper as he looked back to the house and thought of telling his aunt and uncle about the accident. Slowly, he pulled himself to his feet and made the difficult walk back to the house. Lightning snapped and thunder boomed about him, but Lance paid it no heed as he walked toward the other two people whom he had let down.

"Thought I'd find you here." Uncle Joe walked up to Lance as the teenager sat at his usual place on the docks. It had been two months since the storm, and everyone still mourned Brad. "Mind if I join you?"

Lance looked up at his uncle. Sometimes the boy got the impression the salt-and-pepper haired man grieved almost as much for him as for his son. "I don't care."

Uncle Joe sat beside him, letting his feet dangle as Lance did. "You know, I used to sit here like this when I was your age." The tall, forty-three year old man tugged absently on his mustache. "I used to just stare out at the lake and let my thoughts wander."

Lance decided it was time to cut to the chase. "Why haven't you kicked me out?"

"Why in God's name would I do that?" He seemed genuinely shocked.

"Because of what happened." Lance stared out at the water. "I failed. I tried to-" the words got caught in the lump in his throat. The burning sting of tears came to his eyes. His words came out as a whisper. "I tried to save Brad and I couldn't. He'd be here right now if it weren't for me. I let him down like I've let you and Aunt Frieda down."

"All right, now you listen." The man forced Lance to look at him. "If it weren't for you, we wouldn't have any idea what had happened to Brad. And you didn't let anybody down. You did a hell of a job trying to save him. When you stop and think of the distance involved, the wind, the waves, and the rain, it's a miracle you made it as close as you did and still managed to get back to the docks. That's no bullshit, Lance. I don't blame you for what happened, and neither does your aunt. And neither should you. I know you wanted to save him, and I know you tried your best. I don't know many grown-ups who could have done what you did." Their eyes went back out over the water. "So what do you think, Lance? Swimming sound like a plan to you?"

"I haven't been in the water since the accident." Lance still looked glum.

"Well, you can beat it, or it can beat you." Uncle Joe sounded to Lance as if he were trying to impart something that was both wise and inspiring.

"The water." Lance as much stated as asked.

"You're sitting here for a reason. You might as well make it the right one."

Lance nodded. Uncle Joe was right. Why should he sit here and vegetate when he should be practicing? A plan formulated in the boy's mind. He would make sure that if something like that accident ever happened again, he would be ready to atone for his failure. The water had gotten Brad, but it would never get him. Never.

The boy stood up and took off his shoes and shirt. He set his wallet and house keys atop the clothing and dived into the water. Lance glanced back. Uncle Joe seemed surprised at the speed and ferocity with which Lance tore through the now-gentle waters.

Nothing would stop him from mastering the water. Nothing. He wouldn't let himself be weak ever again, and never again let someone die when it was within his power to rescue them. Lance attacked the water as if it were a sentient being that had taken his cousin from him, a being that now had blood on its hands. Brad's blood. It was all around him, drenching him, burning a hole through him...close to his heart...

The Present.

Lance lazily opened an eye. Now he was face down on the floor, lying in a pool of his own blood. *Why am I not dead?* he wondered. The pain began in earnest now. He wanted to scream, but even that effort was beyond him. Spots borne of terrible agony began popping in front of eyes. *Oh goody,* he thought. *Maybe I'll die soon.*

The spots wouldn't let up. They changed in color from blue and green to yellow and tan to an off-white, much like the walls in his living room. That's the way it looked this morning when his wife, Sheila, had flounced in...

Lance P. Dunphy, a little while ago.

Lance stared in shocked disbelief at the empty beige walls in his living room. The repo men had taken the furniture away yesterday, that he already knew. What astounded Lance now was the absence of all his trophies and framed certificates. His high school diploma, his Bachelor's Degree in Education, his awards, medals, and trophies, all in swimming, had disappeared.

"They were just collecting dust." Sheila walked into the room. "So I pitched them. Except for the medals. I was able to hock those."

"What the hell did you do that for?" He was too deep in despair to feel very much anger.

"Well come on!" She had acted as though the answer should have been obvious. "They're foreclosing on the house, they've taken the furniture, and we owe fourteen grand on the credit cards. I mean, really, do you think I'm walking out of this marriage empty-handed?"

Lance felt as though he had been sucker-punched. "What?"

"That's right, I'm leaving you and I'm taking Rodney with me." She spoke very matter-of-factly. "We're staying at mom's until other arrangements can be made."

Lance figured the 'other arrangements' probably involved some guy at some bar she went to. He looked to her, his face and voice revealing only sadness. "I gave up everything for you."

"Bullshit." She huffed. "You wouldn't have had what little you lost without me. How the hell far would you have gotten with a teaching degree? The best thing I ever did for you was convince you to quit that lame phys ed job and get on at the factory."

"I had my dreams."

"The Olympics?" Sheila chuckled derisively. "You would have just lost your ass in front of the whole goddamn world. Hell, you couldn't even save that idiot cousin of yours. How can you even think you ever stood a chance against *real* professionals? It's a good thing I talked you into turning them down. Think of the embarrassment I saved you." She shook her head. "Everything I've done for you, and you still managed to fuck it all up. Debts up to the roof, you've lost our truck, our house, and virtually everything else we own. I don't know why I wasted my time on you. Must've been pity."

"It's not my fault the factory went out of business."

"Save that song and dance for the unemployment office." She sighed impatiently. "Well, at least I still have *my* car. I've got the last of my bags packed. Help me carry them out to the car."

Lance sat down on the bare carpet, silently admitting defeat. There was nothing else, in his mind, to feel. He was barely aware of his wife's angry look, crossed arms, and tapping foot.

"Son of a bitch!" Sheila stomped out of the room. Lance stared out into space as his wife's muffled shouts trailed off as she went into the bedroom. She emerged with a suitcase in each hand. "...should've listened, but nooooo! I had to take up with your sorry ass..." Her voice trailed off as she went outside. She came back in a few moments later. "...pay dearly when my lawyer gets done with you!" She stuck her head in the living room. "And by God you'll never see that kid again until you start sending the alimony and child support checks!" Again into the bedroom. Again toward the front door. "…hope you rot in hell, you lame-ass, cheapskate, no-talent son of a bitch!"

Lance flinched slightly when the front door slammed shut for the last time. He heard Sheila start up her car, put it in gear, back out of the driveway, and shout some last choice words as her tires squealed. He could hear the car speeding down the road. Of all the thoughts that ran through Lance's mind, a single notion stood out and apart from all the rest.

Now he was truly alone.

Lance hadn't seen his mother in twenty-five years, not since the state had stepped in and separated them. Brad was long gone, thanks to him. Uncle Joe had died of cancer twelve years ago. Aunt Frieda passed away three years later. Now Sheila and Rodney were gone. Lance was certain he'd never get to be with his son again. He had no idea how he was going to support himself, much less pass money on for his son's welfare. There just wasn't anyone left. He was as alone now as he had been as a little boy. It was a terrible feeling; the emptiness and loneliness that had plagued him as a child returned to him now with a vengeance.

Tears finally came to the broken man. Lance sobbed as he had not done since Brad's funeral. He had no idea how long he had laid on the floor crying. When the tears eventually stopped, all that was left inside him was a faint hint of despair within a seemingly endless realm of apathy. Nothing mattered anymore. He had tried his best to make his family life work, just like he had tried to save his cousin. Both endeavors had failed horribly. He had let Brad down, and now, he was sure, he had failed as a husband and as a father. Only now did it become clear to Lance what he had to do. The pain of failure had to be put to an end. Only now did the truth of his pathetic existence fully dawn upon him.

Lance calmly stood up and walked out of the room and into the garage. Even now, in the late morning, the room felt cold and solemn. The garage was almost completely empty. The truck was gone, and Lance had sold off most of his tools in a desperate attempt to pay the quickly mounting bills. Lance opened the door that led to the side yard. He walked outside and took in a lungful of mild, fragrant spring air. It was a beautiful day. The sounds, the smells, and the warmth streaming down from the glowing sun urged Lance to make a mental note to keep this moment in mind while he was roasting in hell.

That done, he went back inside and reached over his workbench to a gun rack. Lance barely felt the chill of the metal as he loaded a single shell into the chamber of his twelve-gauge shotgun.

Lance found a spot just in front of a bare wall. He intended to make it as difficult as possible for the mortgage company to sell his house. He'd been paying on it the last eleven years, and it wasn't his fault he was out of work. Normally, Lance would be filled with righteous indignation at the thought. But this wasn't a normal day, and he figured a large bloodstain on the wall and floor would deter most buyers. Lance readied the slide-pump shotgun and pointed it at his chest. There were no more tears, no final words, simply a firm resolve to finish what he had started.

Don't worry, he had told himself silently. You're doing the right thing...

The sound of metal hitting metal was completely obliterated by the deafening explosion that echoed throughout the garage. Before the first waves of sound could blast his eardrums, Lance Dunphy felt the hole being blown into his chest...

The Present.

Lance came around again and saw the daylight, the beautiful day with blue skies, chirping birds, and the aromas of roses and lilacs in the air, all just past the open doorway. It beckoned to his delirious mind as a final beacon of hope. If he could only see the sun, some reminder that there was still something right and good in this world, then maybe there might still be a reason to go on. Perhaps not all was lost. Not yet. If he could just make it outside, one of his neighbors might see him and get help. There was sure to be somebody close by, all he had to do was try. If he dared...

Lance stood on the dock again with Uncle Joe. It was storming now as it had been the day Brad had drowned. The rain fell in sheets, the wind howled like the mournful shrieks of the damned, the waves crashed against the docks; lightning seemed to be everywhere.

"Are you going to let it beat you?" The middle-aged man spoke to a young-again Lance. Despite the terrible clamor, Lance could hear him with crystal clarity. "Now, as before?"

Lance looked out over the violent waters. A hauntingly familiar voice called out to him over the din of the storm. "Lance, help me!" It was Brad. The boy again floundered in a lake that threatened to consume him. Lance looked to Uncle Joe.

"You have to make a decision very soon." The man spoke mildly. "Time is running out."

Lance's breath came heavily. It was up to him. He could either stand by and allow Brad to die again or jump in and try to make things right, for Brad and for himself.

Lance backed away from the edge of the dock, shaking his head. He couldn't bear to see Brad drown again. A shout of pure rage at the waters and at the storm erupted from somewhere deep inside the young man as he took a running leap into the lake. Waves crashed around him, threatening to stop him. Lance attacked the water as fiercely now as he had that terrible day more than twenty years earlier.

Grunting in pain, Lance used one hand to cover the gaping wound in his chest. He used his free arm and legs to pull himself across the cold concrete floor. Immediately, he felt the mind-numbing agony take hold of him, but he refused to surrender. He had to make it into the light. The pain would be over soon and he would be just fine.

The rain stung Lance as he plowed through one horrendous wave after another. Now he could see Brad clearly, struggling now as he had so many years ago. Lance pushed on with even more determination.

Splinters of wood and metal from years of garage projects dug into Lance's right arm. He was halfway to the door. Lance gritted his teeth and kept crawling. Like when Brad drowned, almost meant nothing. It was either all the way or forget it.

Lance could hear Brad's gasps as he fought to remain afloat. He would not fail this time. Just a little closer...

Lance's fingers touched the metal doorway. Sunlight was so very close...

"You can do it..."

Almost there.

Just a little further...

Doctor Royce Barnes lifted the length of the yellow tape strung between two trees and stepped beneath it. The tall, wiry, clean-shaven man paused a moment to look around, then walked toward a cluster of police officers and paramedics.

"Hey, doc." Detective Lee Foster greeted him. The short, squat lawman led the coroner to the body lying face-up and completely within the sunlit side yard.

"What've we got here?" The fifty-ish looking doctor's voice was flat as he knelt by the corpse.

"One Lance Patrick Dunphy." The cop read from a notepad as Barnes squatted to examine the corpse. "Male, Caucasian, age thirty-seven. Height, five-eleven. Weight, about one seventy-five. Brown and blue. Former swimming champ and displaced auto worker. Single gunshot wound to the chest, probably from the shotgun lying near the scene. Recently estranged from his wife, though her prints aren't on the gun or the shell. The blast happened inside the garage, then he was dragged and left outside. Missus Dunphy is down at HQ being questioned."

"Save your time." The coroner looked to his watch, then reached inside a pocket and retrieved a small tape recorder. He hit the 'record' button and spoke as much to it as to the cop. "This was a suicide, plain and simple. The end of the gun barrel was, at most, three inches from the decedent's chest. A murder victim wouldn't stand in the middle of the room waiting to get blown away. He would have tried to run or get the gun back from whoever had it. Multiple puncture wounds, most concentrating in a single area in the chest, is consistent with a shotgun blast. I estimate the time of death was about eleven-thirty this morning. And he wasn't dragged, detective. He crawled outside. See here, the small cuts on his arm? I'll need to do a more thorough examination, but I would say the debris in this guy's arm is the same stuff that's on the garage floor. He was trying to get outside at the time of his death. None of his wounds are postmortem."

"Why would he do that?" Foster wondered aloud. "He blows a hole in his chest, then tries to get help. It doesn't make sense."

Doctor Barnes sighed as he stood up and shut off the recorder. "God only knows."

The two boys climbed up on the dock. The storm had passed, the waters were still, and the sun was shining. Lance and Brad sat there for a moment, eyeing each other curiously. It wasn't clear to either of them which had rescued the other, but now it didn't matter. Both boys had been saved.

They looked back over the waters, now peaceful and inviting. Never again would any storm disturb the calmness of the lake nor the calmness of their souls. That was all behind them now.

Lance and Brad looked back to each other and smiled. They stood up and saw Uncle Joe and Aunt Frieda standing by the house. The boys looked back at the lake, then to each other for a moment. They clapped each other on the shoulder and happily walked toward the house.

It was time to go home.